The Seven-Day Resurrection

Also by this author

Weapons of Remorse

The Seven-Day Resurrection

Chevron Ross

Author Note

Chevron Ross is a pseudonym for this novel's typist.

Its author is God, the author of love and salvation.

Contents

Monday

When Len Holder's mother came back to life, he wasn't completely surprised. She'd been appearing in his dreams lately: emerging from the car with an armload of groceries; sprinkling herbs into a pot of homemade chili; loading the dishwasher, sorting laundry, cleaning the oven. Activities impossible in her last, miserable years. But the dreams were so vivid that each time he awoke, Len had to reorient himself. He was alone in the house and had been since her death.

This particular morning Len awoke not from a dream, but to singing:

"Two little clouds, one summer's day,
Went flying through the sky;
They went so fast they bumped their heads,
And both began to cry."

Rising from his bed, Len followed the voice to the living room. She stood at the window, watching leaves float down from the red oak tree.

"Mom?"

She turned to him, her eyes glazed. "Hi, Len."

"Mom ... what ... where did you come from?"

"Is this my house?" Slowly, she wandered about the room, her fingers brushing the pretentious furnishings. The Ethan Allen sofa. The Stickley lamp table. The swan figurines above the fireplace.

She stopped to admire an Edward Hicks print of Noah's ark. "How beautiful!" she said. "Is this mine, too?"

Len approached cautiously. If she was a ghost, she didn't look like one. Instead of her burial clothes, she wore a Dallas Cowboys warmup suit.

"Mom," he asked, "how on Earth did you get here?"

She didn't seem to hear. Her attention returned to the leaf festival in the backyard. "Is it fall again already? I love this time of year."

This didn't feel like a dream. It had texture, and the haziness of dreams was absent.

Len reached out to touch her shoulder. It was solid. His hand slid down to her wrist. The pulse was steady, her skin was warm.

She drifted past him and sank into the leather recliner. "Do you have any key lime pie?"

"What?"

"Seems like ages since I've had anything to eat."

"I … uh … I'll see what's in the fridge." Numbly, he headed for the kitchen. Her voice followed him, humming the lullaby.

The pie request was a familiar one. In the final weeks before her death, sweets were all she would eat. The hospice nurse said not to worry. "Let her have whatever she wants. It won't make any difference."

Drawing a dessert plate from the cupboard, Len noticed his mother's medical diary lying on the counter. He thought he'd thrown it away seven years ago. Now, it lay open to the last page:

11/01/2013

6:30 p.m. BP 81/41, pulse 101. Still unconscious, but some sort of distress. Chest heaving. Groping gestures for several minutes.

8:30 p.m. BP 79/41, pulse 111. Erratic breathing, gradually stabilized.

10:30 p.m. BP 102/44, pulse 125. More groping. Breathing shallow but regular.

11/02/2013
12:30 a.m. BP 90/42, pulse 133. Frantic gasping and heaving. Hospice summoned.

The nurse had arrived within minutes, giving Mom a light dose of morphine to calm her. "I wouldn't bother recording her vitals anymore," she advised sympathetically. "It should be just a matter of hours."

Meticulous to the end, Len made a final entry that afternoon.

4:36 p.m. No BP. No pulse. No respiration.

The diary said nothing about the sorrow frozen on his mother's face. Nothing about Len and Olivia sobbing in each other's arms. Nothing about the terrible emptiness of her bedroom after the attendants wheeled her away.

Dutifully, Len had phoned Joey, Cindy, and their children. Those who lived in town came over to sit with him. The conversation was awkward. None of them reminisced about Mom or shed a tear.

The sun peeked through the kitchen window, reminding Len that this was a work day. Scrolling through his phone menu, he hesitated. What excuse could he give?

His call went to voicemail. "Miranda, it's me," he said. "Something – uh – unexpected has come up. I'll be at home today. Call if you need me."

Len checked his calendar for November 30, 2020. No appointments, although he did have a batch of open claims on his desk.

He placed a slice of pie on the plate and carried it to the living room. Mom sat in her chair, looking around. "Len, is this my house?"

"Yes."

"Why can't I remember?"

"What *do* you remember, Mom? Where did you come from just now?"

She stared blankly at the pie, as though wondering what to do with it. "What time does *Wheel of Fortune* come on?"

"Late this afternoon, I think." Len hadn't watched a game show since her death and hoped he'd never have to again.

A voice murmured from down the hall. Probably the clock radio. He ignored it and perched on the sofa's armrest. "This is so good!" she exclaimed, tasting the pie. "Did you make it?"

"No, it's one of those frozen things." In her last few weeks, Mom was too blind and weak to feed herself. They had to spoon-feed her like a baby. Sometimes she would sip a nutrient drink, but Len could see that it gave her no pleasure.

Fleetingly, he wondered where the pie had come from. He didn't remember buying it.

A smile crossed her face. "Len, do you remember that song about the two little clouds? My mother used to sing that to me when I got scared of the thunder."

"You sang it to me, too," he said. "When I was little."

"Did I?" She took another bite.

The radio voice grew louder. It sounded like Joey's morning talk show. Len followed it into his brother's old bedroom.

"Aaron Rodgers of the Packers is everybody's pick for most valuable player," said the voice. "But quarterbacks win that award all the time. Who would you choose? Think about it, and we'll start taking calls right after this message."

There was no radio in Joey's room. Nothing but his bedframe and mattress, stripped and left bare since his wedding day in 1962.

Len checked the closet and peeked under the bed. The voice seemed to be coming from everywhere and nowhere.

This *had* to be a dream. He went to the bathroom to splash his face with cold water. It made no difference. Joey's voice droned on. From the living room, Mom's hummed away.

Len had just turned sixty-two when she suffered her first hip fracture. The rehab period was upsetting to both of them. Some of the nursing home residents seemed little more than house plants, cleaned, fed, and watered by underpaid attendants. At supper each evening, Len and his mother watched one of them wheel a shrunken old lady out of her room and park her at a nearby table. Someone brought a tray of food and tried to coax her into eating. The patient stared vacantly into space, ignoring the meal until the aide rolled her back to the room. As far as Len knew, she never ate anything, never spoke, never had any visitors.

The bleak atmosphere brought out the worst in Mom. "They won't leave me alone when I'm sleeping," she complained, "but when I press the call button, they ignore me. The food in this place is terrible. The TV control doesn't work right. These gowns make my skin itch. And this bed's too soft, it makes my back ache." She griped the entire six weeks.

At the end of rehab, Doctor Kirby recommended full-time companionship. "Once they've fallen, they're likely to do it again."

"Please don't leave me in this place!" she begged tearfully. So Len took her home, assuming responsibility because no one else would. Mom and Joey didn't get along. Cindy lived in Pennsylvania, conveniently distant. The grandchildren rarely gave her a passing thought. Len had his own issues, but she *was* his mother. Surrendering his apartment, he moved back into his old bedroom and hired Olivia to watch over her while he was at work. The arrangement lasted five years, until her death.

Len returned to the living room, where she was polishing off the pie. "Mom," he began. How to phrase it? "Mom, I haven't seen you in quite a while. Where have you been?"

She looked around. "Is this my house?"

"Yes, Mom. All yours."

Now he noticed silence from Joey's room. The voice was gone.

Mom clicked on the TV and began watching the *Today* show. Len studied her from the sofa, a tide of dark memories washing over him. Among them, the feeling that something else was amiss. Something more than Joey's disembodied voice and his mother's reembodied spirit.

The Farm Tree

BY LEONARD HOLDER

From where he stood, Gene Driskill could see nothing of his father's face. He lay on his back beneath the tractor, his legs splayed out. If you didn't know better, you'd think he was dead or asleep under there. Dad had a peculiar economy of motion that activated only the parts of his body necessary to the task at hand. When he called for pliers or a wrench, his open palm appeared, gripped the tool, and vanished. The rest of him lay as immobile as the tractor itself. He didn't even grunt as he tightened the bolts.

"Okay son, give her a try."

Gene climbed onto the seat and pressed the starter button. The tractor roared to life. "Throttle back a little." Dad scooted out nimbly to stand beside Gene, listening for misses and backfires. "I was right. Just a dirty filter and plugs. Should be okay now." He wiped his sinewy hands with a rag as his eyes scanned the horizon. "I'd still like to have this section done before dark. You'll have to hustle, though. Think you can handle it?"

"Yes sir."

"You're my man." He clapped Gene on the shoulder. "Tomorrow we'll start harrowing unless we get a shower tonight. Don't forget to strap the tarp over it before you come in." He stowed the toolbox beneath the driver's seat and strode easily across the furrows, toward the late afternoon sun. Dad was everything Gene thought a man should be. Strong, capable, self-assured. He wished he could make his own adolescent body grow faster.

The tractor snarled as he swung it around to line up the plow. Behind him, the blades bit into the earth, ripping up large clods of weeds and soil, the engine spewing gray smoke through the vertical exhaust pipe. The dirt road separating the fields drew slowly closer. If you calculated six minutes for each pass, times twelve furrows per pass, allowing fifteen seconds to turn and realign at each end ... yes, he could just make it before dark.

This was only Gene's second week on the tractor. He was surprised when Dad announced it at breakfast one morning. "John, he can't drive that thing!" Mom protested. "Eleven years old? He's never even driven a car!"

"Sure he can! There's no traffic, no stop signs, no intersections. All he's got to do is make turns and keep it in a straight line. Right son?"

"Yes sir, I guess so."

"I know so. Finish your breakfast and meet me at the fuel tank." John grabbed a biscuit, kissed Mom on the cheek and banged out through the screen door. She sighed. "Gene, do exactly what he tells you. Operating heavy machinery takes practice, and it's dangerous. Last year, Jack Murphy got trapped when his tractor rolled over on him. By the time Dorothy got worried and went looking for him, he'd been lying there for five hours."

"I'll be careful, Mom."

"Your lunch bag's on the countertop. I'd better go wake the little ones." She removed her apron as she climbed the stairs.

Gene dug into his eggs, excited by the challenge. Things were sure different since Dad returned from the Pacific to find Mom cleaning house for several town families while Gene stayed home, babysitting Dina, Terry and Charley.

"Ruth, why isn't this boy in school?" Dad demanded.

"I didn't have any choice, John, with both your parents ailing and mine gone off to Missouri. I didn't write you about it because I didn't want you to worry."

"It's okay, Dad," Gene added. "I don't like school anyway."

"Well, you'd better learn to like it because you're starting back next week. No son of mine is going to grow up ignorant. And no wife of mine is going to be maidservant to anybody.

Gene, put your boots on and follow me. This is a farm family again, starting right now!"

John Driskill set to work as though determined to bury World War II beneath fifty acres of grain as fast as possible. The first time Gene asked how many Japs he'd killed, Dad ordered him to fill the kerosene lamps. The next time he wound up cleaning the hen house. Gene got the message and kept his curiosity to himself.

Meanwhile, Dad sold Grandpa's plow horse, used his GI loan to buy a used tractor, a bull and two cows, labored fourteen hours a day in the fields and put Gene to work after school and on weekends. While the little ones played in the yard, Mom aired the mattresses, scrubbed the sheets in an old metal tub, cranked them through Grandma's wringer and hung them on the clothesline. Gene cleaned and sharpened the plows. He repaired the sideboards on the trailer. He helped Dad build a new livestock tank out of corrugated tin salvaged from the abandoned Thurber farm. In April, when Dina turned six, Mom taught her how to gather eggs, pluck chickens and fill the feed troughs. Everyone was tired but happy at the end of each day. The family was whole again.

Gene glanced over his shoulder. The plow churned steadily behind him. He was still too short to reach the pedals, so he had to drive standing up.

He was embarrassed that first day when he forgot to raise the tractor hitch before backing up to correct his approach. The result was a bent knifing blade that Dad had to hammer straight on Grandpa's anvil. "Don't let it get you down, son," he smiled patiently. "We all make mistakes. The trick is to learn from them."

Two more weeks and they could start planting if the weather cooperated. The *Farmer's Almanac* was predicting a mostly dry spring. "God, please send us a good soaking rain," Dad prayed each evening as they held hands over the supper table. Weeds had conquered the land in Dad's absence, despite government pressure on farmers to increase their yield for the war effort. The bureaucrats seemed to forget that most farm boys were overseas, fighting it.

"It won't be so tough next year," Dad promised. "Chip Woolsey was telling me about this new herbicide, 2,4-D, that kills the weeds without hurting the grain. Gives you a bigger yield, too."

"John, how are we going to pay for all this?" Ruth fretted. "The chemicals, the tractor, cows, chickens, stock feed. Not to mention repairs on the barn. It's too much!"

"We'll do what farmers have done since Adam and Eve got evicted from the Garden. Work hard and trust in God to provide."

Tuesday

Len dreamed he was wheeling his mother into the hospital when a gang of surgeons blocked his way. "Show us your Medicare card!" they chorused. He searched his wallet. There was nothing in it but fast-food coupons. The glass doors closed in his face. Mom shivered in her nightgown.

She'd floated through Monday in the same fog, saying little, ensconced in the recliner as her favorite TV shows babbled away. Len watched her from the sofa, occasionally pinching himself.

As the hours passed, he began to notice details. Her wedding ring was still on her left hand, in accordance with her burial wishes. But she was also wearing glasses again. A few months before her death, Len had thrown them away. Macular degeneration had rendered them useless.

This morning he awoke to the sound of Joey's resonant voice. "Let's have a quiz," it said. "Who scored the only touchdown for Kansas City in the first Super Bowl? That was on January 15, 1967. The first correct answer wins a catered Super Bowl party from Domino's Pizza."

Len entered his brother's room. He still couldn't pinpoint the source of the voice. It drifted in and out, like a weak radio signal. On game days, Joey spoke from TV booths atop football stadiums. He did his weekday call-in shows from his laptop, wherever he happened to be. But he'd never done one from Mom's house before. When she was dying, he didn't come around at all.

As a boy, Len had loved ghost stories, particularly the works of Poe. But one night he awoke screaming from a nightmare about Madeline Usher rising from death, bloody and vengeful. "No more scary comic books for you, young man!" Mom declared, tucking him back in. "Some mothers have to go to work in the morning!"

Her reappearance seemed more an enigma than a ghost story, like Gregor Samsa in Kafka's *Metamorphosis*. Thankfully, Len's mother hadn't returned as a giant cockroach, but she did pose a similar problem. What were you supposed to do when someone arose from the grave? Call the cops? The funeral home? Stephen King? Seven years had passed since he'd settled her estate. How could you reverse all that? Was there a website with resurrection forms to fill out? And what would he tell the rest of the family?

Yesterday, Len had muted the TV during a commercial. "Mom, can you tell me how you got here?"

"Got where?"

"Here. Back home again."

She looked around the room. "This is my house, isn't it? Isn't that what you said?"

"It used to be."

"You mean it's not mine anymore?"

"No. Never mind, I was just thinking out loud."

She shook her head. "I don't think I'll ever understand you, Len. Turn the sound back on." She spent the entire day soaking up TV drivel, as though she'd never been away.

Before her death, Mom and Len had made a nightly ritual of watching a movie together on TCM. Last night it was *You Never Can Tell,* a 1951 comedy starring Dick Powell as a dog reincarnated as a detective to solve his own murder. Mom didn't laugh once, not even when Powell entered a restaurant and demanded a plate of raw hamburger. She just gazed blankly at the screen, as she'd done all day.

When she began to doze, Len escorted her to bed. She drifted off immediately. He sat beside her for an hour, waiting for her to disappear. Once, he put his ear to her chest. The heart beat steadily. The lungs sounded clear. If this was her body, what was buried out west of town next to Will Holder's monument?

"The correct answer is Curtis McClinton," said Joey's voice. "He scored on a seven-yard pass from Len Dawson. Congratulations to Randy Wilson of Twin Falls, Idaho, who wins a catered Super Bowl party from Domino's."

Len once read a magazine article about people hearing voices; solitary old guys like himself, frightened by mysterious noises. Sometimes they talked aloud to people who weren't there. Was this the onset of his own senility?

His mother was almost ninety-four when she began having visions. "I keep seeing my brothers' faces," she told Len. "They look young again, like when I was growing up."

"Do they say anything?"

"No, they're just … there."

Len took her to an ophthalmologist, who wasn't surprised. "When people begin to lose their eyesight, the brain often substitutes visions stored in their memories. The brain can do that when it lacks input from the maculae."

Joey's voice faded away. Len peeked into his mother's bedroom. She lay asleep, still wearing the Dallas Cowboys outfit. Joey had given it to her for Mother's Day one year. Churlishly, she buried it in a drawer, deeming it "inappropriate." Whatever that meant. Now it was back, another mystery. Cindy had donated all Mom's clothes to The Salvation Army after the funeral.

He checked his phone calendar for December 1. No appointments today, thank goodness. Going to the office was still out of the question. He couldn't leave her alone, and he'd never find another competent home health aide like Olivia on such short notice.

Miranda's phone sent him to voicemail again. "Hey, it's Len," he said. "I'm still stuck with the same problem as yesterday. Will you ask Sylvia to check the status on Marvin Haverty's roofing settlement? It's in my pending file. I called the home office before I left Friday, but they didn't have it finalized. Also, can one of you call the hospital and see if Lucia Valdez can have visitors? I salvaged the personal items from her Volvo after I totaled it out. They're in my desk drawer. Someone ought to take them to her, to put her mind at ease. Thanks for your help, Miranda. You know how to reach me if there's anything urgent." Len no longer needed the job, but Miranda would be heartbroken if he retired. Besides, how else would he fill his time? His novel was going nowhere.

Mom slept on. Len showered and shaved, his mirrored face lean and fairly smooth for a man of seventy-eight. Both Len and Joey had inherited their father's superhero jaw and thick brown hair. Poor Cindy wasn't so lucky. She got all of Dad's leanness, but none of her mother's curves.

He returned to the master bedroom, listening to her steady breathing. In a way, it was nice to have her back. For months after her death, he'd harbored mixed feelings of relief and guilt. Relieved to be free of her. Guilty about things unsaid and undone.

Their nostalgia for old movies was about all they'd had in common. Mom liked to say that during the Great Depression, people enjoyed films about rich people dancing in ballrooms and dining on caviar. For ninety minutes they could escape into that world and forget their poverty.

Len himself would watch anything about World War II, like *Casablanca* or *Twelve O'Clock High*. His mother was in her twenties then, following Dad from one army base to another as he trained for combat. Garth was six years old. Cindy was four. Len and Joey were what Mom called "twinkles in your father's eye." Or as Joey would say, "future considerations."

The 1940s were romantically heroic if you believed Hollywood. For Mom it was a struggle, waiting tables at railway stations and bus stops from town to town to earn rent money.

"It was disgusting!" she reminisced. "All those recruits telling dirty jokes while I served them hamburgers and beer. Grinding out cigarettes in their plates for me to clean while they sized me up like I was some dessert that wasn't on the menu. The fact that I was married with two children didn't stop them. They'd tease and paw at me until I wanted to slap their faces. But I needed the job, so I just put up with it."

"Did you tell Dad about it?" Len asked.

"Heavens no! He would have tracked down every one of them and busted their heads!"

When Will Holder shipped off to the Pacific, his wife and children rode the train back to Texas, only to find themselves homeless. The bank had foreclosed on Grandpa's farm. Will's parents were about to lose theirs.

Mom got a job clerking at Teasdale's Drugstore and rented a tired old adobe house beside the main highway running through Chicory. Len and Joey spent their childhoods playing in a weedy vacant lot across the road. They didn't know they were poor.

Len started the coffee brewing, then returned to his mother's bedside. Asleep, she looked as innocent as a child, her angular features hinting at the willowy beauty she'd once been. Touches of gray in her hair made her seem almost regal.

That was another strange thing. Seven years ago, Olivia had stopped brushing Mom's hair when every stroke pulled out more of it. At the end she was almost bald. "Age is so cruel to women," Olivia remarked sadly.

Len shook her shoulder. "Mom, wake up." Her eyes opened. "Good morning. Did you sleep well?"

She looked around. "Is it morning? Why aren't you at work? Where's Olivia?"

"Olivia doesn't work for us anymore."

She blinked at him in dismay. "Why not?"

"Well, she, uh … has another assignment now. Hey, how about some breakfast? That pie was the only thing you ate yesterday."

She sat up. "Len, you didn't fire her, did you?"

"No, of course not."

"Is she never coming back?"

"Well …" He stalled. He hadn't seen Olivia since Mom's funeral. "Tell you what. I'll call the agency today and ask when she's available again."

Rising, she put on her glasses and approached the dresser. "I don't understand. Yesterday, she said 'see you tomorrow' and hugged me goodbye, like always. What day is this?"

"Tuesday."

She peered into the mirror. "Len, how did I get so old?"

"Mom, I think you're a little confused. How about a nice, damp facecloth? That always wakes you up."

"Don't you have to go to work?"

"Not today. You've been … um, you had a sick spell, so I'm looking after you."

"I don't feel sick." Whirling, she seized him, burying her face in his chest. "Len, I'm scared! What's going on?"

"Hey, it's okay, everything's okay." He patted her.

"Nobody comes to see me anymore but Olivia, and now she's gone, too!"

"I'm here, Mom," he sighed. "I've always been here."

After she calmed down, he waited outside her door, listening for a collapse. Instead, he heard footsteps, water running, drawers opening, clothes hangers rattling. Before her first injury, she'd tottered around so alarmingly that Len put his foot down. "From now on, you use the walker wherever you go!" Even then, she parked it carelessly outside the closet each morning while she picked through her wardrobe. The result was an awkward fall, a hip fracture, a bruised elbow, and six weeks in rehab. A year after the implant, she fell again and broke the other hip. In her final two months, she was so crippled and bedbound with arthritis that a hospital gown was the most fashionable dress she could manage.

She emerged wearing her robe and slippers. "How are your knees today?" Len asked.

"Fine. Why shouldn't they be?" She brushed past him, ambling easily toward the kitchen. Thank goodness she didn't need her walker. After her death, Len had donated it to Goodwill.

From the table she watched him scramble a panful of eggs and toast two slices of bread, spreading strawberry jam on them. "No bacon?" she frowned as he brought their plates to the table.

"I gave up bacon," Len said. "I think it was giving me indigestion."

"Well, it wasn't bothering me!"

"I'll get you some on my next trip to the store." He poured two cups of coffee. "Mom, where did you get that warmup suit you were wearing?"

"I don't remember." She munched her toast. "Have you talked to Joey or Cindy lately?"

"No. I did hear Joey's radio show this morning." Without the radio, he added to himself.

"He never comes to see me, never calls. I guess I drove him away."

"Joey's got a very demanding job. I hardly ever see him, either."

"The job's an excuse. He looks for reasons to avoid me. Olivia takes up for him, too, just like you do." Now, she sounded like her old self. Peevish and whiny.

"Mom," Len said, "speaking of not seeing people, where did you come from yesterday morning?"

"What do you mean?"

"Well ... when I woke up, you were standing in the living room."

"So? I got up before you did. So what?" She noticed the clock. "Oh, I'm missing my program!" Rising, she headed for the recliner.

The TV spat out one of those screaming confrontation shows that made Len despair for humanity. Poor Olivia had been a captive audience. Keeping Mom company all day was part of her job, along with house cleaning, laundry and cooking.

At first, Mom had objected to having a stranger in the house. "How do you know she won't swipe my purse and my jewelry?"

"Don't worry," Len said. "All their employees are bonded. Besides, it's this or the nursing home."

"Humph! She'll probably steal my car and run off to Mexico."

Secretly, Len had had his own reservations. He'd expected some ditzy teenager with green hair and nose studs, playing with her cell phone all day while neglecting Mom's medication. To his relief, Olivia was a mature thirty-eight-year-old with teenagers of her own. She had nine years of experience in home health and had just completed twenty-one months caring for a Vietnam veteran.

By the end of the first week, Olivia and Mom were friends. They traded family stories while Olivia bathed her, dressed her and recorded her vital signs every two hours. Best of all, she provided female companionship. When Len got home each evening, Olivia had supper waiting, plus a written report on Mom's condition and behavior. Her agency charged twenty-one dollars an hour, but she was worth it.

"Len, what's wrong with this thing?" Mom fretted, tapping the remote buttons. Apparently, resurrection hadn't improved her TV skills. She'd fumbled around until the screen turned snowy. Len reset the cable connections and found *The Price Is Right*. Different show, same screaming.

He escaped to Mom's room to make the bed. Fluffing the pillows, he froze. Where had the bedclothes come from? He thought Cindy or one of Joey's kids had taken everything after the funeral. Now, a dozen of Mom's old dresses hung in the closet, including the two-piece suit she'd been buried in. And her lingerie drawers were full again.

He checked her bathroom. It contained hand soap, face cream, makeup, a hairbrush, deodorant and toothpaste. The Dallas Cowboys suit lay folded neatly inside the hamper. When you arose from death, did your clothes and toiletries return with you?

Len wandered into his room. "God," he sighed, flopping onto the bed, "please tell me what's going on. Why have you sent her back?"

He considered driving out to the cemetery to see if her grave was disturbed. He pictured his mother clawing her way up through the earth to lurch homeward, zombie-like, in the moonlight. Len shoved the image away. He thought he'd buried all his dark thoughts seven years ago.

He sat up. The wall facing him was a gallery of black-and-white photos right out of *The Grapes of Wrath*. A hazy shot of his grandfather with a mule and plow; his two uncles unloading a rickety cotton wagon; Grandma on the porch working a butter churn. All of them looking as tired and dispirited as the men's worn coveralls and Grandma's flour sack dress. In contrast, Mom and Dad smiled at the camera, nestled against each other in their 1934 Sunday best. "That picture was my parents' wedding gift to us," she told him. "It was all they could afford." Len's only other photograph of Dad, dated February 4, 1942, showed him clean-shaven, stiff and severe in his Army uniform, ready to give the Japanese some payback.

Despite her tattered relationship with her children, Mom was zealous about preserving family history. Len inherited a frayed manila envelope containing Dad's letters from the war years. They offered little insight into the young farmer fighting for family and country. Army censors had turned Will Holder's dispatches into insoluble puzzles:

September 13, 1942

My Beloved Sharon,

Just a quick note before the mail courier from ████████████ returns to the ████████████ We had a little fracas on ████████████ but it turned out all right except ████████████ got killed as we were ████████████ I am doing fine but missing you and the kids. Kiss Garth and Cindy for me.

All my love,
Will

January 30, 1943

My Darling Sharon,

They transferred us out of ██████████████ last week. This is the first chance I've had to write since ██████████████ Everybody in the outfit who survived has dysentery, so we're all pretty miserable. The worst thing is being so far from you and the kids. ██████████████ expects the Pacific War will last until ██████████████ so there's no telling when I'll get to see you again. Please keep writing. Your letters mean a great deal to me.

Love and kisses

Will

The most coherent letter was less about the war, more the musings of a homesick soldier.

June 11, 1943

Dear wife and best friend,

Can't do much today on account of the rain. Reminds me of spring on the farm when it was too muddy to work outdoors, so Papa read to us from the Bible while Mama gave us all haircuts in the kitchen. I sure miss your cooking, sweetheart. The stuff we get here keeps us alive, but that's about all.

Do you ever hear from ███████████ or ██████████? The last I knew, they were at boot camp in ████████████████ Sure hope they don't wind up over here. Tell their folks I asked about them. I wish I'd had a chance to say goodbye before I left. Wonder if I'll ever see them again?

████████████████ just came in to tell us we're going to ████████████████████████████████

██████████████████████████ pretty soon. Makes you treasure a peaceful day like this. Every minute of it.

I got Garth's letter. Tell him I'm counting on him to be the man of the family while I'm gone. Someday when all this is over, I'll take you to a square dance if ████████████ and his fiddle survive ████████████████████ I think constantly of you and the kids, especially the new baby. A big kiss to each, and extra ones for you.

Loving you and missing you,
Will

Any G.I. might have written those letters, but they were all Len had of his father. He reread them hungrily, searching for clues to the man he'd never known.

"Mom," he used to ask, "what were those blacked-out spaces?" Her answers were always the same: "He didn't say," or "I don't remember," or "It doesn't matter now." Persistent questions would kick off one of her griping spells. It was frustrating. Mom was his only source of information about Dad.

After the war, she bought a second-hand Brownie box camera to photograph her children in static poses. The four of them in a solemn row, dressed for church. Garth petting somebody's dog. Cindy smiling tentatively beside a sickly rosebush. Len waiting on the curb for the school bus. Joey sitting in a rusty toy wagon. It seemed that every time Len looked up, Mom was pointing the camera at him. He couldn't understand why the same pose in front of the same shabby house was so important. The only difference was age. Each child a little older, a little taller. Each shot duplicated twice. "The drugstore gives me a discount on extra copies," Mom explained. She was obsessed with bargains to the point of redundancy. How many shots of Cindy in her Easter dress did she need?

The pictures Len wished for didn't exist. Will Holder never returned from the war to pose with his family. "Missing in Action," the telegram said.

"Why do you keep staring at me?" Mom asked.

"Sorry," he muttered. The morning and its wretched TV fare dragged on. He phoned Miranda again but got only her voicemail.

Restless, he opened his laptop. The screen displayed a colorful Peruvian landscape, overlayed with the date: Tuesday, December 1, 2020.

He clicked on the Winslow & Grant shortcut and tried logging in:

INVALID USER NAME OR PASSWORD

That was unusual. Len was zealous about maintaining his credentials. He tried again.

INVALID USER NAME OR PASSWORD

He checked the keyboard. The caps lock was off. The number lock was on.

Bothersome. Len had several claim files that needed his attention. Shelby Chan was bumming rides to work while waiting for him to total out her wrecked Altima. The Kohlers had been living on takeout food ever since a rotted tree limb crashed through their kitchen roof. Daniel Gutierrez was suffering from sports withdrawal because burglars stole his TV.

Everybody has a story, Len reflected. With a wary eye on his mother, he opened his novel and began tinkering with a new scene:

> Ruth slapped Charley's hand as he stood on tiptoes, reaching for the pie. "That's not for you, young man!"
>
> "Why?"
>
> "Because I baked it for the church bazaar. Now stop getting underfoot. I've got a pot of blackberry jam on the stove and a sink full of dishes to wash."
>
> Charley crawled under the table. Rainy days were so boring! Daddy was working in the barn. Gene, Dina and Terry were at school. He couldn't play checkers by himself, and he'd already done all the animals in his coloring book.
>
> A movement between the wall and pantry caught his eye. "Mama! There's a mouse in the corner!" Ruth seized her broom and began swatting at it. "Don't hurt him, Mama! I want to make him a pet!"
>
> "You've got enough pets already. Shoo!" She opened the door and swept the mouse onto the porch. It scampered down the steps, splashed through a rain puddle, and disappeared under the house. "Charley, that cat of yours isn't doing her job. No more table scraps until I stop seeing mice around here."
>
> "Mama, I'm bored!"
>
> "You are? Well, I guess I'll have to find a job for you." She lifted him to the tabletop and produced a pencil and paper. "There. Draw me a picture of that mouse."

"I didn't get a good look at him."

"That's okay. Use your imagination, like your brother does." She returned her attention to the bubbling pot.

Len paused. The scene reminded him of a wintery Saturday afternoon when Mom bundled Len and Joey into jackets, mittens and caps. "Bring me some clean snow, boys," she said, handing each a large bowl. "As much as you can carry." She mixed the snow with sugar, vanilla and a little milk. They sat at the table and snacked on snow ice cream while Mom's vegetable soup simmered on the burner.

The blue flames evoked another, darker memory: Len's kitten, dead from a gas leak. Mom had banished it to the utility closet one freezing night after she caught it stretching its claws on a chair cushion. It was an accident, but she wouldn't let him bury the kitten in the yard. "Put it in the alley," she ordered. "I don't want you digging holes in the lawn." Len glued two Popsicle sticks together and placed the little cross on his kitten's grave. The next day, a garbage truck ran over it.

Another game show was in progress. Mom's eyes had that glazed expression again, as though she was still out of synch with mortality. Or perhaps she was simply bored with TV.

"Do you really like this stuff?" he had asked one day. He was working from home while Olivia attended her grandson's funeral.

"What's wrong with it?"

"It's trashy, Mom. Silly game shows. Frivolous lawsuits. People spilling their guts about their personal problems."

"TV's all I've got," she said reproachfully. "I can't read anymore or do anything. Wait till *your* eyes go bad!"

On the screen, a young woman was taking a shower in slow motion, her back to the camera. Some sort of skin ointment commercial. Len caught himself staring and smiled ruefully. *Act your age, old man.*

Putting the laptop aside, he went to the kitchen to make lunch. The room was spacious, unlike the kitchen of his boyhood home, so cramped and dingy that Mom hung one of Grandma's quilts over the doorway so her lady friends couldn't see into it. Good impressions were important,

Mom always said. She washed the quilt every week to rid it of cooking odors.

The walls around the table still displayed Mom's framed embroidery of the Lord's Prayer and cross stitches of horses, puppies and flowers. A Plains State College football banner hung above the TV. "Home of the Mustangs!" it proclaimed beneath the red silhouette of a charging horse.

The kitchen window still wore the curtains Mom had bought some twenty-five years ago: white batik festooned with cheerful Texas bluebonnets. Cartoon magnets of Foghorn Leghorn, Porky Pig and Bugs Bunny clung to the refrigerator door; ancient gifts from Joey's children, now grandparents themselves. Two ceramic turtles supervised Len's cooking from the knickknack shelf above the stove. After he inherited the house, Len was tempted to box them all up and tote them to the Goodwill drop. He didn't have the heart. It would be like throwing Dad's letters away.

As he stirred a pan of chicken noodle soup, he considered his mother's reappearance in practical terms. Suppose she was back to stay? Len would have to support the two of them. Mom's Social Security and Medicare benefits had died with her. What if she suffered a major illness or injury? Could you check a patient into the hospital if the patient was already dead?

"Is Olivia coming back tomorrow?" she asked over lunch.

"I'll look into it this afternoon," he said evasively.

"I still don't understand why they took her away. Didn't you pay them?"

"You know," he improvised, "I'll bet one of her old clients needed her temporarily. Somebody she stayed with before she came to us. Those home health agencies have a hard time getting good help."

To Len, Olivia was a gift from God. She was good at mollifying cranky old ladies, and a good conversationalist. "She's had it rough," Mom reported as the two women grew acquainted. "Her ex-husband never helps with money and only comes around to make trouble. Her oldest daughter's a high school dropout, unmarried and four months pregnant. The other girl is an honor roll student, but she has asthma. I feel so sorry for them." Len was pleased with the arrangement. Olivia gave Mom someone to worry about besides her own disaffected children.

Her soup spoon froze in midair. "Len, where is this place?" she asked, looking around the kitchen.

"It's your home."

"Why don't I recognize it?"

"Well … try concentrating on something in the room. See that Plains State banner? You made that for the Chicory Garden and Arts Festival."

She peered at it. "I did?"

"Barbara Lazenby loved it. She asked you to make one for her."

"Oh yes, Barbara!" she brightened. "I think I'll give her a call this afternoon." Barbara had been dead for eighteen years.

"Mom," Len asked carefully, "can you remember where you were before yesterday morning?"

Her brow knitted. "Was that when we went to the doctor?"

"No. We haven't seen Doctor Kirby for quite a while."

"That's another thing. I used to see him twice a year. Then later, it seemed I was going to his office all the time."

Before she became bedridden, the doctor was always dealing with mysterious pains and dementia crises. "I think she's just dehydrated," he told Len. "Women her age are prone to urinary tract infections, which sometimes bring on disorientation. Give her cranberry juice and lots of water." Mom mostly ignored the order. Water forced her to go to the bathroom frequently. She needed help to stand up, and the effort inflamed her knees.

Watching Mom finish her soup, Len wondered how much she remembered. He hesitated to ask. Bringing up the past was like lighting a fuse.

"Why don't we take a walk after lunch?" he suggested. "It looks nice and warm outside."

Her eyes clouded up again. "I think I'd rather take a nap." She arose and wandered toward the sofa. Maybe it was just as well. What if Blanche Meadows or Mabel Darby saw them out strolling? Everyone in the neighborhood knew she was dead.

A woman at the home health agency said Olivia no longer worked there. He tried Miranda's number again. "Hey, it's Len," he said at the beep. "You must be busy! Just wanted to make sure you got my other messages. I'll try to be back at work tomorrow."

He phoned Joey. "It's Len. Have you got a minute?"

"Make it quick," he said distractedly. "I'm at the airport, heading for Atlanta. The Falcons game is Thursday night."

"Oh," Len replied. "Well, never mind."

"Why, what's the matter?"

"Joey, I don't know how to tell you this, but Mom has come back to life."

"Oh, for Pete's sake, Len! Is this another one of your dreams?"

"No, not this time. I know it sounds crazy, but I need someone to stay with her so I can go back to work. Olivia's left home health and I don't want to leave her with a stranger."

"Well, obviously I can't."

"What about Janie?"

"She's at some kind of lawyers conference in Houston."

Five children, nine grandchildren, and none of them willing to help out. "Do you mind if I ask Beth?"

"Len, you know she keeps the kids while Hayley's at work. Hey, my flight's been called. I've got to run." He hung up. Not another word about his mother's return. As though it happened every day.

Joey probably wouldn't have stayed with Mom, even without excuses. His last vigil was the night following her second hip replacement. When Len got to the hospital the next morning, Joey looked whipped. "She was on my case all night," he said, "roasting me about my first marriage. My grades in school. Kids I used to hang out with. Repeated every word from every argument we ever had."

"I'm sorry, Joey. I guess it was the medication."

"Yeah, sure." He didn't come around again for almost six months.

Joey's bitterness dated back to high school, when he fell in love with Beth Ferris, a classmate who lived in an orphanage. "Don't you dare get mixed up with that girl!" Mom warned. "Her father's in jail, and her mother's been picking up men at that honky-tonk out on Harvest Road. Evelyn Rose told me all about it." Joey pursued Beth anyway, in a fever of romance and defiance. "We have a lot in common," he confided to Len. "Lousy parents."

But Joey wasn't strong enough to withstand Mom's relentless nagging. "What will the neighbors think?" she argued when he tried to defend Beth. "What about the ladies in my Bridge club? What about our friends at church?" She wore Joey down until he broke up with Beth. The following year he married Whitney Jackson, a pretty but flighty girl in his biology class.

Mom didn't like Whitney either. She brought nothing to the marriage but immaturity and a bundle of emotional problems, the results of an overindulgent father and his two viperous ex-wives. Joey put up with her for five years, just to deny his mother another victory.

"She forgets to buy groceries and feeds our kids pretzels for breakfast!" he fumed privately to Len. "Dresses them in the same clothes every day because she's too lazy to do laundry. Lets them run wild and play in the street while she reads movie magazines. One day she locked them in a closet so she could go shopping with the Wicked Witch of the West." That was Whitney's latest stepmother, who told the kids Joey's whole family was going to Hell because their church used instrumental music.

The divorce put Joey in a bind. He was determined to be a better parent than his mother, but his budding TV career kept him on the road a lot. So he hired a nanny and phoned from his hotel room each night to read Janie and Eric bedtime stories, his menagerie of animal voices sending them into giggling fits. At home, he spent every minute with them. Six years passed before he rediscovered Beth, whose husband had died of pneumonia. They fell in love again and "did what we should have done before Mom interfered."

"He did it just to spite me!" she raged. "He didn't even tell me about it until after they were married!"

"Mom, he didn't tell anyone else either," Len pointed out. "Give them a chance."

But now Beth was a *widowed* orphan with three kids of her own. Joey didn't care whether Mom approved or not, but to Beth the family circle was everything. Eventually, with a little psychology, she won Mom over.

She sought her advice on child-rearing, not because she needed it – Beth was a great parent – but because Mom was a sucker for flattery.

"I wish I'd had a mother like you!" she exclaimed. "How did you manage to raise four kids by yourself? See how much they've accomplished? Joey's a celebrity. Len and Cindy have good business jobs. All without a father, thanks to you!" Tactfully, Beth avoided the subject of Garth. Nobody talked about him anymore.

Over time, Mom mellowed. For the rest of her life, she got along better with Beth than with her own kids. Their friendship placated Joey somewhat. At least he became civil around Mom.

A light snore emerged from the sofa. Apparently, Mom still needed her little catnaps. Len decided to phone the courthouse.

"County Records, may I help you?" a woman answered.

"Yes, I'd like to, um … I guess I need to correct a death record."

"What sort of correction?"

"I don't quite know how to ask this," Len began, "but what do you do when a person has been declared dead, and it's a mistake?"

"You mean the person didn't die?"

"Well … yes and no."

"I don't understand, sir."

"It's my mother. She died seven years ago – I mean, we thought she died but … she came back yesterday," he finished lamely.

The woman hesitated. "May I have your name and the name of the deceased?"

"I'm Leonard Holder. My mother's name is Sharon Denise Holder."

"Her date of birth?"

"September 10, 1917."

"Thank you, one moment." He heard keys clicking. "I show a death certificate for Sharon Denise Holder dated November 2, 2013."

"That's it."

"But you say that's incorrect?"

"Yes. I mean no, the date's correct, but she's alive. Again."

"Was there a funeral and burial?"

"Yes. I'm sorry, I know how this sounds."

Silence. "Sir, I don't know how to help you. You say she was buried and now she's alive? That's not possible."

"I don't understand it myself," he admitted. "Is there some sort of procedure for unusual circumstances, like an inquest? I may have to reverse all the paperwork regarding her death."

"Well, I'm just the records supervisor. The best I can do is transfer you to our chief medical examiner."

"That would be fine."

"Mister Holder, is this some sort of prank?" Walter Garrett asked after Len repeated his story.

"No sir. I promise I'm telling the truth, and I can prove it. I still have my mother's birth certificate and driver's license. Your records will have her fingerprints, won't they?"

"They should, yes. In this county, all bodies are fingerprinted before burial."

"Then suppose I bring my mother and her paperwork to your office? You can take a fresh set of prints."

"Mister Holder," the man said sternly, "I don't mind telling you, all this sounds looney, for lack of a nicer word. What's your purpose here?"

"Mom's Social Security and Medicare benefits stopped when she died. I can't get them restarted until she's declared alive, and I need someone with authority to do that."

"Where is your mother now?"

"Napping in the living room. I didn't want her to hear this. She doesn't seem to know she's been dead."

There was a skeptical silence. "So what happened? Did she just appear out of thin air?"

"Something like that. Look, could we put aside the notion that I'm crazy and focus on the evidence?"

"Mister Holder, before we go any further, I'd like to point out a few things. If I determine that a mistake has been made, I'll have to start an inquest. That will include exhumation of the body – if it's still there – and an inquiry into how an unjustified death declaration and burial occurred. Furthermore, falsification of public records is a civil misdemeanor, but in serious cases, it can lead to heavy fines, even imprisonment. By filing a petition, you could be held liable for the consequences if you held power of attorney at the time of your mother's death."

"I understand. I'm willing to accept the risk."

"Well … all right. Can you bring your mother and her records to my office at 10:00 o'clock tomorrow?"

"We'll be there."

"One last thing, Mister Holder," Garrett warned. "If you carry this request to the federal level, Medicare and Social Security could charge you with attempted fraud."

"I guess I'll just have to chance it."

"In that case, I'll expect you tomorrow morning. Goodbye."

Mom awoke from her nap in time to watch an *Oprah* rerun while Len, having second thoughts, browsed Wikipedia for false death reports. Everyone knew the one about Mark Twain who, when his demise appeared in the *New York Journal,* replied, "the report of my death is an exaggeration." Circus man P.T. Barnum's fake obituary was deliberate. Nearing death at eighty-one, he persuaded the *New York Evening Sun* to print it in advance, so he could read what people said about him. Author Rudyard Kipling, after a magazine announced his death, wrote, "Don't forget to delete me from your list of subscribers." Len remembered a wild rumor from the Sixties that Paul McCartney of The Beatles was killed in a car accident. Fans around the world believed it for years afterward.

Some cases were more serious. John Darwin, a British prison officer, was declared dead after his disappearance in 2002. Five years after his wife cashed in his life insurance, Darwin showed up at a London police station, claiming amnesia. It was a scam that landed both in prison. In 2011 Sarah Moretti, charged with shoplifting in Kentucky, escaped punishment after a fake death certificate claimed she died of a drug overdose. Her second arrest in Nashville the following year exposed the fraud. Federal prosecutors charged Ryan Riley Meganack of Alaska with staging a fatal boating accident in 2016 to avoid imprisonment for assault. In 2017 Tysen Benze of Michigan hanged himself after his girlfriend sent a false text message about her suicide. There was no word about how the girl dealt with her guilt.

There could be other consequences. Though Mom had outlived all her friends, many people at church still remembered her, including Jacob Lawson, the preacher who conducted her funeral. Sooner or later, she'd want to resume attending Sunday services. Imagine the reaction when she walked through the door. What an Easter sermon *that* would make. Word would spread. The tabloid TV shows would be clamoring for interviews, asking her about God, Heaven and Judgment Day.

Questions Len would like to ask her himself.

Bored with TV, he returned to his farm novel but couldn't come up with a transition from the Ruth-and-Charley scene. Len had been struggling with the story for years, with no end in sight. Every time he felt like giving up, a new idea popped into his head, sending him back to his laptop with renewed enthusiasm. Writing, he decided, was the mental equivalent of labor pains.

He searched the house for *Jude the Obscure,* a novel he'd been reading two nights earlier. Unable to find it, he thumbed through an old writers' magazine. "Don't try to be perfect at first," the article counseled. "Just let your imagination run free and let your fingers fly. If you make a mess, you can always clean it up later."

Like many aspiring writers, Len had a computer file full of messes. When *his* imagination ran free, it crashed into brick walls. His alcoholic story was a good example.

It was now 10:45. The liquor store closed at midnight. If Nick waited a little longer, he could claim victory: twenty-four hours without a drink.

The early part of the evening hadn't been so bad. He'd occupied himself with preparing dinner, washing dishes, even catching up on his long-neglected housekeeping. He had one bad moment when he carried out the trash. The last whisky bottle he ever expected to see lay atop the pile.

He lingered over it for a moment. It was like abandoning an old friend. There were a few drops left in the bottom. Nobody would notice if …

No! He slammed the lid down and hurried back to the house.

Seventy-two minutes to go. You can do it, Nick told himself. Just get over this hump and you'll be free. No more hangovers. No more drunk driving tickets. No more sneers from the counterman. *What, you again? I just sold you a quart last night!* Why couldn't people do their jobs without passing judgment?

The minute hand crawled toward eleven. Nick's hands trembled as he placed some Joni Mitchell on the record player. Concentrate on the lyrics, he told himself. By the time the music's finished, it'll be past midnight. But the rhythm only marked the seconds ticking away until the store was locked up.

It would take twelve minutes to get there, assuming the traffic lights were with him. What if he had a flat tire? Worse, what if he didn't have enough money? He checked his wallet. Just enough for a pint. A pint would settle his nerves until morning. That didn't count as drinking. It was therapy.

Raindrops spattered the windows. If the weather worsened, it might slow him down. Even if he left now, the store might close before he got there.

Nick sprinted out to the car and raced through the rain, heedless of red lights. The deluge made the blacktop road almost invisible. Never mind. The store was only a mile away now, and there'd be little traffic under these conditions.

Suddenly, a dim figure swam into view. The man's head turned in time for Nick to see his startled expression as the car bore down on him, the tires skidding on the wet pavement, too late to swerve ...

Then what? Did Nick kill the man? Maim him for life? Or did God intervene at the last moment? Len had abandoned the story. It sounded too much like *The Lost Weekend*.

The idea sprang from Len's memories of his older brother. But Garth wasn't exactly an alcoholic. His drinking stemmed from some inner turmoil that Len had never understood.

At mid-afternoon, a weatherman appeared on the TV with one of those five-second teasers. "Enjoy the sunshine while you can," he said. "There's a big bump in the road ahead for this weekend. Details tonight at 6:00."

"I hope it's not rain," Mom remarked. "Might ruin the cotton harvest."

"I thought farmers were always happy to get rain," Len said.

"They are if it comes at the right time. But a hard rain after the bolls open can destroy your whole crop. That's what finally wiped out your grandfather."

The weatherman was tall and gangly like Mister Teague, Len's seventh-grade science teacher. The class was a major turning point in his boyhood. The students sat in rows of six each. Len's desk was directly in front of Ronnie Hudson, a tall, hulking boy, big for his age. Ronnie cared only about football and spent class time drawing obscene pictures and passing them around the room. After Mister Teague sent him to the principal's office, Ronnie behaved for a couple of days. Then he decided it might be fun to poke Len in the back with his pencil.

"Ow!"

Mister Teague looked up sharply. "What's the matter, Len?"

"Nothing, sir."

The teacher resumed his slide show of oceanic life. A few seconds passed before Ronnie gouged Len harder. "Stop it!" he whispered. Ronnie blew him a kiss. The class giggled.

"What's going on?" Mister Teague demanded. He surveyed the room. "One more disturbance and we'll stop and have a pop quiz! Got it?" He returned to the slides.

Quietly, Ronnie began drawing pictures on the back of Len's new white shirt. Fuming, he weighed his options. His only fight was a no-decision with Dickie Spruell in third grade, when the teacher pulled them apart after Dickie broke Len's glasses. Each boy got ten licks with a wooden paddle. Len also got a lecture from Mom. "Do you have any idea how much eyeglasses cost?" she railed. "I was saving to put new tires on the car. Now they'll have to wait!"

Ronnie outweighed Len by forty pounds. If Len turned and struck him, he'd be a dead duck. If he complained to Mister Teague, Ronnie would finish the day washing blackboards, dusting erasers, or writing an essay on Why I Should Pay Attention in Class. Afterward, Ronnie and his fellow thugs would ambush Len in the schoolyard.

Mom, of course, wouldn't care whose fault it was. "I spend all day working to keep you kids fed and clothed, and look at you! Why can't you sit quietly in school, do your lessons and behave like you've been taught? What will the neighbors say? 'Poor Sharon Holder, widowed and left to raise a brood of delinquents all by herself.'" Len would try to explain about Ronnie, but Mom would find some way to twist everything around. She always did.

He couldn't move to another desk. Mister Teague seated everyone in alphabetical order, to make his roll call easier. So Len sat there and took it, his face burning, the kids stifling their giggles as Ronnie licked the pencil with a flourish and began a new sketch. Len would have to wash the shirt before Mom got home from work. But that wouldn't end the torment. Once Ronnie chose a new victim, he was on a mission. Len prayed for him to suffer a football injury, or appendicitis, or a cerebral hemorrhage.

As Len passed from seventh grade to eighth, then into high school, other persecutors joined in the fun. Whitey Jones poured orange soda over his head in the cafeteria. Mike Toler tripped him in the hallway, the other kids cackling as he crashed to the floor. Two other jocks pinned his arms in the locker room and twisted his fingers until he cried out in pain.

"Why don't you try out for football or basketball?" Joey suggested. "Then they'd respect you."

"Who wants respect from goons and morons?" Len sulked. "Besides, I'm no good at sports." His tryout for Little League catcher had ended when the pitcher's fastball smashed him right in the mouth. As Mom scrubbed the blood from his shirt, she grumbled over the cost of stitches.

"You're not being fair, Len," Joey insisted. "Not all athletes are bullies."

"Easy for you to say. All the guys on the team are your pals."

"That's because I help out at practice every day. You just have to know how to talk to them."

"You can't talk to those Neanderthals! A sock in the jaw is all they understand."

"That's not true. Look at Tim Wesley. He's the best running back we've got, and he makes the honor roll every semester."

"Then he must be a freak of nature," Len retorted. "Remember Dixon Jones, that All-Pro lineman who retired a few years ago? Turns out he graduated from high school with only third-grade reading skills. They gave him a free ride through college because he was a star athlete."

"Len, you're a snob," Joey said. "These guys play sports because they're good at it, just like you write stories because you're good at it. We all have different talents, and they're all gifts from the same God."

"Well, I don't use my talents to pick on people."

Year by year, the injustices mounted. Len withdrew into himself, bitterly pigeonholing all athletes as street punks.

Late that afternoon, Joey's voice emerged again from the empty bedroom. He was talking about the great year Tom Brady was having with his new team, the Buccaneers. Mom didn't seem to notice. She was watching Dr. Phil advise a young mother with a rebellious child.

"Mom, what would you like for supper?" Len asked during a commercial.

"Whatever Olivia makes is fine with me."

"I told you, Mom. She doesn't work for us anymore."

She looked at him sharply. "What? Since when?"

Since your death, he thought. But he couldn't tell her that. "She left the home health agency."

"But ... why would she do that?"

"Don't worry. I'll stay with you until I can make new arrangements."

Unable to bear the distress on her face, he went to the kitchen and put a couple of frozen dinners in the oven. Mom picked absently at hers. Len was both sympathetic and mystified. How could she remember Olivia, her TV shows and her key lime pie, but not remember being dead?

After supper, he endured *Wheel of Fortune* in silence. Pat Sajak and Vanna White must be great actors to smile their way through four decades of the same dull ritual. Len was in no position to criticize. He had squandered his own life in routine office jobs. It was Miranda who had made the past thirty-seven years meaningful.

Tonight's TCM movie was *Death Takes a Holiday,* starring Frederic March. "I remember this," Mom smiled during the opening credits. "It came to the old Prairie Theater when your father and I were courting."

"How long was that before you got married?" Len asked.

"Oh gosh! A month? Six months?"

They concentrated on the film. Death, posing as a visiting prince, tries to discover why human beings cling to life so desperately. He falls in love with a young woman and refuses to return to his job unless she goes with him. She agrees, forsaking the young man who adores her.

The ending disturbed Len. How could she throw her life away so impulsively? How could Death be so selfish?

Len's father was only thirty years old when death took him. Will Holder had left his wife, his children and his farm to defend his country. Growing up fatherless, with the attendant consequences, Len often found it hard to understand God. Look at the way He treated Job, an innocent pawn in a wager with Satan. Job cursed the day he was born, but God wouldn't allow him to die in peace. Yet, He didn't hesitate to snatch away Len's father in a death game between power-mad tyrants.

"You're missing the point, son," Mom had explained. "Job questioned God's authority. It wasn't his place to do that."

Her answer wasn't good enough for Len. To him, God's actions were often cruel and inexplicable.

"Why did God punish Adam and Eve for eating the forbidden fruit?" he asked his Sunday School teacher. "If he didn't want them to eat it, why did he put the tree there in the first place?"

"He did it to test them, Len," Mister Wallace replied. "To see if they would obey him."

"But the serpent told Eve it was okay to eat the fruit."

"She shouldn't have listened to the serpent."

"But if she didn't know anything about good and evil, how could she know the serpent was lying?"

"She didn't have to know. She should have done what God told her."

The other kids looked from Len to the teacher, like fans at a tennis match.

"What about that guy Uzzah, who tried to keep the Ark of the Covenant from falling over? God struck him dead, right on the spot."

"He broke another commandment. God said that nobody was to touch the Ark."

"But it would have hit the ground!"

"God would have stopped it."

"How do you know?"

"That's the whole point of the story, Len. Uzzah should have had faith."

But faith was precisely what Len lacked. Everywhere he looked there was injustice and hypocrisy. People claiming to be Christians banned Negroes from their churches, schools, restaurants, even their neighborhoods. Christians in white robes bombed black churches and lynched Negroes who got out of line.

When he came of age, Len rejected the Church, indignant at its failure to take a stand on civil rights, Vietnam, and other issues of the day. Mom, who had raised him in her parents' congregation, took his decision personally. One by one, each of her children had turned their backs on her.

The final film credits were rolling across the screen. "Mom, what else did you and Dad do when you were courting?" Len asked.

"Wasn't much you *could* do. Nobody had any money in 1934. A movie date was a big deal. Tickets only cost a quarter, but a quarter could buy you two pounds of hamburger, or ten pounds of potatoes. In summer, we took evening walks on the farm roads. We didn't have a radio, so Bess Borden let us sit in her parlor and listen to *Amos 'n' Andy* or *Jack Benny*. On Saturday nights we sat by the fire and read the Bible aloud. Sometimes we attended church socials. It was a happy time, all things considered."

Len was intrigued. She rarely spoke fondly of the past.

"How did Dad propose to you?"

She chuckled. "He didn't, not exactly. I didn't even know he was interested until the day he came over to help us pick cotton. Papa wondered how he could spare so much time when his own family was busy harvesting. Will made some excuse or other until Papa realized he was doing it to be around me. He dragged his cotton sack up one row and down another, wherever I was working, with his sleeves rolled up so I could see his muscles. Papa couldn't pay him, so he invited him to supper."

"So he never said, 'Will you marry me?'"

"It was later, after Will's daddy fell off a horse and broke his leg. His mother was poorly, so they had to move in with her sister. Will dropped out of high school and took over the farm. We were sitting on the porch one evening when he said, 'Sharon, farming's awfully hard work. I think I need a good wife to help me. What do you think?' I told him it made sense to me, and that was that."

"And that was his proposal?" Len asked. "Doesn't sound very romantic."

"It was to me. I was afraid he'd never propose at all!"

Len thought of those YouTube videos. Suitors in superhero costumes showing up at the girl's office with diamond rings. Football players dropping to their knees on the fifty-yard line. Surprise parties. Airplane banners and skywriters. Disconcerting for the girl if she hasn't decided yet about the guy.

"Where did Dad get the money for your wedding ring?" Len asked.

"It's just glass," she smiled, holding it up to the light. "Your father bought it at the dime store. He promised to buy me a real one someday, but we were always just barely getting by. Then Pearl Harbor came along." Will Holder was drafted immediately into the Army. For several months, Mom, Garth and Cindy followed him around the country, returning home after he shipped overseas. Len and Joey were conceived during their father's brief furloughs.

After the fateful telegram came from the War Department, Mom removed the ring. Decades later, when she drew up her will, she asked to be buried with it. "We'll still be married in Heaven," she assured Len.

It was past nine o'clock. "I'm not sleepy yet," she said. "How about some cocoa?"

"Sounds great." They went to the kitchen. Len warmed some milk in a pan while Mom sat at the table, her eyes roving over the cross-stitch figures on the wall. "Did you say Barbara Lazenby made these for me?"

"No, you did it."

"When?"

"Oh, long ago. Back in the 1980s." He brought two steaming cups to the table.

"I could have sworn Barbara got a newspaper writeup for winning the arts competition at the county fair."

"She did, but that was for china painting." Len studied his mother closely. That haze was clouding her eyes again. "So you don't remember all these cross stitches?"

"Well, they look familiar but … I don't know."

"You used to spend hours working on them, especially after you left the VA."

"The what?"

"The Veterans Administration. Don't you remember that either? You were office manager in your last sixteen years."

"The VA! Oh, yes." She frowned and sipped her cocoa.

"After you retired, you and Barbara met for lunch every Thursday, then spent the whole afternoon right at this table, working on crafts."

"Well … if you say so." Her eyes grew wistful. "Len … Barbara's dead, isn't she?"

"Yes."

"I thought so. After you mentioned her name during lunch, I got to thinking about her, but I just didn't want to believe it." She sighed. "I miss her."

"So do I."

They finished the cocoa in silence. Mom took her cup to the sink, washed it, dried it, and lined it up neatly beside its mates in the cupboard. "Good night, Len." She shuffled off to bed without a hitch in her walk.

He went to his room to dig her records out of the file cabinet. There was a death certificate dated November 2, 2013, and a burial certificate dated four days later. He studied them, trying to imagine tomorrow's conversation with the medical examiner.

That night, he dreamed Miranda was sinking in a bog. Unable to reach her, he tried phoning 911. His finger kept pressing the wrong keys.

The Farm Tree

BY LEONARD HOLDER

"All right," John said, "calm down and tell me what happened."

"I wasn't doin' nothin'! I just —"

"Anything. You weren't doing anything."

"Anything." Terry rubbed his eyes to unblur his vision of Dad, kneeling before him. "And Joe Waddell came up and punched me right in the stomach!"

"Then what?"

"He pushed me down in the dirt and dared me to do something about it. Everybody was standing around us yelling until Miss Perkins sent us both to the principal's office. After that, Joe yanked my ear and said he was gonna fix me for getting him in trouble."

"Why didn't you hit him back?"

"Mom said not to."

"I told him to stay out of fights, John." She dried Terry's tears with her apron.

"Ruth, the boy has a right to defend himself."

"I don't want him to grow up like that Eli Carson. They finally had to put him in reform school and he still turned out rotten."

"That whole family's rotten." John returned to Terry. "Son, are you afraid of Joe Waddell?"

"Yes," he sniffed.

"Your brother's not afraid of anybody."

"Gene's older than me. And Joe's big and mean! Make him leave me alone, Dad!"

"Well ..." John turned thoughtful. "I guess I could do that. I'm bigger than he is. I'll bet I can punch him in the stomach harder than you can."

"Do it, Dad! He deserves it!"

"But that would make me a bully too, wouldn't it? Now, I could complain to the principal or Joe's parents. But what do you think would happen then?"

Terry slumped. "All the kids would call me a sissy."

"That's right. Terry, Joe picks on you because he thinks he can get away with it. You have to show him he can't."

"But he'll hurt me!"

"He's hurting you right now! Do you want to go through life being afraid all the time?"

"No sir."

"Terry, let's try something." John raised his palm. "Make a fist. That's good. Now, hit my hand as hard as you can."

Terry hesitated, then struck it. "You can do better than that. Put your shoulder into it."

A loud smack followed. "Ouch!" John flapped his hand. "Terry, if you hit Joe like that, he'll never bother you again."

"How do you know?"

"Bullies are mostly cowards underneath. I've seen my share of them."

"What about Mister Marsh? He chewed me out today, and it wasn't even my fault!"

John took the boy's small hand in his large one. "Son, I'll make a deal with you. The next time Joe Waddell picks on you, you've got my permission to clobber him. And if you get in trouble, I'll fix it with Mister Marsh. Now, go wash your face and do your chores."

Ruth waited until Terry left the room. "John, I don't want my boys fighting!"

"Neither do I. Let's wait and see what happens."

The next afternoon, Harlan Waddell drove into the farmyard. Gene and his dad were out front, fixing the water pump.

"Driskill, your son busted my boy's nose at school today. I want to know what you're going to do about it."

"I've already done something about it."

"What?"

"Told him to aim for his teeth next time."

Harlan's face turned red. "You belong to the same church I do! Is this your idea of being a Christian father?"

"Is it yours?"

"What are you talking about?"

"Harlan, you know Joe's been bullying other kids the whole school year."

"He's no bully! I just taught him to stand up for himself!"

"Well, that's what I taught my son."

Harlan glowered. "Driskill, I can make a lot of trouble for you. I'm a Mason and a charter member of the Rotary Club. The mayor's a personal friend of mine."

John grabbed the man's shirt and pulled him within an inch of his nose. "Harlan, I didn't spend three years in combat to mince words with some draft-dodging car salesman. Now, you shove off before I get a notion to stand up for *my*self!"

"Can he really make trouble for you, Dad?" Gene asked as Waddell's car sped away.

"Let him try. God doesn't bring us into this world to be victims." He turned back to the water pump. "Let's pull this piston valve. I think it's corroded."

Wednesday

During the night Len crept into his mother's room to see if she was still there. In the darkness, he could hear her breathing. He went back to bed and lay awake for an hour, listening to Joey's voice.

"I'd have to go with Justin Herbert as Rookie of the Year," it said. "He's been phenomenal since he stepped in for Tyrod Taylor."

Joey went on to rave about Davante Adams, describing his pass-catching as "a work of art." Len snorted. If a literary critic called *The Scarlet Letter* a touchdown, people would laugh at him.

Three o'clock in the morning. Why was Joey on the air so early? His show was timed to catch rush-hour commuters.

After a while, the voice went silent, either because Joey stopped talking or Len fell asleep.

Shortly before dawn, he dreamed that hordes of slobs were invading the house, digging through Mom's closets and looting her cabinets. Two of them ripped out the fireplace and turned it into a barbecue pit. A guy in a sweaty undershirt sank into Mom's favorite chair, cracked open a beer and lit a cigar. His kids jumped up and down on the sofa. "Stop them, Len!" Mom pleaded. He tried to chase them away, but his arms and legs were paralyzed.

He awoke with a sense of failure. Daylight peered through the window. Through Mom's door, he could hear her humming "Two Little Clouds" and filling the tub with water.

While she bathed, he tried phoning Cindy again. She still didn't answer. Neither did Miranda. This wasn't like either of them.

Len's appointment calendar for December 2 was blank, although Wednesday was the day for weekly staff meetings. He called his office number and got a recording. Too early, he supposed. Chad was probably dropping his wife off at her job. Sylvia would be at the gym for her morning workout. Still, the phone forwarding should have kicked in. This was Sylvia's week to be on call.

While making coffee he turned on the local news. "Good morning!" the anchorwoman chirped. "Here are today's top stories. Police break up a drug ring operating out of an abandoned building downtown. The Chicory City Council votes today on next year's budget. And a powerful cold front will invade our region late Sunday night."

Mom stayed in her room so long that he finally knocked on the door. "Come in!" She was digging through her dresser drawers. "Len, I can't find my Bible."

"Why are you looking for it?"

"For Sunday School, of course!"

"Mom, this is Wednesday, not Sunday. We're going downtown this morning."

"Oh!" She looked up blankly. "I got all dressed up for nothing."

"That's okay, you look nice." She wore a lavender dress with a white sash and matching shoes. Mom had always been a fanatic about appearances, even in the old days. "Just because we live in a renthouse doesn't mean we have to dress like hobos," she told her children. She browsed fabric shops for discounts and used Grandma's old treadle machine to make dresses for Cindy. She used bluing to keep the boys' jeans looking new and hung them on stretchers to prevent wrinkling. In those lean years, Mom spent little on herself. A plain skirt and blouse were sufficient to draw stares and whistles from men she passed on the street.

Even after her promotion to secretary boosted her earnings, she continued to check the newspaper ads for bargains. By the time her children were grown she was an executive, able to afford the upscale boutiques. She added prim little hats and matching gloves to her Sunday morning ensemble. Through the Seventies, she clung to formal attire while younger women opted for jumpsuits, peasant dresses and bellbottoms.

Then she got old. Arthritis rose up to defeat her in battles with pantyhose and high heels. "I never thought I'd see the day when women wore pants and flats to church," she remarked sadly. "Now, I'm one of them."

As she entered the kitchen, Len suddenly remembered her medical diary. What if Mom saw those hospice entries?

The diary wasn't on the kitchen counter where he'd last seen it. "What are you looking for?" she asked as he searched the cabinet drawers.

"Did you see a spiral notebook around here?"

"No. Why are we going downtown?"

"Oh. There's, uh, some sort of mix-up in your records at the courthouse." He peeked into the laundry room. No diary.

"Why do I have to go? You've been handling my business for years."

"They might have questions about you that I can't answer."

He hoped she was still confused enough to absorb the lie. Mom's first symptom of dementia appeared shortly after her eighty-fifth birthday when he found her at the kitchen table, trying to balance her checkbook. "I don't know what I'm doing!" she wailed.

"Don't worry, Mom. I'll take care of it." The checkbook, normally accurate to the penny, was a chaos of miscalculations and omissions going back four months. The debits were in the credit column, and she had added when she should have subtracted. It was the start of a gradual slide into memory lapses, confusion, and finally, helplessness.

He couldn't find the medical diary. Maybe it was in his room.

"Can Olivia come downtown with us?" Mom asked.

"Olivia's not working for us anymore. Don't you remember?"

She sank into a chair. "Len, did I do something to make her mad at me?"

"I'm sure there's some other reason."

"She was my friend. Who's going to stay with me now, while you're at work?"

"I'll find somebody else."

"I want Olivia," she murmured.

"Come on. Let's have some breakfast and you'll feel better."

"I'm not hungry."

He persuaded her to eat a yogurt cup and had one himself. Lately, Len was inclined to soft foods to soothe his indigestion. Nothing – Rolaids, Alka-Seltzer, Maalox – could pacify it. Another old-age malady, he supposed, like backaches, high blood pressure and liver spots. Thank God his brain still worked.

Mabel Darby waved at them from across the street as Len backed out of the driveway. Mom waved back. Mabel didn't seem surprised. She sat in her usual spot on the porch, sipping coffee.

Mom brooded silently during the trip downtown while Len felt the old burdens descend on him: drive her to appointments, fill her prescriptions, buy her groceries, take care of her house repairs and yard work. Pay her bills, handle her investments, file her tax returns. Keep track of her vital signs, watch over her every free minute. Meanwhile, his job had demanded attention, often at night and on weekends. The tug of war lasted for years, the pressure and responsibilities draining. There were recurring urinary tract infections, emergency hospitalizations, two lengthy hip rehabs, special medical supplies to buy. And the tedium of sitting through hours of television with her, when he could have been writing. For the first time, Len appreciated what it must have been like for Mom, raising four kids by herself.

It occurred to him that somewhere along the line, he'd forgotten how to have fun. Not the spontaneous fun of childhood, but camaraderie. By the time he was a teenager, Len had little in common with other boys. While they played sports, he read novels. While they danced to rock and roll, he listened to Mozart. While they bragged about backseat seductions, he dreamed of chaste kisses under moonlit skies. On Friday nights, Len's classmates formed caravans to the drive-in movies, speeding joyfully past Turcot's Market where Len worked, bagging groceries. He was a world unto himself until his senior year, when Loretta Weaver entered his life.

As he drove into the parking lot Len said, "Mom, we'll have to wear facemasks in the courthouse. There's a virus going around."

"A virus? What is it?"

"COVID-19. It's like the flu, only worse. Masks help prevent the spread."

"I haven't heard a thing about it," she said. "When did it start?"

"About a year ago." He opened the glove compartment. There were no masks. "That's funny," he said. "I bought a new package of them last week." He searched under the seats.

"I don't see anybody else wearing masks," Mom said.

She was right. Bare-faced people were coming and going through the courthouse doors.

"I wonder why?" Len said. "Masks are mandatory on county property, and the vaccinations haven't started yet."

"So what do we do?"

"Show our faces like everyone else, I guess."

For someone so important, Walter Garrett was hard to find. The medical examiner's office was buried – appropriately – in the courthouse basement, at the end of a shadowy hallway. The wooden outer door had a frosted glass pane with no name or number. An unmasked receptionist directed them to a small inner office whose only advantage over a cubicle was a single glass wall reaching all the way to the ceiling.

Forensic and toxicology books filled the shelves behind Garrett's desk. Len barely had knee room to sit across from him. The furniture was ancient. The splintery wooden chairs creaked. It was like walking into a Dashiell Hammett story.

Garrett looked a lot like Don Stern, Len's old boss at Gaston Publishing. He was stout, with a ruddy face and bushy hair. Gaston was one of several tedious jobs where Len found himself counting the minutes until five o'clock each day. His coworkers piddled, dozed at their desks and ignored each other. Don himself rarely spoke, except when dumping a fresh pile of manuscripts on Len's desk. "I need these out by Friday," he said gruffly.

Garrett was courteous at least, shaking Len's hand in violation of another COVID restriction.

"This ID expired fifteen years ago," he said, examining Mom's driver's license.

"Yes, but you can still check her thumbprint against your records, can't you?"

"Possibly."

"The mug shot's a good one," Len said. "You can tell it's her."

Garrett peered through the glass at Mom, seated beside the secretary's desk. The girl had fetched Mom some coffee and was chatting with her.

"What happened to the mask requirement?" Len asked. "I thought you'd be up to your neck in death certificates."

"What are you talking about?" Garrett said.

"The pandemic. Don't you have to certify all the virus deaths?"

The man eyed him warily. "What virus? The only virus I know about is the flu, and the death rate is normal for this time of year."

"Never mind," Len said hastily. He already sounded like a nut. "What about my mother's paperwork?"

Garrett inspected her death certificate. "This seems to be in order. I recognize Harley Bishop's signature. He's the deputy M.E. Where's she — where *was* she buried?"

"Perpetual Care Gardens."

"She looks mighty healthy for ninety-six." He flipped through the funeral home documents. "Mister Holder, you said on the phone yesterday that your mother just popped up out of nowhere. How can you expect anyone to believe that?"

"I wouldn't believe it myself if I hadn't been there."

"Tell me how it happened."

"It was Monday morning. I woke up and found her standing in the living room."

"Were there any heavenly lights or noises, like the movies?"

"Nothing. Just Mom, singing an old lullaby."

"Did she say anything about being dead?"

"I haven't asked her about it. Not directly, anyway. She seems disoriented, like she doesn't know where she's been. I don't want to scare her."

Garrett put the papers aside. "Tell me about yourself, Mister Holder."

"Like what?"

"I want to know who I'm dealing with. I've got a reputation to protect. You're asking me to do something very bizarre."

Len nodded. "Fair enough. I'm a claims adjuster for Winslow & Grant. My supervisor is Miranda Thomas. Here's our office number if you want to verify my employment." He produced a business card. "I'm seventy-eight years old. I've been with the company for thirty-seven years. It's a small regional office; Miranda, myself and two other agents."

"Seventy-eight? Why aren't you retired?"

Len smiled. "I like the people I work with."

"How'd you get into insurance?"

"It was a roundabout thing. After college, I discovered that a bachelor's degree in English Literature is worthless unless you become a teacher, which meant slave wages in this school district."

"Couldn't you teach at a university?"

"Probably, if I got a master's degree. But I didn't have the money for graduate school, so I took whatever jobs I could get while I worked at home on my novels. My first job out of college was clerking at the city library. Then I wrote ad copy for local radio and TV. My brother helped me get that job."

"Oh!" Garrett's eyebrows rose. "Is your brother Joey Holder?"

"Yes."

"Gosh, he's great! I see him on the football broadcasts all the time. You must be proud of him."

"I am." He meant it, despite the way Joey fawned over jocks.

"Sorry, you were saying?"

"Anyway, advertising was a good creative opportunity, but there was no chance for advancement. So I tried various other jobs. I spent eight years at Gaston Publishing, proofreading textbooks."

"Sounds dull."

"It was," Len said, with feeling. "Winslow & Grant was my salvation."

"Do you have a family?"

"My coworkers are my family."

Garrett drummed his fingers on the desk. "English major, eh? And you write novels. Anything I might have read?"

"No, I'm sorry to say. I've never been able to finish one."

"I see." The man eyed Len dubiously. "This thing with your mother isn't some fantasy, by any chance?"

"Mister Garrett, I wouldn't know how to make up a story like this."

The examiner returned his attention to Mom, who was still chatting with the secretary. "Do you mind if I ask her a few questions?"

"Well … try not to upset her. She's a little confused."

Len fetched his mother. "Mom, this is Mister Garrett. He's helping me clear up some problems with your paperwork."

She took a seat. "What's the trouble?"

"Sometimes records get mixed up, Mrs. Holder. I need you to verify some things about your personal history. Can you tell me when you were born?"

"Certainly. September 10, 1917."

"Which hospital?"

"There weren't any back then. Paxton Memorial got built in 1928, during the oil boom. I was born in our farmhouse, two miles north of town on County Road 21."

"Did you attend school here?"

"Sometimes, when the family could spare me. Farm chores kept us busy, especially at harvest time."

Garrett made notes as Mom named her grandparents, parents and two brothers. "Our family brought in the first bale of cotton three years in a row during the Great Depression. The prize was only fifty dollars, but that was a lot of money in those days."

"So I've heard."

"That land was in our family for three generations."

Len had seen the farm only once, back in the early Fifties, when Mom drove her children north of town one Saturday to show them where she grew up. Vast stretches of cotton blanketed both sides of the dusty road, peppered here and there by houses and barns. Dozens of braceros roamed the fields, shoving handfuls of cotton into long canvas sacks.

"See that section over there?" she said, pointing through the windshield. "Cindy, that's where I used to spend my days working when I was your age. All that land was ours before the bank took it."

54

Mom's face fell as they approached their destination. The old farmhouse stood at the end of a potted road, its yard overgrown with weeds. The porch sagged, the chimney was crumbling, and all the window glass was broken. Rotted wooden siding littered the ground, exposing patches of tarpaper. The barn roof had caved in, and the big wagon door hung lopsided from a single hinge.

"What happened to it, Mom?" Len asked.

"Looks abandoned. I guess the bank took a partial loss, anyway." A tear trickled down her cheek. "My poor Mama and Papa." She turned the car around and drove home without another word.

Garrett was still scribbling. "Mrs. Holder, what's your address?"

"1217 West Colgate."

"How long have you lived there?"

"Fifty-three years. Remember that, Len?" She turned to him. "We moved in on October 1, 1957, right before the Sputnik scare."

"I remember," he said, surprised by her sudden acuity.

"Did your husband sign the mortgage agreement?" Garrett asked.

"No, we lost Will in World War II. I got a job with the VA a few years afterward. Widows of servicemen got preferential treatment back then. That's how I raised my children and saved enough to get out of that old rental house off the main highway. After we moved, Dave Gutersen turned it into an ice cream parlor."

"Oh, I remember that place," Garrett smiled, "before the redevelopment. It had little holly trees, and a nice green lawn around it."

"That's because I wore myself out fertilizing, watering and keeping it trimmed," Mom said grimly. "Unlike some neighbors I could mention."

"Such a shame, too. There's a strip mall there now."

"What?" she exclaimed. "When did that happen?"

"Seven or eight years ago, I think."

She frowned. "Seems like only yesterday we stopped by for milkshakes."

Garrett returned to his notes. "Mrs. Holder, do you belong to any civic organizations?"

Len listened in amazement as Mom rattled off a list of ladies' clubs and volunteer groups, plus her lifelong church membership. Yesterday, she didn't recognize her own house. Today, she was an encyclopedia. And that hazy look in her eyes was gone.

"Why do you need all this information, Mister Garrett?" she asked.

"Just to make sure your file doesn't get mixed up with someone else's. Would you mind if I took your fingerprints?"

"What?"

"All our records include fingerprints. That way if there's any confusion, we can tell whose records belong in which file."

"Fingerprints are for criminals!" she declared indignantly. "I've never done an illegal thing in my life!" She turned to Len. "Why did you bring me here? Am I accused of something?"

"Mom, don't you remember being printed when you got your driver's license? It's the same thing."

"Mrs. Holder, you're not in any kind of trouble. This is a routine procedure. Look." Garrett drew a fingerprint scanner from his desk drawer. "We don't even use ink anymore, so you won't have to clean your hands."

She eyed the thing resentfully. "All right."

The sensor beeped as Garrett pressed each digit to it. "You have such soft hands, Mrs. Holder! Do you use skin cream?"

"Yes. Back on the farm, we used lard. It worked just as well."

He smiled. "That's what my mother says."

"Did your mother grow up on a farm, Mister Garrett?"

"My grandparents had an orange grove in California. They had to lease it out, though, during the war. Grandma got a job in an aircraft factory while my grandfather was off fighting the Germans. After the war, they returned to farming. My mother still says the oranges in the grocery store are pathetic. She got spoiled picking them fresh off the trees every day." He took Mom's other hand.

"Len has no idea what his grandparents and I went through in those years. Are yours still living?"

"No. My mother owns the farm now, although she's got a tenant manager running it. Grandpa bottled his own orange juice and sold it at a roadside stand every weekend. He used the same orange press to the day he died."

"Len's generation doesn't know what hard work is. They sit around in air-conditioned offices and torture each other with computers."

Garrett laughed. "Sometimes I think I'd rather pick oranges for a living." He put the scanner away. "You've been very helpful, Mrs. Holder. If you'll wait outside for a moment, I'll wrap things up with your son. Thanks for coming in today."

Len turned her over to the secretary. "Well, what do you think?" he asked, closing the door.

"This information should help confirm her identity," Garrett said. "We may want to contact the school system, the VA and her church. And the funeral home, of course."

"Please don't tell them any more than necessary. I don't want a bunch of rumors to get started."

"We'll be discreet. Say, is she right about buying her house in 1957?"

"Yes, why?"

"She said she's owned it fifty-three years. That only brings us up to 2010."

Len calculated on his fingers. "You're right. That's three years before she died."

"Doesn't she know what year this is?"

"I don't know. It hasn't come up until now."

"Hmm. Well, let me do some checking and I'll get back to you." Garrett read over his notes. "I don't know how much good I can do you. Medicare and Social Security are inundated with fraudulent claims. Even with documentation, you'll never convince the federal government that one of its citizens is back from the dead."

"There's something you're not telling me," Mom said in the car.

"What do you mean?"

"I'm not a child, you know! I was dealing with the government before you were born. Who do you think took care of all *your* paperwork when you were a kid? Who was that man? Why was he asking all those questions? And having your mother fingerprinted!" Shadows of old resentments crossed her face. "You think because I get confused sometimes you can put something over on me. Nobody asks questions like that unless there's something wrong."

"Mom," he lied, "the other day I got a letter from Social Security. They're threatening to stop your benefits unless we can clear up a paperwork mistake in Washington."

"How did that happen?"

"Maybe it was a computer glitch. It'll be all right after I fill out a form and provide some documents."

"Well, why didn't you say so in the first place?"

"I didn't want you to worry. You've had your share of problems."

She snorted. "You kids! You keep everything to yourselves. You didn't even tell me about Olivia until I dragged it out of you. Garth was the same way. After we lost your father, he stopped talking to me. Acted like I drove Will away! I couldn't do a thing with him. Always sneaking away from school, the truant officer showing up at my door with all the neighbors watching. Smoking cigarettes, stealing soda pop and candy from Turcot's Market. Nothing I could do straightened him out. I'd paddle him, and he'd just laugh at me and run off with his hoodlum friends. The next thing I knew, he was shoving a permission letter in my face so he could join the Marines. I signed it for his own good, figured they'd make a man out of him. Meanwhile, I had you, Cindy and Joey to take care of. 'God, where did my life go?' I asked Him. One minute I was an innocent farm girl, the next I was a slave to a houseful of ungrateful kids."

It was an old lament, with additional verses castigating Len, Cindy, Joey, dead relatives and ex-neighbors. Mom had a volcanic streak that could erupt without warning. Arguing with her only made it worse. She seemed to relish complaining.

"The Marine Corps went in one ear and out the other," she continued. "Garth spent his separation pay on liquor and chasing girls. That slutty Billie Jo Riley! She gives him a son neither of them wanted, then takes up with some motorcycle bum and runs off to Montana. Garth leaves Danny with me while he bounces from cotton gins, to roofing, to ditch digging, to roughnecking, one hard-labor job after another. No wonder the boy grew up feeling rootless."

The only things worse than Mom's tirades were her silences. When Len was a child, they frightened him. "What's the matter, Mom?" he would ask timidly. "Just leave me alone," she muttered as she grimly cooked meals, mopped the floor, or scrubbed the bathtub. Then the house was thick with apprehension, the kids tiptoeing around fearfully or hiding in their rooms, wondering what they'd done wrong now.

Oh God, he prayed. Don't make me go through this again.

"Mom," he interrupted as she paused for breath, "I'll take care of the paperwork problem. You don't have to worry. Say, why don't I take you to lunch? You've always liked The Tea Garden."

She sighed. "I guess so. Yes, that would be nice."

There were no "Takeout Only" signs outside the restaurant and no masked people inside. Len dismissed the virus from his mind and seated his mother at a table.

He always felt out of place in The Tea Garden, with its pink wrought-iron furniture, frilly wallpaper and artificial greenery. It was primarily a lunch spot for businesswomen. They eyed Len suspiciously, as though he'd blundered into the ladies' room.

The waitress reminded him of Marilyn Travis, his first date in high school. Sixty years later, the memory still embarrassed him. Cheerfully, the girl took their order, complimenting Mom's dress and recommending a new quiche-and-salad combo. Mom's gloom lifted. She enjoyed being fussed over.

A nearby clamor drew their attention. A dozen young women sat around two tables pulled together. One of them was opening a package covered with bassinets and teddy bears. From the box, she withdrew a hands-free baby carrier and slipped it over her shoulders. "AWWW!" the ladies cooed. A fleeting smile crossed Mom's face.

While awaiting their food, Len decided to test her again. "Mom, do you remember who won the last Presidential election?"

"Obama, of course. I hope John McCain runs again next time. We haven't had a war hero as President since John Kennedy."

After lunch, she asked, "Are you going to the office this afternoon?"

"No. I don't want to leave you alone. They'll call if they need me."

"In that case, how about taking me to the manicurist? My nails look terrible."

Another female sanctuary. With an inward sigh, Len proceeded to the salon. In former days he had tried dumping this errand on Olivia. She had to turn him down. The home health agency forbade her to chauffeur clients. Liability reasons, they explained.

"I'm going to try a different girl this time," Mom said as he parked the car. "The last one left the edges ragged and they snagged my nylons."

For forty-five minutes he sat in a plastic chair while an Asian woman filed, buffed and polished Mom's fingernails. To pass the time he scanned news headlines on his phone browser. In Georgia, masked volunteers were recounting election ballots. Meanwhile, emergency distribution of a new COVID vaccine was due to begin within the next two weeks.

COVID and the Presidential race had been the dominant stories for almost a year now. Why had there been nothing about them on TV this morning?

He looked around. The only people wearing masks were the manicurists, protecting themselves from nail dust and chemical vapors. All of them looked Vietnamese, a byproduct of the war that had defined Len's generation. After the fall of Saigon in 1975, actress Tippi Hedren helped establish a beauty school for Vietnamese women. It was a huge success, with more than 130,000 nail salons scattered across the U.S. To Len, it was a small atonement for the brutality his country had inflicted upon theirs.

The manicurist was finished. Mom approached the cash register. "Len, look in my purse," she said. "There should be a coupon in there, and I don't want to chip my nails digging for it."

In her wallet, he found a coupon for a free manicure. There were also two credit cards. Len searched his memory. Hadn't he cut those up after she died?

"Sorry," the manicurist said. "This coupon not good." She pointed to the expiration date: December 31, 2010.

"What do you mean?" Mom snatched it away from the girl. "Look, it says right here, good till the end of this month."

"She's right, Mom. This coupon is ancient."

"You stay out of this!" Mom glared expectantly at the woman, who hesitated, then smiled. "Is all right. You long-time customer. We honor it anyway." Mom headed for the door. Embarrassed, Len slipped the woman fifty dollars. "I'm sorry," he whispered. "She's not feeling well."

"That was ugly, Mom," he said on the way home. "That lady's probably as poor as you used to be."

She ignored him. "Look at this. The polish is starting to chip already. They never use enough topcoat. That's the last time I go back to that place!"

After changing clothes, she conked out on the sofa. In her last five years, the naps had lengthened into mysterious lethargies. Len would return from mowing the yard to find the TV silent and his mother in bed, in the middle of the afternoon. "Do you feel sick?" he asked. No, just a little tired, she said. But the naps gave her headaches, and the headaches made her depressed, especially on weekends, when Olivia wasn't around.

As she slowly declined but hung onto life, she adding whining to her criticisms. "Why is it so cold in here? Why do my knees hurt? Why do I have to take so many pills?" Then she'd start dragging up old conflicts again, picking at Joey, berating Cindy, every word dripping acid. "Mom," Len would sigh, "I've heard all this before. What makes you think I want to hear it again?" Pouting, she would slink off to the bedroom for another nap. A secret part of him wished she would expire in her sleep and set him free. But she always woke up, sometimes in good spirits. "Let's have some of that key lime pie!" she'd exclaim brightly, or "Let's go to the park!" Then Len felt ashamed.

Shaking off the mood, he tried calling Miranda. Voicemail again! Now he was worried.

He phoned his office. "Winslow & Grant," a man's voice answered.

"Chad, this is Len."

"I beg your pardon?"

"Is this Chad?"

"No sir, this is Ron Stokes. May I help you?"

"Oh, I must have – wait, did you say Winslow & Grant?"

"Yes sir."

"Uh … is Chad or Sylvia there?"

"I'm sorry, we don't have anyone here by those names. Are you sure you've called the right number?"

"Yes! I'm Len Holder. I work there."

"Maybe you want the sales office. This is the claims department."

"That's right, that's my department."

Phones rang insistently in the background. "I'm sorry sir, can you hold please?" There was a brief silence. Who in the world was Ron Stokes?

"Sir, we're in a kind of crisis here today. May I take your number and call you back?"

"What crisis?"

"Our office manager got hurt in a traffic accident last week. It's a small staff, so as you can imagine –" more phones rang. "I'm terribly sorry, would you mind calling back later? I've got to go." He clicked off.

Len checked his contacts menu. The number for Winslow & Grant was correct. What was this about an accident? Was that why Miranda didn't answer?

A crisis, the man said. Len should be there to help. But he couldn't leave Mom alone.

Redialing the number gave him a busy signal. He browsed the web for local accident reports. A few collisions, but no victims he recognized. Len phoned the hospital. There were no Miranda Thomases listed as patients.

He texted Chad and Sylvia:

Worried about Miranda! Where R U?

What Len had told Walter Garrett was only half the truth. He did like his coworkers. But that was Miranda's doing. Before she took over the little claims office, he'd forgotten what it was like, looking forward to seeing another person each day.

"Len?" Mom sat up. "How long have I been asleep?"

"About twenty minutes. Do you feel better?"

"Better how?"

"Never mind." Maybe she'd slept away her bad mood. Before her death, Olivia told him she often broke into monologues while he was at work, rehashing old family squabbles. Olivia took them in stride. Listening to dyspeptic old people was part of her job.

Even in childhood, Len had sensed a fundamental sadness about Mom. He wished he knew how to comfort her but couldn't think of what to say. He thought he found a solution in second grade when his teacher's storybooks began to spark his imagination. Perhaps he could write a story for his mother; something with a happy ending, like *Cinderella* or *The Little Engine That Could*. He pictured her reading it with pride, her face growing brighter with each page until she put the story aside to embrace him.

One day after school he sat at the kitchen table, writing with pencil in his Big Chief tablet:

Leonard And The Fox Box
A Story By Leonard Holder

Once upon a time, there was a Boy
hoo lived by the side of a Big Rode.
He lived in a nice howse with his Mom
and his Brother and his Sister. They
were very hapy until one day a big
truk came roring down the rode and a
Large Box fell out the back.

The boy opened the box and fownd 4
Foxes inside. There was a Mama Fox
and a Daddy Fox and too Little Baby
Foxes.

The boy hoos name was Leonard
asked the Foxes to come live with him
and his Mom and his Brother and his
Sister. But the Daddy Fox said, "Foxes
cant live in howses like people. We
want to live in the vakant lot across
the rode."

So the boy hoos name was Leonard karried the box across the rode to the vakant lot. But the Mama Fox said, "Foxes cant live in a box. I have to cook dinner in the ovin, and the ovin will set the box on fire."

So the boy searched the vakant lot for a place to bild a howse. But there wasnt inny wood. So he asked the Daddy Fox what to do.

"I will ask my Baby Foxes to bild a Fox Din." So the Baby Foxes crawled out of the box and used their claws to dig a Din in the durt. Soon they had a big Din with a roof made of grass and weeds that groo in the vakant lot.

The Mama Fox and Daddy Fox were prowd of the Baby Foxes. But the Mama Fox said, "There are no beds in the Din for us to sleep." So the boy hoos name was Leonard tore the flaps off the box and made them into beds. There was a big bed for the Mama

Fox and the Daddy Fox and too little beds for the Baby Foxes. And every day, the boy hoos name was Leonard browt food for the Mama Fox to cook in the ovin that she made from a tin can she fownd in the vakant lot.

And the Baby Foxes groo up and went to skool and made lots of munee so the Foxes didn't have to live in the vakant lot innymore. They bilt a Big Fox Din next door to the boy hoos name was Leonard and lived hapully ever after.

It took Len three afternoons to finish the story. "Mom, look what I wrote for you!" he announced when she got home from work.

"Don't pounce on me the minute I walk through the door!" she snapped. "Give me a chance to catch my breath."

He followed her to the living room, where she collapsed on a chair and took off her shoes. She stretched out and closed her eyes with a heavy sigh. Len fidgeted beside her, shuffling the papers noisily. "Oh, all right, give it to me." She leafed through it rapidly. "Your spelling's terrible! What are they teaching you kids in school these days?" She cast the story aside and went to her room to change clothes.

Len gathered up the pages and showed them to Cindy. She praised his work, gently corrected his spelling, and urged him to keep writing.

Len's earliest memory of Garth was watching him unpack a duffle bag following his Marine Corps discharge. There was no room for him in the old renthouse, so he slept on the sofa and went off each morning to whatever job he could find. In the evenings he listened to country music on the radio while Cindy helped Mom with the supper dishes. Sometimes he played checkers with Len and Joey on the living room floor.

Having a man around the house was a new experience for the boys. Garth was lean, tanned, and muscled. Standing erect, he could lift Len with one hand and Joey with the other. He smelled like sweat and cigarettes. Sometimes he smelled like whisky.

Mom nagged him about his habits, demanding that he put on a shirt to cover up his Marine Corps tattoos. She reproached him for setting a bad example until he yelled at her to shut up. The kids gaped at him. You didn't dare talk that way to Mom. Tight-lipped, she went about her business as Garth lit another cigarette and studied the checkerboard, pretending to be stumped.

After their marriage, Garth and Billie Jo moved into a garage apartment near the warehouse district. Mom wouldn't let her other kids visit them. "Shantytown trash," she called Billie Jo after learning about her daughter-in-law's barroom escapades and the couple's violent quarrels. It wasn't long before Garth was back on Mom's sofa, with his infant son Danny sleeping on his chest.

By the time Len was ten, Garth was far down the road toward perdition. On his infrequent visits, he was usually drunk, out of a job or both, begging Mom for another of the loans he never repaid. The scenes always ended with Garth storming out of the house, Mom weeping in the kitchen, the younger children cowering on the front porch.

The last time Len saw him, Garth was distraught, asking Mom if she knew where Danny was. "Billie Jo got a custody order," she explained. "I couldn't stop her. The judge said parenthood rights outweighed everything else. I don't know where she took him." Garth hugged Cindy and his little brothers and left. Forever, as it turned out.

The next day, Mom lined up Cindy, Len and Joey in a row like soldiers. "I want it understood that I'm not going through this again!" she barked. "Your father may be gone, but I've still got his leather belt, and if you ever pull any stunts like Garth did, I'll wear you out!" The belt remained in her closet, untouched. Mom's tongue was a much more fearsome instrument.

Len came to dread her return home each evening. The smallest things could set her off. "Who left this wet towel on the floor?" she would screech. "What are your shoes doing in the driveway?" "Why hasn't somebody taken out the trash?" Her discipline went far beyond the usual demands like "Don't talk with your mouth full" and "Get your elbows off the table." It was a rage that tore through her children like a buzzsaw, leaving wounds that never healed.

She had stern rules. Only Mom could open the mail. Only Mom could answer the phone. Those were grown-up jobs. And never tell any family secrets. "People love to gossip," she warned, "even if they don't know what they're talking about."

In Len's day, children expected to be disciplined. They went to school each morning with the knowledge that misbehavior would result in severe consequences. But with Mom, there was no reward for good behavior. No praise, no hugs, no warmth.

"Don't think people are going to love you for doing what's right," she told them. "Nobody praises me for showing up for work and doing my job every day. All I get for that is money to keep a roof over our heads and put food in our stomachs."

One evening shortly after Mom began working at the VA, she came home, marched straight to her room and closed the door. The minutes ticked by, the silence growing heavier.

An hour passed. "What are we supposed to do about supper?" Joey asked Cindy.

"I don't know." The three of them sat anxiously in the living room, afraid to move, watching the sunlight fade. The house was almost dark when she finally emerged, her face haggard and tear-streaked. At the sight of her children, she sighed. "Cindy, come help me, please." They went to the kitchen to prepare a late meal.

Twenty-four years after Garth vanished, his son appeared at Mom's door. Danny didn't remember his grandmother but had always wondered about her. Mom was thrilled to see him. He looked so much like Garth, who looked so much like Dad.

"What happened to your father, Danny?" Len asked.

"I was hoping you knew," he answered sadly. Billie Jo had dragged her son around Montana from one boyfriend to another, growing plump, then fat until none of them wanted her. She worked in cafés and truck stops, Danny mothered by the other waitresses, tolerated by the owners, cleaning tables and learning the business as he grew. Billie Jo, an unrepentant smoker, died of lung cancer at forty-six. "She never amounted to much," Danny admitted, "but she'd do anything for me." He was prosperous now, owner of a small West Coast restaurant chain. He kissed Mom and left her some pictures of his wife and children. After that, he kept in touch for the rest of her life. Mom cherished every letter and phone call.

While Mom watched her afternoon TV shows, Len stepped into the kitchen to phone his office again. He got a busy signal. Further texts and calls to Chad and Sylvia went unanswered. Something terrible was happening.

He tried phoning Miranda's husband. There was no answer at his office or their home.

"God, please bless Miranda," Len prayed to the sky outside the kitchen window. "Please let her be all right."

"Did you say something?" Mom called.

"No, nothing."

Before Miranda became his boss, Winslow & Grant was just another paycheck. Each day Len worked his claim files, left at 5:00 o'clock, and spent the evening alone in his apartment, reading the latest prize-winning novels. On weekends he went through the motions of a dutiful son: keeping Mom's lawn trimmed, cleaning the rain gutters, watering the shrubs, fixing leaky faucets, and trying his best to keep her company. That was the hard part. Mom didn't want to hear about his job. Len didn't want to hear her gripe about the past. So they let TV fill the void, like strangers in a doctor's waiting room. Sometimes Len suspected that his visits just made her lonelier.

Len himself preferred solitude. He had little in common with his coworkers. Both were twentyish and single. Chad Norris was a night owl, restlessly cruising bars and looking for Miss Right Now. His eyes were always bleary, and he often nodded off at his desk while filling out claim forms.

Sylvia Torrejo was a workout fiend, with a grim intensity that Len found unsettling. She harbored a smoldering hostility toward men, the result of an incident she wouldn't discuss. She wore sweats to the office and spent every free moment training for marathons and lifting weights, as though she had something to prove. One day, Len almost tripped over her doing pushups in the hallway. "Sorry," she panted, "there's not enough room in my office. Fifty-two … fifty-three … fifty-four …"

The claims office was a ship with no rudder. Bill Taggart, the manager, had lost a son in Vietnam and rarely came to work anymore. Eventually, he simply disappeared, leaving a muddle of jumbled files and lost paperwork.

When Miranda was hired to replace Bill, Len resented her at first. He didn't mind working for someone half his age. But her exuberance overwhelmed him.

"This place needs some personality!" she declared to the blank walls and industrial carpet. She stayed in the office all that first Saturday, transforming the bland workspaces into mini-galleries, at her own expense. When Len arrived Monday morning, he found silk flowers on his desk. Prints by Matisse and Monet surrounded him. Chad's walls were full of tapestries and mosaics. The mountain biking posters in Sylvia's office now coasted through a jungle of hanging ferns, ivies and spider plants. "I've been attacked by *Better Homes and Gardens*!" she exclaimed.

From the start, Miranda took a personal interest in her staff. "You look tired," she told Chad. "Why don't you settle down? You're too old to be burning the candle at both ends."

"I like hanging out," he shrugged. "It's fun."

"What you need is a steady girl," Miranda decided. "Someone who'll make you a good wife, and I know just the right one. Marylou Reed, a soprano in our church choir."

"Church!" he exclaimed.

"Don't look at me that way! She's cute! You'll like her."

"Is this a job requirement?"

Miranda ignored Sylvia's muscles and concentrated on her face. "You have such beautiful eyes and healthy skin! What kind of makeup do you use?"

"I don't," Sylvia scowled. "Makeup's for attracting men. They're not worth the trouble."

"Well, I think you're gorgeous. You remind me of the women in those old Renaissance paintings. You ought to be a professional model."

"Thank you," said Sylvia, thawing a little.

"How'd you get into claims?"

"I wanted a job that didn't chain me to an office. I like fieldwork."

"Oh, I'm so glad to hear that!" Miranda trilled. "Some insurance adjusters hate that part of the job."

Ignoring Len's reticence, she settled into the chair beside his desk to pry personal information out of him. "Joey Holder's your *brother*? That's so cool! I've never met anyone famous. You'll have to introduce him to Frank. Joey's his favorite sports announcer."

Unprompted, she regaled him with stories about her college friends and her courtship with Frank. "He was a graduate assistant to one of my business professors. I asked him to help me study for finals. Then we started dating. Finally, he introduced me to his parents, and I just fell in love with his whole family."

Miranda always dressed in bright colors. Her rosy cheeks and round physique prompted Chad to dub her Mrs. Santa Claus. Fittingly, she wore an elf hat to work at Christmastime and put gift baskets of homemade fudge and cookies on everyone's desk. Exactly the wrong kind of boss for an introvert like Len.

But as the months passed, his defenses crumbled under Miranda's cheery assault. Shyly, he told her about his English Lit degree and his fruitless efforts at novel writing.

"Oh, I wish I had a talent like that," she said wistfully. "My mother made up her own fairy tales when I was a little girl. I can't even write a coherent sentence. Len, from now on you're my editor!" She made him proofread her business letters and memos. A good thing, too. They often contained unintentional humor.

Dear Mrs. Nichols:
I wish to convoy to you my wishes for your prompt recovery.

Dear Mr. Thurston:
Rest assured that none of your problems are insolvent.

To Claims Staff:
Headquarters advises that your next pay increase will be retrogressive to January 1.

Miranda's grammatical weaknesses belied her passion for organization and efficiency. "Look at this!" she cried, sorting through a mountain of documents that her predecessor had left behind. "Some of these people have been waiting five or six months!"

"I know," Len replied. "Bill sort of let things go after his son died."

"What happened to him?"

"Vietnam. He stepped on a landmine."

"Oh, how terrible! The poor man!"

Miranda kept long hours those first few weeks, refiling claims and apologizing over the phone to neglected clients. Sometimes she took a break, bursting into Len's office with tidbits about her family.

"Guess what? My dad bought a Harley! Mom's furious about it, she thinks he's going through his second childhood. Speaking of which," she added, digging through her purse, "look at this picture of Vic feeding Darla her bottle. Aren't they both cute?" She refreshed her lipstick. "I'm taking a long lunch break today. Frank's taking me to Harrigan's for our anniversary. It's the same place where that waitress spilled water on him last time. He feels sorry for her and wants to give her another chance. Isn't that sweet?"

Occasionally, Miranda brought Vic and Darla to work. They ricocheted around the office like pinballs. Over the years Len watched them grow from toddlers to teenagers to parents. Then Miranda brought her grandchildren to show off like trophies. Len came to miss her during vacations and business trips. The office was dreary without her.

Miranda worried constantly about her weight but seemed powerless to control it. Each time she showed up with paper plates and plastic forks, Len knew what was coming. "I'm starting a new diet tomorrow, so you guys have to help me finish this coconut cream pie." The next morning she'd exclaim, "I lost half a pound overnight, even with the pie, so I'm already on a roll! Starting today, I'm on yogurt and carrots." But Miranda was a stress eater. By Friday the pressure would get to her, and Len would spy a half-eaten Hershey bar on her desk. "It's just for today," she'd grin sheepishly. "I'll get back on my diet next week when things calm down." Which they never did. The lapses didn't discourage her, though. "I'm going to get this weight off, you watch. In another month you won't recognize me." Len smiled. He liked her just as she was.

The afternoon waned. Len ignored Joey's voice drifting in from his empty room and threw together a supper of tuna sandwiches and potato chips. He'd never been much of a cook. Before moving in with Mom he'd relied largely on frozen dinners and fast food. Then he read a magazine article claiming that people who ate seafood tended to live longer.

Detesting the smell of fish, he compromised with canned tuna or sardines, slathered with mayonnaise or mustard to kill the taste.

After Mom died, he missed coming home to Olivia's evening meals. Grilled chicken with a tossed green salad. Cheese potatoes and onion soup. Homemade tamales smothered in chili. Olivia always had the table set for Len and his mother, sometimes with a lighted candle for ambience. He felt like the husband in a 1950s sitcom.

Mom frowned at the sandwiches as she took her seat. "Why are you using my best china? Wedgwood is for guests and special occasions."

"Well, it's not much use sitting in the cupboard."

"Len, this is expensive bone china!" she insisted. "I don't want it to get chipped like our old dishes. The way you kids banged them around in the sink, they weren't fit for serving ourselves, much less our guests."

Kids. It was always "you kids," even after he turned sixty-five. Sometimes Len felt he had never grown up in Mom's eyes, and never would.

"These chips are stale," she grimaced, reaching for another one.

"I guess they've been in the pantry too long."

"We didn't have nice dishes when I was a girl," she recalled. "Just dingy old glassware that I washed outdoors at the hand pump."

"Yes Mom," he sighed, "you've told me all that before."

"That was my first job. Three meals a day, except when I was at school."

"I know that too, Mom."

"On Saturdays, I scrubbed my hands raw doing laundry with lye soap and a washboard. Oh, there was no *end* of chores! I used to wish we had school year-round so I could sit in a classroom instead of hoeing weeds in the cotton fields. In winter I froze my fingers milking cows at 4:30 in the morning. Mama was on her feet all day, cooking and cleaning the house. The only time I saw her relax was to sew patches on Papa's overalls or darn his socks by the light of a kerosene lantern. Later, the Depression came, and that made things even worse. When the war started, your uncles Alvin and Clyde enlisted. I was married by then, so that left Mama and Papa to run the farm alone."

Len hadn't heard that part before. "Didn't they feel guilty, going off like that?" he asked.

74

"Papa insisted. They would have been drafted anyway after Pearl Harbor. He didn't want his boys to wind up in the infantry. Volunteers could choose the Navy or Army Air Corps, where they had a better chance of surviving. Papa was right. Both boys came home safe. Too bad he didn't live to see it."

"I always wished I could hear Dad's war stories," Len said. "What did he talk about while he was home on leave?"

"Oh … I don't remember," she shrugged.

"Didn't he tell you about his missions? Fighting the Japanese?"

"It was a war, Len. Some things are best forgotten." She reached for another chip.

The evening news had nothing about COVID or the accident Ron Stokes mentioned. Len worried about Miranda all through the weather report, sports news, and *Wheel of Fortune.*

Tonight's movie classic, *A Guy Named Joe,* starred Spencer Tracy as a dead bomber pilot, jealously watching another pilot woo his grieving sweetheart. Len and his mother had seen it before, so he put on a DVD of *The Lawrence Welk Show.* Corny, but one of Len's few pleasant family memories, the kids gathered around the Philco on Saturday nights, listening to Big Band tunes while Mom ironed their Sunday dress clothes.

Ken Delo appeared on the screen, singing to the camera:

*"So rare, you're like the fragrance of blossoms fair
Sweet as a breath of air, fresh as the morning dew."*

"That was your dad's favorite song," Mom beamed. "Will used to sing it to me across the cotton rows. He had a beautiful voice."

Len smiled at the thought of his parents as teenagers, stealing a moment of romance amidst the toil of harvest. What could have turned that lovestruck young girl into this bitter old woman?

Lawrence's gang sang their goodnight song. Len followed his mother to the bedroom, watching for danger signs as she drew a fresh nightgown from the bureau. "You don't have to fuss over me," she insisted. "I'm not helpless."

"I'm worried about you falling. Remember, the doctor told you to dress sitting down."

"I'm okay. You go do whatever it is you do at night." He returned to the living room, half expecting a loud thump and a cry of pain from the bedroom. It had happened twice before.

What a day! A resurrection crusade with a bureaucrat. A tongue-lashing from his dead mother. Chaos and mystery at the office. And a pandemic that had disappeared from TV but was still viral on the internet.

It was funny, Len reflected, how the human mind worked. When confronted with a miracle, like your mother's return from the grave, people scoffed. But when the Harry Potter fantasies appeared, everyone rushed out to buy them. "Willing suspension of disbelief," Len's college professor called it.

Len himself had always loved fiction. It contained a substructure of truth where he could find shelter from reality. People baffled him. His moody mother, his bullying schoolmates, grouchy teachers, aloof girls — he didn't seem to belong anywhere. The people in books were often puzzling too, but their creators understood them, and they helped Len to understand. Fiction was a welcome balm in an ugly world.

Len had always been the reader of the family, even more than Cindy, their best student. He excelled in his English Lit courses, identifying as he did with disillusioned characters like Jude Fawley and Holden Caulfield. In high school, he read *The Catcher in the Rye* to tatters.

Mom's resurrection is fictional, too, he decided. And I'm waiting to see how the story turns out.

He searched the house again for *Jude the Obscure* but still couldn't find it. He'd boxed up all his books when he gave up his apartment to live with Mom. Her own shelves contained nothing but old Harlequin paperbacks, neglected as her vision deteriorated. After Len inherited the house, he kept meaning to discard them to make room for his own collection. He never got around to it. Like the refrigerator magnets and cross stitches, the paperbacks were part of the house, and the house reflected its owner's personality. Seven years after his mother's death, Len still felt like an intruder.

Returning to the living room, he thought how cozy it was. The plush beige carpet. The patterned accent curtains on the windows. The matching guest chairs whose arms seemed to wrap around you like a blanket. When Mom was alive, all the furnishings and decorations had seemed frivolous to Len. To Mom, they formed a barrier against her hard-scrabble past. Now they were merely relics destined for an estate sale.

On the coffee table lay *Catch-22,* Joseph Heller's irreverent novel about a World War II bomber squadron. Strange that he hadn't noticed it before. He didn't remember digging it out of storage.

He opened it to the first chapter. Captain Yossarian was faking illness to avoid flying combat missions. While the doctors puzzled over him, he enjoyed meals in bed and censored the enlisted men's mail. Outside the hospital, other airmen prayed to be sent home before the Colonel decided to raise their mission requirements. No chance; the Colonel was campaigning for promotion to General. Heller's air force was a bedlam of cowardice, corruption, incompetence and petty ambition, a shocking rebuttal to the heroic war movies of Len's youth.

During his mother's decline, Len had cherished late night as his private time. With Mom in bed and the TV silenced, he could read or work on his novel until he got sleepy. In college, he had quickly learned that most artistic people lived and died in obscurity, recognized, if at all, only after their deaths. He tried writing a few short stories but couldn't finish them, uncertain of what he was trying to say. To his dismay, Len discovered that his greatest talent lay in performing routine office tasks. Even Winslow & Grant wasn't fulfilling until Miranda took over, so he continued to dream of becoming a prize-winning novelist.

He skimmed through *Catch-22.* The mess officer was using American combat planes to run his own business, buying up farm products and reselling them in a shady profit scheme. He even made a deal to let the Germans bomb his own airbase.

The novel's flight surgeon had a problem similar to Mom's, declared dead because he was mistakenly listed with a lost bomber crew. The doctor wandered around insisting he was still alive, ignored because the flight roster said otherwise. Paperwork ruled the world of *Catch-22,* controlled by a demoted mail clerk named ex-P.F.C. Wintergreen.

Though Len admired Heller's wit, *Jude the Obscure* struck him on a personal level. If Jude wasn't meant to be a scholar, maybe Len wasn't meant to be a writer. Only his novel about the farm family showed promise. His other efforts seemed shallow or trite.

In college, Len had tried crafting a story reflecting his romantic frustrations. To his horror, the result read like one of Mom's paperbacks:

> Wendy chewed her nails nervously as the arriving passengers deplaned. Fifteen years had passed since she and Michael said goodbye at this very gate. She still remembered her crippling sense of loss.
>
> "I love you more than anything, darling, but my mother's condition is serious," he explained, embracing her as others crowded around them, clutching their tickets. "She has no one else. It's up to me to do the right thing."
>
> "Michael," she wept, "if you leave like this, we'll never see each other again!"
>
> "I'll write you. I'll call you."
>
> "No, you won't. She'll turn you away from me and swallow you up!"
>
> "What else can I do?"
>
> A voice rang through the terminal. "Final call for Flight 283 to Milwaukee." The tragic longing in Michael's eyes was her last glimpse before he vanished into the departing crowd.
>
> What would he think when he saw her now, middle-aged and sagging? Would he still want her after a life of meaningless affairs? Passengers streamed through the gate, but there was no sign of Michael. Perhaps she'd pinned her hopes on the wrong man …

Len had filed the story in the trash, with the coffee grounds and banana peels.

The Farm Tree

BY LEONARD HOLDER

Dina and her mother sat at the kitchen table, shelling black-eyed peas for supper. Outside, Charley lay on his stomach in the dirt, chirping at a brood of baby chicks and tempting them with bits of grain. In the distance, John steered an orange Massey-Harris harvester over thick rows of maize. The machine had put the farm in hock and cost more than Ruth's grandfather earned in his entire life. But it was worth it.

"You're awfully quiet today," Ruth observed. "Something on your mind?"

"It's nothing."

"Is that so? Do you know what a contradiction is?"

Dina thought for a moment. "It's when you say something that's the opposite of something you said earlier."

"That's pretty close. It's nothing is a contradiction, too."

"Huh?"

"If 'it' was nothing, there couldn't be an 'it'. So when I ask what's bothering you, don't tell me it's nothing."

Dina dropped her pod into the bowl. "Mom, why can't I wear lipstick to school?"

"At your age? Why would you want to?"

"Because Jeanette Booth does. She uses rouge too, and her mother paints her nails every Saturday night after her bath."

"Hmm." Ruth's fingers liberated peas while her eyes studied her daughter. "Twelve's a little young for makeup. Does anyone else wear it, besides Jeanette?"

"No, and that's why all the boys look up whenever she walks into a room, like she's Elizabeth Taylor or somebody."

"Any boys in particular? Ricky Williams, for instance?"

Dina moped quietly. "That's what's really bothering you,

isn't it? Don't you think he already likes you the way you are? Without lipstick?"

"Everything was fine until I got these darned glasses. Now, I look like an owl with pigtails. And all these chores are making my hands rough. Girls are supposed to be soft." Tears welled in her eyes as she ripped savagely into another pod.

"We'll put some lard on them when we get through. Let me show you something." Ruth went to the bedroom to retrieve her picture album. "This is me when I was your age."

Dina's eyes widened. "That's you? It doesn't even look like you!" Ruth's monochrome face was a mass of freckles and blemishes.

"Back then, girls didn't wear makeup until they were sixteen. Your grandma said it looked trashy on a young girl. And she was right. Anyway," Ruth kneeled beside her daughter, "by the time I finished high school, my skin had cleared up. Then I looked like this." She turned the page.

"Wow!" Mom's face was clear and smooth, surrounded by luxurious, wavy hair. Her eyes and teeth sparkled. "No wonder Dad fell for you!"

"Oh no. Dad and I were best friends even when I looked like this." She turned back to the first page. "The romance part came later. Come here." She guided Dina into the bedroom and stood her before the mirror. "That's you on the outside. The part behind the glasses, under the skin, is the part that counts. If you stay true to the person you are on the inside, you won't need makeup to be attractive. Even to Ricky Williams, if he's worth anything." She squeezed Dina's shoulders. "Now, what do you say we get back to those peas?"

They returned in time to see Laura galloping toward the house aboard Silky. She and John waved at each other. "What's she got draped over that horse's neck?" Ruth wondered.

The girl dismounted, patted Charley's head, and swept into the kitchen with a bundle of white fabric. "Here it is, straight from the Sears catalog!"

Dina ran her hands over the cloth. "I thought you decided on tulle."

"Sherry Fincher talked me into organza. It's supposed to be more comfortable for an outdoor wedding in summer." Laura turned to Ruth. "How soon can you start on it?"

"Next week, if Dave Sievers fixes my sewing machine like he promised. Did you find a pattern you like?"

"Right here." She produced a thick McCall's envelope with a bridal sketch on the front.

"Why don't you wear your mother's dress?" Dina asked. "It's beautiful."

"Too old-fashioned. This one's going to be long and slinky." Laura winked seductively at Dina. "Ruth, can I leave this with you? Gene wants me to haul some stock feed out to pasture."

"Sure, go ahead." Laura galloped back up the road as Ruth laid the fabric on the dining table. "Six weeks until the wedding, and Gene's made a farmhand out of her already." She went to the screen door. "Charley, leave those chicks alone! They've already got a mother!"

"I'm teaching them how to hunt for food!"

Ruth sighed. "That boy! No wonder my vegetable garden's all wrecked, with him digging up worms for his babies." She resumed her assault on the peas.

"Mom," Dina asked, "when did you know you were going to marry Dad?"

"Oh, my stars!" she laughed. "I thought he was never going to ask. We'd be sitting on his family's porch after supper, and I could feel him sneaking glances at me, fidgeting, trying to work up the nerve. Then he'd walk me home without a word, and I thought, 'He's waiting until we get to the house.' But he just said goodnight and left. Most timid man you ever saw."

"Dad? Timid? How'd he finally get around to it?"

"One evening we were on the porch, listening to the radio from the living room. Fred Astaire was singing 'Night and Day.' Your dad starting singing along with it. Then I joined in. Somewhere around 'no matter darling where you are,' we looked at each other. His eyes asked the question, and I said 'yes' out loud." Ruth chuckled. "You should have seen the relief on his face."

"What about the wedding? Was it in our church, with bridesmaids and music and lots of flowers? Who picked out the ring?"

Ruth smiled. "I never knew anybody my age who had a big wedding. Everyone was so poor. We couldn't even pay the minister, so Mama invited him to Sunday dinner. Afterward, he married us in the parlor. Your father put his grandmother's wedding ring on my finger and said, 'Until better times.' Then we all had apple pie and milk. He didn't buy me this ring until five years after the war ended."

"You didn't even have a honeymoon?"

"I'm still waiting for that. Maybe after we pay off the loan on the harvester." She studied her daughter. "Why are you so interested?"

Dina sighed. "Weddings. They're so romantic. I can hardly wait!"

Thursday

Len's first act upon waking was to text Chad and Sylvia again. They didn't reply. He explored the internet for news about Miranda's accident. There wasn't any.

The radio show in Joey's room was already underway. "The oddsmakers pick Alex Smith for comeback player of the year," he said. "But for many of us, Ben Roethlisberger is a sentimental favorite. What do you think? Send me a text message with your vote, and I'll announce results at the end of the show."

Len searched the empty closet and peeked under the bed. Nothing. *It's a poltergeist,* he decided. *This house is haunted, and the ghosts are Mom and Joey. Only they're not dead.*

At 8:00 o'clock he phoned his office. An answering service intercepted. "They're closed today," the woman said. "I don't know the circumstances. Our instructions are to take messages."

"I think I'd better drive over there and find out what's going on," he told Mom at breakfast. "You'll have to come with me."

"Why?"

"Something's happened to Miranda. I don't want to leave you here alone."

"Who's Miranda?"

He sighed. "My *boss,* Mom. My boss for over thirty years now."

"I thought you worked for somebody named Bill."

"That was ages ago. Miranda's the one who sent you that nice potpourri basket while you were in the hospital."

"I don't remember." She watched him cut up some strawberries and spread them over two bowls of cornflakes. "I'd rather have bacon and eggs."

"We're out of bacon. Try the cereal. It's better for you anyway." *Listen to me. Preaching healthy eating to the undead.*

She regarded her breakfast morosely. "Len, why can't Olivia come stay with me?"

"I told you. She quit her job."

"Did I say something to hurt her feelings?"

"I'm sure it has nothing to do with you."

"She could have at least said goodbye."

She did, Len wanted to say. She kissed your cheek when you were unconscious, and again as you lay in the coffin.

When Olivia entered their lives, Len had no idea that she and Mom would become so close. Olivia was divorced, trying to support two daughters. Selena was in seventh grade. Delia was sixteen, pregnant and unwed. The culprit, Lucas Gomez, was an overgrown adolescent with no job or sense of responsibility. He hung around when there was food in the house. The baby was Delia's problem. As her delivery time drew near, Lucas found reasons to be elsewhere.

The child died during labor. Olivia, who had looked forward to being a grandmother, was devastated.

Mom tried to console her. "Maybe Delia can get married and have another child."

"I hope so," she replied tearfully. "Even so, your first grandchild is special." She bought a little headstone for the baby's grave with the inscription *Pequeño Precioso:* Precious Little One.

A few months later, Mom was disgusted to learn that Lucas was back. He sat around watching TV with Delia or playing baseball with other idlers in the park across the street. At night he slept outside on Olivia's porch swing.

"What's wrong with that girl?" Mom complained to Len. "Doesn't she know a parasite when she sees one?"

"Stay out of it, Mom," he advised. "It's none of your business."

"If I were you, I'd kick that bum out of the house," she told Olivia.

She shook her head. "It has to be Delia's decision, not mine."

Olivia never let her problems interfere with her job. Except for the baby's funeral, she didn't miss a day in five years, not even the morning she showed up with a black eye.

"What happened?" Mom gasped.

"Oh, just a little memento from my ex-husband."

"Len, get some ice and a dishtowel. Did you call the police?"

"It wouldn't do any good. He'd just lose his job again, get court-ordered counseling, then be back at my door demanding money."

"Why did he hit you?" Len asked as Olivia applied the cold compress to her eye.

"Mateo has bipolar disorder. Or severe schizophrenia. The psychiatrists aren't sure. He only gets violent when he's been doing drugs."

"Olivia, you don't have to put up with this," Mom insisted. "Go to court and get a restraining order."

"That would only make him worse. Anyway, I've got the girls to think about. Usually, Mateo's very gentle and loving. They worship him."

Mom brooded for days. "We've got to do something for her!"

"Like what? We can't call in the law if she won't."

One day Len asked Olivia why she married the guy. "Take a wild guess," she replied sardonically.

"Oh. Sorry. What attracted you to him in the first place?"

"Well, you know how it is when you're a teenager. Mateo had all these ideas about becoming a Latino rock star. He had a terrific voice, and he played guitar like a pro. I believed in him."

"So what happened?"

"No gigs. The nightclubs around town wouldn't book him. The other guys in the band got discouraged and gave up. Then Delia came along, and the bills piled up. We moved from one rent flop to another. Mateo had already dropped out of high school, so he couldn't get a decent job. It was after Selena was born that he started getting delusional. I filed for divorce to protect the girls. It went downhill from there."

"I'm sorry, Olivia," Len said. "You deserve better than this. For whatever it's worth, I hope you know that Mom loves you very much."

"I know," she smiled. "I love her, too."

During breakfast, they watched the news. A typhoon had struck the Philippines, killing at least 5,700 people. The Pope was meeting with Israel's Prime Minister. There was a brief clip of President Obama proclaiming tomorrow a Day of Remembrance for John F. Kennedy.

Len wondered why Obama was speaking. He wasn't President anymore. And what was special about tomorrow, December 4? Kennedy's assassination had occurred on November 22, 1963.

Len remembered that day well. He was in college, listening to a lecture on Henry James, when a weeping coed burst into his classroom with the news. The image of Jackie Kennedy walking to St. Matthew's Cathedral behind her husband's coffin was seared in his mind forever.

Locally, the weatherman forecast a few more mild days before Sunday night's cold front. In sports, Joey recapped an NBA game from last night.

"He looks like he's put on weight," Mom remarked.

Len agreed. "Probably his diabetes."

"Diabetes?" she exclaimed. "Since when does Joey have diabetes?"

"Oh ... umm ... several years now."

"Why haven't you mentioned it before?"

"Well –"

"See what I mean? You kids never tell me anything!"

I've got to watch what I say, Len thought. A lot has happened in the past seven years.

Mabel Darby waved again as they left the house. Mabel's routine never varied. She believed fresh air was the key to good health. Even in winter you could look out the window and find her on the porch, bundled up like an Eskimo on guard duty, her coffee fogging her glasses.

"How bad is Joey's diabetes?" Mom asked.

"He's okay, as long as he takes his insulin and watches his diet."

"I told him that job was going to make him sick. Living on hamburgers and hot dogs in those football stadiums. Sometimes I think he does it just to worry me."

The autumn flowers outside Len's office building looked dejected, awaiting the inevitable. Mom stayed in the car while he took the elevator to the third floor.

A handwritten sign on the Winslow & Grant door said "Closed Temporarily" and referred queries to the home office. Len inserted his key. It wouldn't turn.

"I know this thing works!" he muttered. He knocked several times, in vain. There were no windows to peer through.

After a few more struggles with the key, he phoned Los Angeles headquarters. "Yes, we're aware of Mrs. Thomas's accident," a woman told him.

"Do you know what hospital she's in? The one here in Chicory has no record of her."

"It was my understanding that she had severe head trauma and had to be airlifted to a special facility."

"Oh, no!" Len groaned. "Do you know which one?"

"No. That's all the information we have."

He tried Chad and Sylvia again. Neither of them answered.

Len hadn't wept since his mother's death. Now, his eyes blurred as he rode the elevator back down and stumbled outside. "What's the matter?" Mom asked.

"Miranda's in the hospital. It sounds bad."

"Who's Miranda?"

"My boss, Mom!" he cried. "Can't you remember that?"

"Well, don't bite my head off!"

"I'm sorry, I'm worried about her." Wiping his tears, he took a deep breath and slid behind the wheel.

"Len, it sounds like you're needed here. Why don't you take me home? I can manage by myself."

"There's nothing I can do. My key doesn't work and nobody answers the phone. I'm sorry I dragged you over here for nothing."

"It's all right. I like being out on such a pretty day. Why don't we go visit your father's memorial?"

"Uh … maybe some other time." Mom was buried next to Dad's monument. Len couldn't imagine how she'd react to the sight of her own grave marker. Still, the thought of returning home and sitting through *Family Feud* was too much. "I'll tell you what," he suggested. "Let's go to the park, like we used to. We'll pick up some birdseed on the way over."

"Oh, good idea!" Len headed for the pet store, wondering why Chad or Sylvia hadn't phoned him about Miranda.

They sat on a bench near the pond. Months of dry weather had reduced it to a puddle. A flock of geese and several ducks competed for swimming space. A half dozen doves strutted hopefully around Mom as she opened the seed bag. "You got the wrong brand," she complained. "This isn't Pennington."

"They were out of it," Len replied.

"You should have gone to another store."

"Birdseed is birdseed."

"I like the other kind better."

"You're not the one eating it."

"Oh, you're so stubborn!" She scattered the granules over the dry grass and cooed at the birds. Len brooded about Miranda, lying helpless on some operating table, surrounded by doctors, nurses and beeping equipment.

He once asked why she didn't apply for an executive position at company headquarters. "Who wants to live in Los Angeles?" she said, wrinkling her nose. "Are you trying to get rid of me?"

"You're too smart for a little branch office like this. You can do better."

"So can you."

He shook his head. "I'm too old for career climbing."

"That's not what I mean, Len, and you know it. I know you've got a book in you somewhere."

Miranda had other reasons to remain in Chicory. Her husband ran a successful trucking business. Their children, Vic, Darla and Josie, were active in church and devoted to their school friends. "Besides," she told her three employees, "you guys are my second family."

"We have another family," she declared at their first staff conference. "They're our customers. They're at the mercy of disasters, accidents and criminals. They depend on us to come to their rescue when trouble strikes.

From now on, we're going to treat our customers like members of our own families, and their losses as our own."

Miranda divided their clients into four groups, assigning one group to herself. They phoned all of them to introduce themselves, then followed up with a letter explaining claims procedures. "For faster service," it said, "please call the local number listed above." Miranda hated automated phone menus and suspected her customers did, too. She was right. The claimants were grateful to talk to human beings instead of a recording. Word spread quickly about Winslow & Grant's personalized service. By the end of Miranda's second year, the sales office had logged a twenty-five percent uptick in new Chicory clients.

Miranda set up a rotating system in which the four adjusters worked the big cases in pairs. When a claim involved death, injuries or major damage, one agent handled the paperwork while the other helped the family with emergency cash, food, or lodgings.

The agents took turns being on call and covered each other's absences. The arrangement succeeded because Len, Chad and Sylvia liked Miranda and wanted to please her. In time, they grew to like each other. They shared lunches in the conference room. They celebrated each other's birthdays with candles stuck in cupcakes. Miranda and Frank hosted a Christmas party for their employees every year in their home. Often, their kids dropped by the office after school. Over the years, Miranda's daughters must have charmed Len out of two hundred dollars' worth of Girl Scout cookies.

Miranda's warmth gradually drew Len out of his shell. He went on field visits with her, listening to claimants tearfully describe personal treasures lost to house fires, tornadoes and thieves. Often, Miranda cried with them.

One day they sat by Melanie Carter's hospital bed. Len was totaling out the lady's car after her husband's death in a head-on collision.

"Mister Holder," she whispered weakly, "is there any way you can total out a broken heart?" Len put his claims book aside to embrace the widow as she wept on his shoulder.

To Len's surprise, Chad fell in love with Marylou Reed, Miranda's choir soprano. He stopped bar-hopping and became a regular at her church. The first time Marylou visited the office, Len decided Miranda was wrong.

Marylou wasn't just cute; she had a joyful glow about her that made Len wistful for his own departed youth. Chad beamed like a schoolboy as he showed her around the office, though there was nothing to see but desks, file cabinets and claims manuals. Smitten, as Mom would have said. Len sat with Miranda and Sylvia at the couple's wedding. The following year, Chad and Marylou became parents.

Sylvia continued her bodybuilding but switched to business clothes during work hours. Len approved. Skirts and ruffled blouses cushioned the impact of her massive body. Even her attitude toward men began to soften after she met Demetri Baros, a weightlifter at the gym. Demetri reminded Len of those giant teddy bears you could win at carnivals; big, cuddly and warm-hearted. He worked at his father's Greek restaurant and held moussaka-eating contests on Saturday nights, invariably winning due to the energy he burned up in his daily workouts. Sometimes he brought lunch trays of spinach pie and Greek salad to the office as an excuse to visit Sylvia. He measured his biceps against hers and challenged her to arm-wrestling matches until she broke down in a rare smile.

But Sylvia was a tough catch. It took Demetri almost three years to get her to the altar. "He'd better not try any rough stuff with me," she glowered at their wedding reception. "I'll put him in traction."

"Why aren't you married?" Miranda asked Len one day.

"I'm not very good company," he said. "Besides, both my brothers had marital problems. I didn't want to end up like them."

He was ashamed to tell her the truth: that he'd never known how to approach girls, although as a teenager he was obsessed with them, hardly able to pay attention in class with nymphs like Chelsey West and Tanya Kruger sitting nearby. Girls were mysterious. They formed little cliques and gathered around the lockers between classes, whispering and giggling. They dolled themselves up to attract boys, but sneered if you looked at them.

His first date wasn't even his idea. Marilyn Travis plopped down beside him in Music Appreciation class one morning. "Say, Len, what's your favorite pizza place?"

"Uh ... well, actually, I've never been to one," he stammered.

"You're kidding! You've never had a pizza in your whole life?"

"Just Chef Boyardee." Mom never took her kids to restaurants. Eating at home was cheaper.

"That's terrible!" Marilyn exclaimed. "Why don't you pick me up around 7:00 Friday night? We'll go to Luigi's. They've got this wonderful cheesy crust."

Len was tongue-tied. It was 1960. Girls weren't supposed to ask boys out!

"Well, I ... I guess so. I'll have to ask my mother if I can borrow the car, though."

"Great! Friday night then." She returned to her regular seat as the bell rang. Len's heart raced. Marilyn wasn't as beautiful as Chelsey and Tanya, but she wasn't bad-looking. In fact, as she sat there, listening to a lecture on Brahms, she began to look enticing.

Mom was delighted. Marilyn's father was a prominent dentist and president of the Lions Club. She gave Len the keys to her Plymouth and a twenty-dollar bill, extravagant for a teenage date in 1960. "Have a good time," she said, "but be home by ten."

Marilyn was ready when he arrived. Len escorted her to the passenger seat and got behind the wheel, sweating nervously. He had never sat in such intimacy with a girl before. A light perfume filled the car. Petticoats rustled when she moved. Late evening sunlight glistened through her tawny hair.

Thankfully, Marilyn took charge of the conversation as they headed for Luigi's, merrily repeating school gossip while Len rehearsed his manners. *When you get there, help her out of the car. Open the door and let her enter first. Pull the chair out for her.*

Things went all right until the waiter left with their order. Then Marilyn smiled expectantly across the table. Len's mind went blank.

"How did you like the school play?" she prompted him.

"I, uh, didn't go."

"Well, you didn't miss much, unless you consider *Death of a Salesman* a comedy. The acting was hilariously bad. Do you like drama?"

"I like Shakespeare."

"Blah!" Her nose wrinkled. "I'd like to be in a play sometime. I would have tried out for that one, but I'm behind in History and I've got a paper to write for Civics."

"Oh." Len couldn't think of any other response.

Marilyn tried another subject. "How come you're not in the band?"

"I don't know how to play any instruments."

"Not even percussion? Even my brother can do drum rolls, and he's the laziest person you ever saw."

Len wished the pizza would arrive. Maybe it would give him something to talk about. His necktie choked him. He kept his hands below the table so she couldn't see them trembling.

"How's your mother?" Marilyn asked.

"She's fine."

"You have a married sister, don't you?"

"Yes, but she doesn't live here anymore."

"Do they have any kids?"

"Yes, two daughters."

"How nice! So that makes you an uncle, doesn't it?"

"Yes … yes, it does." Actually, Len was already an uncle to Garth's son, Danny. Mom forbade Len and Joey to talk to outsiders about Garth or Cindy. Garth was the black sheep of the family, and Cindy was struggling through an impoverished marriage.

The waiter brought the pizza. Len placed a slice on Marilyn's plate, then tried to cut his own with a fork. She laughed. "Don't you know how to eat pizza?" She was already chewing away, holding her slice in midair.

"This is the way we eat at home," he replied defensively.

"That's too much trouble. Here." She held a fresh piece to his mouth. As he bit into it, melted cheese slopped over his chin. "Whoops, my fault!" she laughed lightly. Len blushed, humiliated, wiping his chin with a napkin. "Oh, well. Good thing it wasn't tomato sauce falling on your clothes. Your mother would probably have a fit."

"Yes. She would." He lowered his head in shame.

Marilyn's smile faded. "I'm sorry, Len," she said helplessly.

He retreated into himself, concentrating on his plate through the rest of the meal, his first date disintegrating in silence. Neither of them spoke as he drove Marilyn home. "Thank you, Len," she said. "I had a nice time. Don't bother getting out. I'll see you at school." She closed the door and scampered into the house.

"How was it?" Mom asked as he returned the car key.

"Okay."

"Did you ask her out again?"

"I'm tired. I think I'll go to bed." Mom pumped him again the next morning, but his evasiveness told her all she needed to know.

Afterward, Marilyn was polite to him at school, but it was clear that she wanted nothing more to do with him. Len checked out a library book on dating etiquette. It seemed he'd done everything right, except talk.

In November of his senior year, Loretta Weaver approached him in the cafeteria for help with *The Great Gatsby*, their latest reading assignment. Literary conversation always drew him out. Their discussion led to a Coke date after school, then a movie, and Len's first goodnight kiss. For days he walked on clouds. Loretta was plain-faced, but slender and graceful, with light blue eyes and long auburn hair that flared in the sunlight. Len liked to imagine her as Aphrodite, floating among the ruins of Athens in a diaphanous gown.

Unlike Marilyn, Loretta was gentle, probing for topics to make him relax and confide in her.

"Len," she asked as he walked her home from school, "do you think Romeo and Juliet got married just to aggravate their parents?"

"Why would they do that?"

"Think about it. The whole play revolves around a feud between their families. If it weren't for the feud, they might not have gotten involved."

"So you think they married out of spite?"

"It's possible."

Len thought about that. Cindy's marriage had resulted from a rebellion against Mom.

"You've got a point," he conceded. "But I still think it was love. Otherwise, they wouldn't have married in secret."

"Maybe their romance was just a physical attraction," Loretta said.

"But look at the dialogue! There's so much passion in it."

"Oh, well," she said dismissively. "People will say anything in the heat of passion."

The remark bothered Len. He knew Loretta had dated other boys. He couldn't help wondering how far things went.

Len's mother seemed to approve of Loretta. At least she never criticized her, and she was cordial when Len brought her home for dinner one night. Maybe Cindy's elopement had taught her a lesson.

They dated regularly until May when Loretta began talking about the senior prom. They were sitting on her parents' porch, watching the sunset. Loretta's eyes sparkled as she described the dress her mother was making for the occasion.

Len had never considered attending the prom. He was an outsider, he didn't know how to dance, and he was uneasy in crowds. "Let's go see *Exodus* instead," he suggested.

"We go to movies all the time," Loretta said. "The prom is special, something you remember your whole life."

"It'll just be the same football idiots and snobs we see in school every day. I can't wait to graduate and get away from them."

"But Len," she said anxiously, "my mother's already spent a week sewing my dress. What'll I tell her?"

"That's not my fault. You should have asked me first."

"It doesn't work that way. Boys are supposed to do the asking."

He clammed up, the years of abuse and taunts still boiling within him.

"Please, Len. All the other seniors will be there. Won't you do it, just for me?" Loretta pleaded until her tears turned to anger. She rushed into the house, leaving him alone on the porch.

At school the next day she refused to speak to him. All her girlfriends roasted him with angry glares.

"Look, I'm sorry," he said, confronting her in the hallway. "I'll escort you to the prom if it's that important."

"You needn't bother," she replied icily. "I've already been asked."

"By whom?"

"Larry Simmons."

"Simmons!" Len sneered. "That loudmouth? He's got the IQ of a gnat!"

"Well, he's certainly more of a gentleman than some people I know!" She turned her back on him and left. Len spent prom night watching TV with his mother while Aphrodite danced in the gym with Larry Simmons, who couldn't have gotten a date with Medusa.

He lay awake half the night. Was she doing it to punish him? To make him jealous like Jude Fawley, manipulated into helping Sue Bridehead rehearse her wedding to a middle-aged man?

> How could Sue have had the temerity to ask him to do it
> – a cruelty possibly to herself as well as to him? Women were
> different from men in such matters. Was it that they were,
> instead of more sensitive, as reputed, more callous, and less
> romantic; or were they more heroic? Or was Sue simply so
> perverse that she wilfully gave herself and him pain for the
> odd and mournful luxury of practising long-suffering in her
> own person, and of being touched with tender pity for him
> at having made him practise it?

Whatever Loretta's motive was, it worked. "Can we forget the prom?" he begged. "Go back to the way we were?"

"I still like you, Len," she admitted. "But maybe it's best that we see other people for a while."

"I don't want anyone else."

"It'll be good for both of us, to see how serious we are about each other."

"I've always been serious. Aren't you?"

She regarded him frankly. "Len, what do you plan to do with your life?"

"I don't know yet."

"If we got married, how would you support us? You don't like to do anything but read."

"We're just finishing high school! I've got my whole college career to decide."

"I don't want to wait that long."

So it was that on graduation night, Len sat despondently in the auditorium with the rest of his class. Ronnie Hudson slouched beside him, capped and gowned despite flunking almost everything but Physical

Education. Loretta sat two rows back, torturing Len with her presence. On stage, the band accompanied Chelsey West and Michael Jeter in a duet:

> *"When other nights and other days*
> *May find us gone our separate ways*
> *We will have these moments to remember."*

That summer, Len saw Loretta around town with Todd Morgan. He began to stalk them, lurking in the night shadows outside Todd's apartment, watching their silhouettes against the window and waiting fearfully for the lights to go out. But Loretta always left after a couple of hours. Then one night, the lights went out and stayed out. Len trudged homeward, trying not to imagine what was happening in Todd's dark bedroom.

He suffered depression all through his first college semester. In January, Loretta phoned to see how he was doing. Could they go out to dinner? He told her to ask Todd's permission and hung up. That was their last conversation.

Len's few college dates were mismatches. The girls wanted to talk about Fabian, Pat Boone and Jackie Kennedy. Len wanted to talk about Rosa Parks and Martin Luther King. Convinced he had some disqualifying flaw, he sought refuge in literature. "You're going to end up an old bachelor!" Mom complained. So be it. Celibacy was painless compared to the miseries of love.

But nature still held sway. One day he was in the university library, skimming through the card catalog when he noticed Chelsey West at one of the reading tables. With her deep brown eyes and chestnut hair, Chelsey resembled Natalie Wood. In her senior year, she'd been homecoming queen and the star of *My Fair Lady,* the spring musical. Half the gorillas on the football team pursued her. Back in high school, if Len the bookworm had dared speak to Chelsey West, the news would have been a schoolwide joke. But now, away from the old pecking order, she was fair game.

Chelsey glanced up from her reading and smiled. Len smiled back. Her eyes lingered briefly, then returned to the page.

He hesitated. The thought of approaching Chelsey West made him dizzy. What could he say to her? She was The Queen, he was a peasant. He gathered up his books and left the building.

A few days later he saw Chelsey in the student cafeteria. She sat alone by a window, sipping Dr. Pepper through a straw. School talk, that was it! He could ask what she was majoring in. What classes she was taking. How her parents were doing. Build a relationship gradually. Would she like to take a walk? Go to a movie? Marry him?

As Len started across the room, a burly guy in a letterman's jacket brushed rapidly past him and slammed his palms down on Chelsey's table. She looked up, startled. Len couldn't hear their conversation, but their intense whispers, the guy's red face, and Chelsey's fearful eyes left little doubt. It was Link Endicott, an old classmate with an explosive temper. Len watched the drama build until Link grabbed her arm and hustled her out of the cafeteria.

Len felt obliged to intervene, but how? Link could have demolished him with one punch. Anyway, was it any of his business? Maybe they were engaged or something. For days afterward, Len kept his eye out for Chelsey, but that was the last time he ever saw her.

"What could I have offered her?" he rationalized. "What could we possibly have in common to make her want me?" His answer both times was nothing.

Throughout college, Len saw many other attractive coeds but never made a move, fear of rejection burning through him like poison. He decided the only way to cope was to stop looking at them. If you didn't look, you didn't get hooked. He developed the habit of walking across campus head down, averting his eyes from everyone. Still, he never forgot those few idyllic months with Loretta. He missed the comfort of belonging to another person.

The English Department gave Len a job typing notes and researching journal articles for his professors. He used the money to rent a small apartment across town from his mother. To celebrate his escape, he deliberately left the cap off his toothpaste tube. Left the bed unmade. Went from room to room without turning off the lights. Let dishes pile up in the sink. But after a week he felt foolish and returned to the fastidious habits he'd been taught.

Each night he set aside two hours for writing. At first, he sat staring at his typewriter, waiting for ideas to sprout. Nothing came. "Write what you know," Mark Twain had suggested. Len knew only insecurity and ridicule. He imagined himself slugging Ronnie Hudson back in seventh grade, like the hero of those Charles Atlas body-building ads.

He cranked a sheet of paper into the machine.

Johannes Brahms was lying on the beach when Beethoven walked by. "Scaredy-cat!" he taunted, kicking quarter notes in Johannes's face.

"Why do you let that jerk bully you?" Clara Schumann asked as Ludwig strutted away, laughing.

"I can't help it. He's bigger than I am. Thirty-two piano sonatas, sixteen string quartets, five piano concertos, and nine symphonies. And look at the fortissimos on that fifth one!"

"So what? I'll bet if you took Richard Wagner's composition course you could beat the cadenzas out of him."

"How does it work?"

"Wagner uses *leitmotif,* a fundamental component of opus-building. That's how he created the Ring Cycle operas."

"Ring Cycle? Sounds like a washing machine."

"You'd better stick up for yourself, Johannes, or I'll dump you for Franz Liszt!"

Johannes couldn't stand Franz, so he ordered Wagner's workout program and spent an hour each day flexing his crescendos. After six weeks they were bulging.

He went back to the beach. "Hey, Ludwig! Put up your fugues!"

"Say what?"

"Don't play deaf with me!" He threw a D-sharp rondo that caught Beethoven on the downbeat, knocking him into a pile of sheet music.

"Encore! Encore!" Clara swooned. She kissed Johannes passionately as Ludwig sank into obscurity.

Len was proud. He thought he had the foundation for a good satire. All he needed was some reader feedback. But he had no friends. Jeff Tarbox, his coworker in the English Department, was even more reclusive than Len.

So he tried showing it to his mother.

"Who's Clara Schumann?" she asked.

"She was a composer's wife. Brahms was in love with her."

"What's Richard Wagner got to do with this?" she frowned, mispronouncing the name. "He works at the post office."

"It's pronounced 'REE-kard VAHG-ner,'" Len said. "He was a German composer."

"I don't understand all these big words. And why does he need a credenza?"

"That's *cadenza*." Too intellectual, he decided. Mom was poorly educated, but she wasn't stupid. If she couldn't grasp the humor, no one could.

That evening Joey phoned from New York with some exciting news. The network had assigned him to cover the sixteenth hole of a pro golf tournament. It was a big break for him. Len promised to be watching.

He discarded the Brahms manuscript and started over.

It was golf, not ambition, that destroyed Tony Morelli's life. Ambition was a natural impulse. Golf was an unnatural sport.

Throughout his corporate apprenticeship, Tony envied the executives who spent their afternoons on exclusive golf courses, talking business deals over putts and clinching them over drinks in the clubhouse afterward. On the tee they looked confident and relaxed, whacking their drives in long, lazy arcs, then strolling along to the next shot.

It felt awkward when Tony tried it. "Line yourself up," his brother coached. "Keep your back straight. Bend your knees slightly. Grip the handle like this. Square up your shoulders. Keep your right elbow inside as you come back. Tuck in your chin. Shift your weight on the follow-through. Keep your eyes on the ball."

It was too much to think about. Tony whiffed it. He skidded it through the grass. He bounced it off his shinbone. "Just relax!" He loosened his grip a little and threw the club thirty feet up the fairway.

To be a player in business, you had to play golf with the big guys. Tony was too busy working sixty-hour weeks to learn. Then one day, his boss invited him to a business tournament at Pinewood Links. It was the advancement opportunity he'd been waiting for. He blew a fortune on a fancy golf bag, clubs, shoes and clothes. Each evening after work, he smacked three buckets of balls across the driving range. That was how he discovered he needed lessons more than practice. But there was no time. The tournament started tomorrow.

After handshakes with the fat cats he'd come to impress, Tony snapped his opening tee shot neatly off the toe of his club into the adjacent fairway. The ball narrowly missed another golfer and bounced into the rough. By the time he found it and chopped his way back to the first hole, the other men were waiting impatiently on the green.

Every stroke drove him deeper into discredit. His total score, which he didn't bother recording, included four double bogies, six triple bogies, and eight pickups.

"You're a good man, Tony," his boss sympathized after the promotion went to Phil Dorsey. "It's just that Phil plays scratch golf. Keep working on your game. We'll see what happens."

So he increased his hours on the driving range. He took lessons from the clubhouse pro. He read instruction booklets. Nothing helped.

From his failure, resentment grew. Then bitterness and anger. From anger, a sinister plan.

Len showed the first chapter to his mother. "I'm not interested in golf," she said.

"It's not about golf," he explained. "That's only the catalyst."

"Another big word! Why can't you speak plainly?"

Len decided the story needed further development. He tried several approaches. Tony spied on the golfers and blackmailed the ones with skeletons in their closets. He sabotaged their sales figures to wreck their careers. He became a serial killer and beat them to death with his putter. Dissatisfied, Len tore up each new draft.

Between classes and work, he daydreamed about Tony and rushed home each evening to a fresh start.

> James Alderson smiled at the documents spread across his mahogany desk. "Tony, this is a very impressive stock portfolio! None of the other brokerages have offered me anything with so much potential. Where do you get your information?"
>
> "It's all about keeping your ear to the ground," Tony replied. "Mister Alderson, if you let me manage your investments, you'll be able to retire at fifty, take your wife to Europe and build that lake cabin you've been dreaming about. And all the while, your money will be working overtime to keep you both comfortable through your golden years."
>
> "Tony, let's talk about this away from the office. How's your golf game?"

Len trashed the page and started over.

> "You can't do this to me!" Tony protested. "I've spent the past five weeks setting up this account. I'm right on the verge of bringing Alderson on board. He trusts me."
>
> "I understand your frustration," the boss replied. "You shouldn't take it personally. Alderson's a big fish, too big for us to risk on a junior broker. It's time to turn this account over to an experienced executive like Mort Reagan. When Alderson realizes that a corporate vice-president will be handling his investments personally, we'll have him hooked."
>
> "But Mort will get all the credit, plus the five hundred dollar closing bonus I'm entitled to. It's not fair, Mister Wentworth!"

"Who said life is supposed to be fair? You're part of a team, Tony. We all work together to do what's best for the company." Wentworth arched his brow. "You *are* a team player, aren't you, Tony?"

Len ripped the paper from the carriage. Tony was a loser, just like his creator.

He tried a few short stories. A street guitarist swindled by a crooked music producer. A movie fan trapped in an elevator with a snobby actor. A secretary with a hopeless crush on her boss.

"Len, you'll never make a living at this," Mom said. "Why don't you apply for a job at the newspaper?" Out of the question. The thought of asking people for interviews terrified him.

One Saturday morning he slumped at his kitchen table, staring at the typewriter. It stared back, daring him to start something else he couldn't finish.

"God," he pleaded to the walls, "writing is the only thing I care about. Why can't I be good at it?"

What's your purpose, Len? God asked.

"I want to express myself."

What are you trying to express?

"That I feel cheated!" he cried. "That I don't belong anywhere! That my life isn't supposed to be like this!"

Lots of people feel despair, God reminded him. *Many of them have written about it.*

"But they were great authors! I'm just a mediocrity."

I don't create mediocrities, God said.

Desperately, he began a story about a character suffering from writer's block. "Write what you know," he muttered cynically. Predictably, it went nowhere.

Len hauled the smirking typewriter to the closet and stashed it on the top shelf. He made himself a pot of coffee, stretched out on the sofa, and spent his Saturday reading a collection of short stories by Anton Chekhov, Eudora Welty, Carson McCullers and other writers he admired. "Reading is pleasure. Writing is pain," he announced to God that evening as he crawled into bed. "Let someone else do it." God was silent.

Years went by as he drifted from one clerical job to another, correcting textbook errors and typing manuscripts for other writers. When a colleague invited him to a party or a drink after work, he politely declined. If a woman offered him a tempting smile, he slunk away. Everyone learned from his glum posture to leave him alone. Most of the time, his only human contact was his mother, who couldn't seem to stop griping.

"That boy at the filling station didn't check my tire pressure, and he left smears on the windshield!"

"The phone company charged me for a collect call last month! That's twice in a row!"

"Len, you haven't said a single word about my new blouse!"

He ignored her, preoccupied with his own frustrations. On weekends, he interrupted his reading only to watch Joey's sports broadcasts. Joey couldn't write, didn't even like to read. But he was witty and engaging. "I got the passion, you got the talent," Len grumbled at the TV.

The darkness between the day Len gave up writing, and the day Miranda came into his life, was like a spell of amnesia as he coasted out of the idealistic Sixties and through the disillusioned Seventies. Suddenly he was past forty, with only a history of dead-end jobs and no friends. He'd squelched his emotions for so long that he'd forgotten what feeling felt like. Miranda's personality stirred something dormant in him.

"You need to have more faith in yourself," she insisted. "You're intelligent and clever with words. You're polite, disciplined, hard-working. You'd be surprised how many women would gladly swap the monsters they married for a nice guy like you."

Nice? Where'd she get that idea? Couldn't she see he was boring and antisocial? "I'm too old and it's too late," he told her. "I'm okay the way I am."

Miranda tried to change his mind. She showed him pictures of attractive divorcees who attended her church. Invited him to her house for dinner with her unmarried cousin. Introduced her to Frank's widowed sister. Her campaign failed as Len imagined himself married at fifty, his wife at the mercy of his cantankerous mother. Both Garth and Joey had been divorced, at least partly because of Mom. The fictional Jude Fawley was a victim of *two* failed marriages. Len preferred the safety of his paper castle, the fellowship of paper characters who shared their deepest feelings with him, who were never too busy for him, never lost patience with him, never criticized him, betrayed him, or demanded anything of him.

Eventually, Miranda gave up her matchmaking. Now, Len wondered if he'd hurt her feelings. He yearned to be at her bedside instead of sitting in the park beside someone who was supposed to be dead.

"Don't you just love birds?" his mother asked, tossing more seeds to the growing flock. "They're so skittish until you feed them. Then they trust you right away."

She napped again after lunch. Len paced the floor, worrying about Miranda. Then he began to worry about his claim files. He had twelve cases open, and he hadn't touched them all week. What would his policyholders think?

He took his laptop to the kitchen table and tried logging into the Winslow & Grant database.

INVALID USER NAME OR PASSWORD

It *had* to be right! Lord#of#the#Flies wasn't something you forgot easily.

Frustrated, he went to his room and tried Cindy's number again. "Hi, Len," she answered.

"I've been trying to reach you. Is anything wrong?"

"I just muted my ringer. What's on your mind?"

He hesitated. Convincing the medical examiner was one thing. His sister was another. "Cindy, you're not going to believe this, but our mother has come back to life."

She gasped. *"You too?"*

"What?"

"That's why I quit answering. She's been phoning me. At first, I thought it was some kind of scam, but it's her voice!"

Len was stunned. "Cindy, she hasn't called anyone. This house doesn't have a landline, and she doesn't know how to use my cell phone."

"I'm sure it's her! She picks at me the way she always did, about things nobody else could possibly know. That time the milk delivery spoiled because I forgot to bring it in from the porch. The scratches you and Joey made on the table with your toy cars. Our arguments about Brandon. When I hang up, she calls right back. Finally, I just stopped answering."

"When was this?" Len asked.

"It started Monday morning. The caller ID shows a different number every time, so I never know if it's her or somebody else."

Len checked his "Recent Calls" list. The only calls to Cindy were his own.

"Len, are you there?" There was a tremor to her voice that he hadn't heard since her blowup with Mom, over sixty years ago.

"I'm here. Cindy, are you sure you're not imagining this?"

"Are you?"

"No, she's too real. Her body's solid, her skin's warm, she has a pulse. We go places, eat in restaurants, have conversations."

"How can that be?" Cindy asked. "We buried her two weeks ago."

"Two weeks?" Len said. "What are you talking about?"

"After the funeral, I thought I was finally free of her. Now she's haunting me."

"Cindy, you're not making sense. Maybe I should put her on the phone."

"I don't want to talk to her! Len, I'm scared, aren't you?"

"No, just ... baffled."

"Have you told Joey?"

"I tried to. He said I was just dreaming."

"When did you start seeing her?"

"Monday morning. She's the same as before, except her health seems better. She can see again and get around without a walker. No arthritis or other symptoms. Let me put her on the phone. Maybe it'll help."

"Help who? I'm sorry, Len. Maybe if I ignore her, she'll stop calling." Cindy hung up.

Two weeks? he puzzled. *Mom's been dead for seven years.*

"Who were you talking to?" she asked as Len entered the living room.

"Oh … it was just insurance stuff."

She sat up, refreshed from her nap. "Let's call Cindy. I haven't heard from her in ages."

Len eyed her suspiciously. "Didn't you talk to her a couple of days ago?"

"If I had, don't you think I'd remember?"

He rang Cindy's number again. "She's not answering."

"Then let's call Joey."

"He's gone to Atlanta. He'll be prepping for tonight's NFL game."

She sighed. "I wish you kids communicated more. You've all turned into a bunch of strangers. I hear from Danny more often than I do from Cindy or Joey."

"Well, you know how it is. People get busy with jobs and kids."

"And they forget all about their parents!"

"I haven't forgotten you, Mom."

"I don't mean you, it's just that … we don't feel like a family anymore!"

A family? Len thought. *When were we ever a family?*

It was the summer of 1951. Mom crouched on the floor, scrubbing the rug with a wet sponge. "How do you think you're going to survive marriage someday if you can't keep two little boys out of the mud?" she yelled at Cindy. "These stains will never come out! What will the Bible class ladies think when it's my turn to host? You've got one thing to do while I'm at work, that's babysit your brothers, and you can't even do that right!"

Len and Joey huddled in a corner, ashamed for getting Cindy in trouble. She wept while Mom banged around the kitchen, preparing supper and snapping at the boys. "Wash your hands! Set the table! And don't you dare break anything!" An angry silence hung over the meal, making the food as unpalatable as paste.

Cindy was fifteen; skinny, freckle-faced, and shy. Her only friend was Martha Hayes, whose father had lost an arm in the war and scraped out a living in the barbershop, polishing men's shoes one-handed. Mom tolerated Martha but urged Cindy to make other friends. "You'll always be judged by the company you keep," she advised. "Martha's a nice girl, but she's poor, fat, and ugly. No girl who cares about her reputation wants anyone to think she's desperate."

That was why Mom made Cindy walk about the house with a book balanced on her head to improve her posture. She sat her at the kitchen table with a Maybelline kit, applying mascara to her eyelashes and showing her how to use makeup and face powder. "You'll never get a boy to notice you without makeup," she warned as she applied rouge to Cindy's cheeks. "Keep your eyebrows plucked, your hair combed and your nails smooth and polished. Speak softly, and always smile when a boy speaks to you, no matter how you're feeling. Let him control the conversation. Most boys are afraid of intelligent girls like you."

After Cindy got her driver's license, Mom sometimes let her keep the car during the day to run errands. But she always checked the odometer when she got home.

"Who have you been visiting?" she demanded.

"Nobody. I picked up the dry cleaning and drove out to the fruit stand for peaches like you told me to."

"The fruit stand's only half a mile down the road. You've put four miles on the car today. Now where did you go?"

"I had to detour around a roadblock. They were repaving the highway."

"That's a likely story. You're grounded!"

Part of Mom's irritability grew out of embarrassment. She could barely afford to pay rent on their decaying house beside the highway. Her only furniture was musty relics salvaged from her parents' farmhouse. Friends who came to visit pretended not to notice the odor. Mom tried scrubbing the sofa and chairs with white vinegar and baking soda. It didn't help. "If it's the last thing I do, I'm going to move out of this dump," she grumbled.

She applied for a secretarial post in the VA's benefits department. The job required a typing speed of sixty words per minute, so she scrounged garage sales until she found an Underwood typewriter. It was so old that Theodore Dreiser could have used it to write *Sister Carrie*. She practiced at home each evening until she passed the test and moved into a higher pay grade.

In 1954 Cindy graduated from high school with honors. But in those days, girls aimed for marriage, not careers. At Mom's insistence, she enrolled in Plains State College in hopes of finding a husband. She lived at home and paid her tuition by working in the cafeteria, where she met Brandon Wygant, another freshman. Brandon was from a coal mining family in Hazleton, Pennsylvania. He'd come to Texas because he'd always wanted to see a rodeo and meet some cowboys. He was disappointed to find only farmers. "We've got plenty of those back home!" he complained to the kitchen staff.

Unlike Cindy, Brandon was cheerful and outgoing. He was also mischievous. He loosened the caps on the syrup bottles to make the students drown their pancakes. He mixed chili powder in the scrambled eggs. He topped the lemon pies with shave cream. The food supervisor went crazy trying to figure out who was doing it.

Brandon could spot a promising victim by instinct. One day, he took advantage of Cindy's nervous nature by dumping a scoop of ice down her back. It worked better than he'd hoped. With a screech, she hurled a tray of macaroni into the faces of three students waiting in line. While they cursed and grabbed for napkins, she fled to the kitchen, where Brandon found her sobbing atop a stack of flour bags.

"That was when I knew," he told the family after he apologized. "That was when I realized how it felt to be on the receiving end of a prank." He reached for Cindy's hand. "And I decided it was time to get serious."

Brandon was too poor to take her out on dates. He'd barely earned enough money to pay his tuition by working in the coal mines all summer with his father. So he came to Mom's house for study sessions with Cindy. But Brandon had been the class clown in high school and wasn't used to buckling down. He spent a lot of time playing Monopoly with Len and Joey and teaching them how to make paper airplanes.

"What are you majoring in?" Mom asked him.

"I haven't decided. What I'd like is to have my own TV show someday. But guys like Milton Berle and Red Skelton already have that sewed up. I don't know. Maybe I'll major in business. Open a novelty shop or something."

"Cindy, that boy has no direction," Mom said after he returned to the dorm. "You should concentrate on school and keep your options open. There are other fish in the sea."

"They aren't biting," she responded.

Dissatisfied, Mom kept up a running commentary on Brandon's faults. He was short and homely, with coarse, sandy hair that defied combing. His jeans were faded, his shirt cuffs were frayed, and his toes poked through his only pair of shoes. Often, he had dirt under his fingernails from his weekend landscaping job. But he was always a polite guest, saying grace at the dinner table and volunteering to help Mom with the dishes. He fixed a flat on Joey's bicycle, repaired Mom's electric fan, and changed the oil in her car. And he spent hours entertaining the boys. Brandon was the closest they ever came to having a father.

As the first semester progressed, Brandon became more dependent on Cindy. She sat at the kitchen table typing his botany report while he dazzled Len and Joey with card tricks. Mom glowered as she ironed the bed linens.

At the end of his freshman year, Brandon took the bus home to Hazleton, to earn next year's tuition money. Throughout the summer he wrote to Cindy every week. Len had never seen her so happy.

When Brandon returned in September, she dropped out of college to help him with his studies. Mom was outraged. "You're the one with brains!" she argued. "*He* should be supporting *you!*"

The afternoon wore on. Mom was watching a talk show. Len's thoughts shifted back to Miranda. Was brain trauma curable? He looked it up on the internet. The prognosis ranged from dizziness and slurred speech to irreversible coma. He went to his room, sank to his knees, and prayed.

To pass the time, he opened Mom's file cabinet and sifted through her yellowed newspaper clippings. Pearl Harbor. D-Day. Roosevelt's funeral. Hiroshima.

The file also contained old family recipes scribbled on index cards. Grandma Holder's apple cobbler. Aunt Beulah's coleslaw. An uncredited recipe for white gravy. Len dimly remembered Granny Sullivan serving him and Joey dishes of banana pudding. She was a widow, too. Grandpa had wrecked his health during the Great Depression, trying to make a go of the farm. After the foreclosure, he died while Len's dad was overseas. Mom couldn't support her own mother, plus four children, so Granny moved to Waco to live with her sister. She rarely came to visit, unable to afford the bus fare.

Here was a clipping Len hadn't noticed before: his article about Chicory recruits killed in World War II. He'd written it for the school newspaper during his junior year, partly to honor his father. An editor at the *Chicory Gazette* saw the story and republished it under Len's byline. Mom had never mentioned it. But she'd obviously considered it worth saving.

As he put the souvenirs back in the envelope, a small card fell out. One side read *USS West Point,* stenciled in blue. Beneath it was a faded ink scrawl: "April 14, 2300 hrs."

Len took it to the living room. "Mom, do you know what this is?"

She examined the card. "Where'd you find it?"

"It was in that envelope of clippings you saved from the old days. What does that date mean?"

She turned it over. Something flickered in her eyes. "I have no idea." She handed it back to him.

"Do you think Dad might have put it in his pocket while he was home on leave?"

"I don't remember. Be quiet, I'm watching this." She turned back to the TV.

A web search revealed that *USS West Point* was a troop transport ship during the war. Dad must have written himself a note, reminding him when to report. Len wished he knew which year the date referred to. It would be nice to have the card matted and framed.

That evening, Mom volunteered to prepare supper. Len declined. She had given up cooking as dementia transformed her meals from homey delights to burnt offerings. "Why don't we order some takeout and watch the game tonight?" he suggested. "Joey's doing the commentary."

The Falcons were hosting the Saints. "Home field advantage is about the only thing going for this team," Joey told the camera. "The Falcons began this season as Super Bowl favorites. Now, with a 2-9 record, they're trying to recover from an embarrassing blowout last Sunday against Tampa Bay. Their best receiver, Julio Jones, is out for the year with a foot injury. If that's not enough, their offensive line has played poorly and their starting safeties, Thomas DeCoud and William Moore, have been widely criticized for subpar performance. Mike Smith was NFL Coach of the Year last season, and team owner Arthur Blank has given him a public vote of confidence. But if the Falcons don't win their remaining games, they won't even make it to the playoffs, much less the Super Bowl."

"I have to watch TV just to see my own son," Mom groused. "Maybe he'd pay me some mind if I was a football star."

Len was puzzling over Joey's remarks. They were full of errors.

He had mixed feelings about his brother's job. If not for Joey, Len wouldn't have wasted a moment of his life watching sports. Cardinals versus Packers. Bears versus Eagles. Human beings split into artificial tribes to battle over artificial turf. What was it about people, that they couldn't get enough conflict? Whites versus Blacks. Liberals versus Conservatives. Jews versus Muslims. No wonder there was always a war somewhere. If you didn't have a reason to fight, you made one up and called it sport. If you were clever enough, you even turned a profit on it. People sucked up tribalism like an opiate and worshipped their heroes like Greek gods. Even mean ones like Ronnie Hudson.

Of all the nations on Earth, Len thought, Americans had the poorest sense of values. Some athletes earned enough money each year to fund a dozen small school districts. While millions of people around the world suffered in poverty, Americans quarreled over a referee's call in last Sunday's game. While African refugees drowned in the ocean, Americans worried about a quarterback's shoulder injury. Sometimes Len wished Joey had grown up to be Walter Cronkite.

Atlanta got off to a good start, scoring first on a ten-play, seventy-yard drive. The camera showed Falcons fans cheering the touchdown. None of them wore COVID masks.

Then the home team stalled. By halftime, New Orleans had recovered and taken a one-point lead. "The Falcons have lost four games in a row," Joey commented. "It's hard to believe this is the same team that ended last season with a 13-3 record."

Len was bewildered. He had watched enough of Joey's broadcasts to remember that Atlanta had a losing record last year. In fact, he thought

Coach Smith had been fired. Yet there he was on TV, prowling the sidelines.

The Falcons trailed 17-13 late in the game when they drove to the Saints' 29-yard line. But defensive pressure forced them to attempt a field goal. The kicker failed, and the Saints held on to win.

As the dispirited players trudged to the locker room, the screen showed a grim-faced owner leaving the VIP box. "Mike Smith has built one of the NFL's healthiest careers in Atlanta," Joey said. "But now, with a 2-10 record, I'd say his condition has gone from critical to hospice."

Hospice! That was the word that had gotten Joey in hot water during one of his telecasts. But that had happened years ago.

Mom didn't seem to notice any of Joey's remarks. "Doesn't his suit look nice?" she commented. "I wonder where he bought it?"

After she went to bed, Len did some online research. His memory was correct. The Falcons had fired Mike Smith on December 29, 2014, after two disastrous seasons. Following a brief stint as defensive coordinator for Tampa Bay, he'd been fired again. Now he was retired from coaching.

The Falcons team roster for this season listed Raheem Morris as head coach. The two defensive backs Joey mentioned, Thomas DeCoud and William Moore, were long gone.

Len looked up Mike Smith's NFL record. He'd been Coach of the Year all right. But that was in 2012.

On a hunch, he browsed through the entire history of Thursday night NFL games. The Falcons had lost to the Saints 17-13 on November 21, 2013.

Len and his mother had just watched a game played seven years ago. Why would the network rebroadcast an old football game?

He sat up for a while, leafing through *Catch-22*. Yossarian was complaining about a dead man in his tent. There was no body; the poor guy had just transferred to the squadron and stowed his gear in the tent before flying off to die on a bombing mission. His possessions remained unclaimed, his name unknown, his very existence lost in a paperwork muddle.

This was the hour Len used to relish in Mom's last years. Working claims all day and pampering her all evening robbed him of his precious solitude. The best nights were when she felt lousy and retired early, giving him time to work on his farm novel.

By then, macular degeneration had robbed his mother of the only pleasure she and Len had in common: reading. Mom's collection of Harlequin romances gathered sad layers of dust. Len bought her an audiobook device, but she couldn't see well enough to operate it. He tried reading to her at night, but his throat always tightened up, tired from talking to claimants all day.

"It's just as well," she said. "It's not the same as seeing the words on the page."

Her growing memory lapses spoiled their evenings of classic movies because halfway through them, she forgot what had happened in the beginning. Action films were worthless; she couldn't see the action.

Len couldn't think of any other way to entertain her. Modern TV dramas were too fast-paced for Mom. The actors mumbled, and the abrupt scene changes confused her. So he bought her some DVDs of old shows like *Perry Mason* and *Marcus Welby, M.D.*, which were slow-paced and mostly dialogue. Mom enjoyed them at first but eventually got tired of hearing the same ones over and over.

What she needed was someone to talk to. Olivia was good at this, but Len and his mother just got on each other's nerves.

"That hailstorm we had last week is keeping me busy," he remarked one evening. "I had to total out four roofs today."

"Be thankful you don't have to do the labor," she retorted. "Your father had to keep up repairs on the house and the barn, in addition to farming."

He tried telling her about his coworkers. "Sylvia runs forty miles a week, and she's competed in seventeen marathons."

"Humph! Women in my day were too ladylike for such foolishness!"

Other topics only rekindled bitter memories. One night, Len asked her what high school was like in the 1930s.

"I had to miss a lot of days because we were picking cotton," she recalled darkly. "Mrs. Floyd thought I was playing hooky and tried to trick me by assigning our class to write down all the Presidents' names. I got them all perfect, but Judy Wheeler accused me of copying off her paper. So Mrs. Floyd made me recite them aloud, in order, in front of everybody. I was so embarrassed! Judy Wheeler was always out to get me, jealous because Will chose me over her. She and her sister thought they were better than everybody else because their father owned the feed store."

Len tried another subject. "Did you ever date anybody else before you met Dad?"

"Like who?" she scoffed. "Who else was there, in a dusty town in the middle of cotton country? Eddie Wicks was a pimple-faced mama's boy, and Max Harvey was a drunk like his no-good father."

She turned on Len. "That's why I don't understand you kids. You've had all the advantages your father and I never had. Garth could have done anything he wanted, but he had to go and marry that Billie Jo Riley tramp. Then Cindy ran off to Pennsylvania with that scatter-brained coal digger, and Joey chased after Beth all through high school, just to get my goat!"

"I thought you liked Beth now," Len said.

"I do!" she snapped. "That's not the point. And you! You're as bad as the others!"

"Why? What's wrong with me?"

"You don't have any friends. You never go anywhere or do anything but sit around reading books and tapping away at that computer thing of yours. What kind of life is that? I think you hang around my house just to make me feel guilty!"

"Guilty? For what?"

"You treat me like I'm some cross you have to bear. Some chore you have to do. Waiting for me to die so you can go back to being a hermit!"

Len's temper flared. "Mom, I'm doing this so you won't have to live in a nursing home!"

"See what I mean? I'm nothing to you but an obligation!"

He bit his tongue. Scenes with Mom never solved anything. He turned on the TV to fill the silence.

Each night as she struggled off to bed with her walker, Len parked a baby monitor in her room. He kept one ear on it while he worked on his novel. Sometimes Mom couldn't sleep. She tottered back to the living room to sit with him, staring into space as Len pecked at the keyboard.

"You want a sleeping pill?" he offered.

"No."

"Some cocoa?"

"No."

"Want me to sing you a lullaby?"

She glared at him. "Are you trying to be funny?"

He closed his laptop. "Mom, what's wrong?"

"Nothing." She hauled herself up and returned to her room.

In her final months, when she could no longer walk, Len accomplished little. Bedfast and confused, she mostly slept during the day and cried out for Olivia at night.

"She's not here, Mom," Len said, "she's at home."

"It's time for my bath. I need her to help me."

"Your bath can wait until morning. Here, let me adjust your pillows."

"I want Olivia, not you!"

"Mom, I'm all you've got right now."

"Then leave me alone! Go work on those darned books of yours, since they're so important!"

Later, he would be drifting off to sleep when she called for Olivia again.

"Mom, it's after midnight. Olivia's at home."

"When's she coming back?"

"First thing in the morning."

"Where am I?" She looked around blindly. "Is this my house?"

"Yes, Mom. Don't you recognize it?"

"I don't know!" She tugged restlessly at the bedclothes.

"Would you like some water?"

"I want some key lime pie!"

"It's late, Mom. Try to get some sleep."

Back to bed for a few minutes before she cried out for Olivia again. And again.

Her deterioration uncapped a geyser of bottled-up grievances. "You think you're so superior because you went to college and I didn't," she declared at 3:00 o'clock in the morning. "If you're so smart, why are you so cold and smug that nobody knows how to talk to you, not even your own mother!"

It's dementia speaking, he told himself. But the accusation rang true.

The stress showed in his face. "Take some time off!" Miranda urged. "We'll cover for you. You can't do us any good if you're constantly exhausted." She didn't know it was shame as much as fatigue. His inner voice kept praying that Mom would die in her sleep.

Some nights he came home to find her propped up in bed, listless and defeated. "Are you hungry, Mom? Olivia made us some enchiladas." With her vision almost gone, she could hardly find her plate with a fork. Len would try to feed her, but the spoonful was too big, or the food too hot, or he was too clumsy. "I'm not hungry anyway," she'd say. "You go do whatever you want."

"Can't I get you anything? Some Ensure, or fruit juice?"

"No, I'll be all right."

"Well, call if you need me." His duty done, he left her alone to sleep or think whatever a dementia patient thought. He worked on his novel as Mom's restless moans filtered through the baby monitor.

As she grew worse, Olivia sat by the bed all day, monitoring her vital signs, making notes in the medical diary, feeding her pills, emptying her catheter bag, cleaning her, changing the sheets, holding her hand, and patting her face as she groaned her way through aches and hallucinations. Len took over at night, the duties cutting further into his sleep.

The final night was all Mom. Though she'd been unconscious for three days, her body functions continued. "I had to change her bedding six times," a weary Olivia reported when he got home. Len spent the evening at her bedside, feeling helpless and inadequate. She was quiet until midnight, when she began gasping and heaving with her mouth closed tight, something Len hadn't seen before.

Panicked, he summoned a hospice nurse. "It's some sort of internal stress," she observed. "There's nothing we can do except keep her comfortable." The nurse increased the morphine drip and sat up with Len all night.

The heaving episodes diminished, replaced by groping gestures, her hands reaching out, opening and closing on air. Finally, they sank to her lap. Her respiration calmed. "She's trying to let go," the nurse concluded as she left at dawn. "Just watch her and keep the room quiet. I doubt she'll last through the day." Olivia arrived at 7:30, but Len skipped work. They sat beside Mom until her final breath escaped late that afternoon.

Afterward, he could never bring himself to occupy the master bedroom. For seven years now, he'd entered only to vacuum and dust, leaving Mom's furniture and wall hangings in place. Forgotten exhibits in a lonely museum.

He crept into her room. She slept on her right side as she'd done all her life until arthritis forced her to lie on her back, with pillows tucked under each knee to relieve the stress. How pitiful she'd looked after her last hip replacement, her legs so stiff that she couldn't cooperate with the nursing home therapist, struggling desperately to move her walker just five steps, finally exhausted, wheeled back to her room, discharged by Medicare rules, sent home to wallow in a bed of misery until God decided she'd had enough.

Watching her now, Len remembered a night long ago when a thunderstorm disturbed his childhood slumber. As he cried out, his mother came to hold his hand and sing softly:

"Two little clouds, one summer's day,
Went flying through the sky;
They went so fast they bumped their heads,
And both began to cry.

"Old Father Sun looked out and said:
'Oh, never mind, my dears,
I'll send my little fairy folk
To dry your falling tears.'"

In a hospital somewhere, Miranda's family kept vigil by her bedside. Len pulled up a chair and sat beside his mother, listening to the ghostly murmur of Joey's voice from down the hall.

The Farm Tree

BY LEONARD HOLDER

By 1960, John Driskill was the most successful farmer in the county. After the co-op elected him chairman for a second term, he persuaded the town's three bank presidents to build a grain elevator to serve the tri-county area. Gene Driskill, the only man around with an agribusiness degree, was their choice for its manager. He and Laura built a house in town. The following year, they made John and Ruth grandparents.

Gene still helped with the farm. It was bigger now. Dad had purchased one hundred fifty acres from the Nelsons after the aging couple moved in with their son's family. He also hired the Finch brothers to build the Driskills a new farmhouse. When it was finished, John installed Matt Brady, his new farmhand, in the old one. The Bradys were a young black couple with two children of their own. Ruth and Annie Brady quickly became friends.

At first, Terry was proud to replace Gene as Dad's right-hand man. A week of moving irrigation pipes took the shine off that. He was so sore he could hardly walk. "It'll wear off," Dad promised. "Then you'll have muscles like your brother. The girls will be fighting over you."

Terry grinned, but he had other things on his mind besides girls.

Today he and Dad were building a screen over Mom's vegetable garden to keep the critters out. Mom was in the kitchen, baking pies for Dina's wedding reception and listening to *Ma Perkins* on the radio. Charley kneeled beside the water pump, grooming his pet raccoon in the washtub while his pet squirrel and pet kittens chased each other around the yard. A frustrated blue jay scolded them all from the red oak tree.

Terry watched his father measure a section of chicken wire. He figured now was as good a time as any.

"Dad ... would you be disappointed if I didn't go to A&M?"

John glanced up. "I thought you wanted to go to college after you graduate next year."

"I do, but not to A&M." Terry drew a deep breath and took the plunge. "Dad, I want to go to art school."

"Art school? You mean like painting?"

"Yes sir."

"Where'd you get that idea?"

"Remember those sketches I made for my class project last semester? Mister Bolton thinks I've got talent. He says I can probably get a scholarship if I maintain my grade point average through my senior year."

"He got all this from a few pencil drawings?"

"No, I also did some watercolor posters for the Christmas party. A dozen of them. Scenes of Jesus in the manger. The Magi bringing gifts. Angels with the shepherds. Mister Bolton said he'd never seen a student with such a captivating style or mature grasp of composition."

Terry watched his father apprehensively. This was a conversation he'd dreaded for weeks.

John put his wire cutters aside. "So you don't want to be a farmer?"

"No sir." He lowered his head. "I'm sorry."

"You don't know how glad I am to hear this. I thought I was raising a family of serfs."

"Sir?"

"Terry, I'm proud to be a farmer. This is what I was meant to do. But who needs a world full of them?"

"You're not disappointed? I thought you wanted all of us to be farmers."

"I wanted all of you to learn how to work hard and take responsibility. You've done that. What you do with your life is up to you." He resumed snipping wire. "So how do you make a living as an artist? Did Mister Bolton have anything to say about that?"

"Well, actually, I haven't thought that far ahead. I guess I'd want to be like Pablo Picasso. He shows his work in art galleries all over the world, and there are library books full of his paintings." He sighed. "I guess there's only one Picasso, though."

"Just like there's only one Terry Driskill, right? Son, if you want to study art, you have my blessing. But I'd like you to do one thing before you go."

"What's that?"

"Paint a portrait of your mother, for her fortieth birthday."

Terry grinned, relieved. "Sure, Dad. I'll be glad to."

"And make it flattering. Ladies are sensitive about their age."

A clattering roar drew their attention as Matt Brady drove the tractor into the yard. "You done with that section already?" Dad asked.

"Naw, I 'bout run outta gas." Jumping down, he grabbed the fuel hose and began filling the tank. "This old machine makes a lotta noise, but she still runs good."

"Yeah, we got our money's worth all right."

"Mistuh John, whatcha want me to do tomorrow? I figure to have them west acres cleared before dark."

Dad wiped his brow and studied the sky. "Looks like dry weather for the next several days, at least. Why don't you start on the south section tomorrow?"

"Awright."

"And Matt, I told you before, I'm not Mister John. It's just John."

Matt grinned. "Sorry. It's the way I was brung up."

"Well, quit making me feel older than I already am. Ruth made a big pitcher of lemonade. Go inside and cool off before you start back."

Matt headed for the house, pausing to kneel beside Charley. "Is that a boy or girl raccoon you got there?"

"Boy. His name's Pancho."

"Pancho? Like that guy on 'The Cisco Kid'?"

"Yeah." Charley poured rinse water over the animal. "He'll wash his hands before he eats, but he never takes a bath. So I'm giving him one."

"Whatcha gonna do with him?"

"Raise a family. But first I have to find him a wife."

"First things first, huh? Well, I'll keep an eye out for a lady raccoon while I'm out in the field." Matt removed his hat as he entered the kitchen.

"Terry, come hold this in place for me." John began tacking the final section of wire onto the frame. "So. This Picasso. Is he the one with the melting pocket watches?"

"No, that's Salvador Dalí. Picasso's the one with the angular shapes. *The Three Dancers. Avignon. The Weeping Woman.*"

John nodded. "I saw an art book once while I was overseas. A guy in my outfit carried it in his field pack wherever he went. I didn't understand much of it."

"Mister Bolton says it takes a while to develop your artistic sensibility," Terry said, "unless it comes naturally."

"Hm. I guess I lost my artistic sensibility in the war."

Terry studied his father's lined face. He had a stoic bearing, like Dana Andrews in "The Best Years of Our Lives."

"Dad, how come you never talk about the war? Did something bad happen to you?"

John's hammer paused. He closed his eyes. "Some things are best forgotten, Terry." He drove the last nail home and stood up. "Go call your mother. Let's see what she thinks about this carrot coop."

Friday

Sunlight poured through the window. Filtered through the red oak's bare branches, it drew a gnarly pattern of finger-shadows on Len's face. He stirred and sat up. He must have slept in the chair all night. Mom lay beside him, breathing softly.

His anxiety about Miranda arose with him. Chad and Sylvia hadn't responded to his messages. He tried phoning them. The endless ringing didn't make sense. Both were used to being on call. Emergencies came with the job.

"Will you run over to Walmart?" Miranda pleaded one morning, her call rousing Len from a deep slumber. "I need clothes for two adults and three kids."

"What's wrong?" he yawned. The clock read 4:15 a.m.

"The Jeffersons' house burned down. They lost everything, even their cat."

"Was anyone hurt?"

"Just a little coughing from the smoke. They're getting oxygen at the fire station."

"I'm on it," Len said, fumbling for some clothes. "Where are you?"

"The Hospitality Motel on Decker Street. Len, it's freezing outside. Buy some heavy coats and warm-up suits. One large, one medium, and three smalls. And get some toothpaste, brushes, combs, things like that. They've only got five dollars in cash, and Mister Jefferson's job starts at 7:00."

It wasn't the first time Miranda had gone out of her way in an emergency. She kept a cash fund for disasters like this one. When you needed help, she reasoned, you needed it now. The home office never complained. The Chicory branch had the most loyal clients in the company.

Miranda was waiting when he arrived. "I got them a suite instead of a room," she said as Len dumped his purchases on the bed. "Mrs. Jefferson has a job too, babysitting four kids. She's phoning the parents now."

Miranda took the family to breakfast in the diner, then drove their children to school. They stayed in the motel at company expense until they found a new home. On the day they moved in, Miranda presented the children with a new kitten. The Jeffersons gathered around and hugged her, Winslow & Grant customers for life.

It was about this time that Len began having dreams about a different family. They lived on a farm. Each evening they sat around the supper table holding hands, their heads bowed in prayer. It was a pleasant vision that lingered after he awoke each morning, through the workday, and at night as he tried to sleep. The family grew in his imagination until finally, early one Saturday, he fetched his typewriter from the closet and began to write, for the first time in twenty-three years.

He poked his head into Joey's old room. "COVID has made it almost impossible to plan anything," said the voice. "The NFL is working on a day-by-day game schedule."

Len checked the internet for NFL news. There was no game last night. The Cowboys-Ravens match had been postponed due to COVID. The Falcons weren't scheduled to play until this coming Sunday.

Maybe last night's broadcast was a last-minute replay, to fill the time slot. If so, they could have picked a better game, like the classic Buffalo Bills comeback of 1993. The Bills had rallied from a thirty-two-point deficit to defeat Houston. Even Len had been impressed.

Hearing Mom stir, he went to the kitchen to make breakfast. As he sliced pears and apples into a bowl, he wondered for the umpteenth time how and why his mother had returned to life. According to his Sunday School teachers, you went to Heaven if you'd been good; to Hell otherwise. But what if there was no Heaven or Hell? What if you were reincarnated; not as a different person, but as yourself, fated to live the same life over and over until you got it right? Was the universe merely a cosmic recycling factory? If so, why hadn't Mom returned as an infant instead of an old lady?

"God," he pleaded to the sun rising through the kitchen window, "I don't understand this. What am I supposed to do about her?"

The situation was forcing Len to relive painful memories, like the night Brandon came to the house to ask for Mom's blessing. Len and Joey were sprawled in front of the TV, watching *Cheyenne* while Mom mended holes in their socks.

"Cindy's not ready for marriage," she responded.

"I love her, Mrs. Holder," Brandon pleaded. "I promise I'll take good care of her."

"How? You don't even have a job, and you flunked two courses last semester."

"I guess I'm not college material," he admitted, staring at his feet. "But lots of people without degrees have successful careers."

"Doing what? Washing dishes in the cafeteria? Where would you live?"

"We'll move to Hazleton. My parents will take us in for starters."

"Nonsense! Cindy, you don't have to take the first offer that comes along. You can do better."

"Don't say that!" she cried. "Brandon's the best thing that's ever happened to me."

"Why? Because he makes you laugh? How does that put food on the table? What if you have kids? Do you have any idea how much it costs to raise a family? Look at what I went through, and I've still got Len and Joey to support."

"You don't like him because he's not some big shot!" Cindy blurted, her face flushed. "You don't give people a chance, you never have!"

"You mind your tone with me, young lady!"

"Maybe I should leave," Brandon said.

"Yes, leave!" Mom snapped. "And don't come back until you've made something of yourself!"

"If he leaves, I'm going with him!" Cindy shouted.

"Where? To the coal mines? He's got no future!"

"At least he'll get me away from you!" She fled to her room.

"I'm sorry, Mrs. Holder," Brandon mumbled, edging quietly outside.

Len and Joey traded uneasy glances as Mom followed Cindy. Angry voices clashed behind the door. Cindy, her cheeks damp, emerged with a suitcase. At the sight of her brothers, she put it down and embraced them. Then she was gone.

Joey's hospice remark from last night was all over the TV news.

"Comparing a football coach's job to terminal illness is an insult to suffering seniors everywhere," a hospice spokesman declared. Indignant families of dying patients had flooded the network with demands for an apology. "Twitter has already logged more than seventy-four thousand comments," the anchorman reported.

Now Len was really confused. If Joey's hospice remark was seven years ago, why was it leading this morning's news?

"If he'd studied in high school instead of wasting his time on that radio stuff, he might not be in this mess," Mom said, sprinkling granola on her fruit. "Now, all our church friends will be gossiping about it."

"Mom," Len sighed, "you worry too much about what other people think."

"You wouldn't say that if you'd been at those parent-teacher conferences. The whole faculty acted like I was an unfit mother because of Joey's grades. What was I supposed to do, take his tests for him? Was it my fault that he neglected his homework so he could fool around on the practice field after school and blabber about sports on the radio?"

"But look how he turned out! Joey's got a career most people would kill for."

"Your father wouldn't have stood for it," she insisted. "Before the war, Will was the best student in our school and one of the best farmers in the county. Everyone looked up to him, even the Tiptons. Remember them? Merle served two terms as mayor, and Phyllis was president of the Garden Club. Their daughter was Demolay princess, and their oldest son went to medical school."

Len let it pass. In high school, the princess was a pothead. The medical student was a kleptomaniac.

He understood Mom's concern, though. Her generation clung to standards dating back to Thomas Hardy's day. In *Jude the Obscure*, Jude and Sue become outcasts when word gets around that they're living in sin.

"After breakfast, why don't we run over to Schoffner's?" Mom suggested. "Maybe we can find you a nice suit like Joey's. It's my treat."

Len rolled his eyes. "Mom, I've been buying my own clothes for quite some time now."

"I know, but you haven't had a new suit for ages, and you look so handsome all dressed up. I was thinking you could wear it to church Sunday."

He was afraid of that. How could he explain her return to the pastor and others who'd attended her funeral? "I'd rather not, but thanks just the same."

"I wish you weren't so prideful," she complained. "Whenever I offer to do something nice for you, you take it as an insult."

"It's embarrassing, Mom! A seventyish old man being dressed by his ninetyish old mother!"

"Well! Excuse me for embarrassing you!" She hacked at a pear. "Why don't you cut these things into bite-size pieces?"

The truth was that Mom's gifts always came with a price tag. When Len was sixteen, she bought him a Cross pen and pencil set, then acted hurt because he didn't carry them around in his shirt pocket. Len couldn't make her understand that enough people already thought he was a nerd. For his graduation present, she gave him her old Plymouth but nagged him if he didn't keep it washed and waxed. She bought him new clothes for college, then kept asking what his classmates said about them. "They didn't say anything, Mom. College isn't a fashion show." Thank goodness she hadn't lived in Biblical times. She would have scolded Aaron for getting sacrificial blood on his beautiful new ephod.

After Len got his own apartment, Mom came over to check it out. Silently, she inspected the flea-market chairs with stained cushions; the wobbly lamp table; the wooden crates containing his books.

A few days later a delivery van arrived with new furniture, including a handsome oak bookcase with glass doors. It was the nicest thing she'd ever given him. Still, it made him uneasy. The next thing he knew, she'd be filling the shelves with romances and detective stories.

She didn't, though. Instead, she gave him a bottle of wood polish and a lecture on house cleaning. That was the price of the furniture.

After doing the dishes he phoned his office again. "Winslow & Grant," Ron Stokes answered. "How may I help you?"

"This is Len Holder. I called a couple of days ago."

"I'm sorry, Mister Holder. We've had a problem here that put us behind on our claims. May I have your policy number?"

"I'm not a claimant!" he insisted, "I work there! We talked about this."

"We did?"

"Who are you, anyway? I've worked there for thirty-seven years and I've never heard of you."

Stokes cleared his throat. "I don't know what to tell you, sir. I've been with this office the past eight months."

"Who's your supervisor?"

"Well, it *was* Miranda Thomas. That's the problem I mentioned. She died yesterday morning."

Len's knees buckled. He sank into a chair. "She died?"

"Did you know her?"

"She ... oh, God!" he wept.

"I'm sorry to be the one to tell you. She was in a car accident on her way home last Friday."

The man waited patiently as Len struggled for control. "Did she suffer?" he choked.

"I don't think so. They airlifted her to a neurological facility for emergency surgery. She never regained consciousness."

"When ... where ... what about the funeral?"

"We don't know yet. Mister Holder, suppose I call you back when I find out? We're awfully busy today, trying to catch up, but I'd like to clear up this confusion."

"Yes. Thank you, I'd appreciate that. I'm sorry I was rude."

"Don't worry about it. We're all upset, too. Goodbye, Mister Holder."

Len sobbed into his hands. *Why didn't God take me instead? Miranda had someone to live for.*

"What's wrong?" Mom called from the living room.

"My boss died."

"Oh!" She came to sit beside him. "That's too bad. What happened?"

"It was a car accident. I don't know the details."

Mom watched him wipe his tears. "Well, I'm not surprised, the way people drive these days. When I was a girl, we had to memorize the driver's handbook and take a written test before we even got behind the wheel. Still, some kids practically got away with murder. I don't know how many times Garth got stopped for drunk driving, and the police brought him home in broad daylight with all the neighbor ladies watching. 'I brought you up better than that!' I told him. 'What would your father say to you, shaming the family like this?' He either ignored me or talked back to me in language that would have earned him a whipping if Will had been here."

I don't need this, Len thought as she prattled on. I need a hug.

His last memory of Miranda was a quiet Friday afternoon at the office. Sylvia had left early for the weekend to compete in a triathlon. Chad was out on a field visit. Len was replacing a toner cartridge in the copier while Miranda cleaned the minifridge.

"What are you reading these days?" she asked.

"*Jude the Obscure.* We studied it in high school, but that was so long ago I'd forgotten most of it."

"What's it about?"

"A young man who sacrifices his dreams for two women who betray him."

Miranda eyed him dubiously. "And you *enjoy* a story like that?"

"Sure. It's a classic."

"Sounds depressing."

"No, not really. It's ... I don't know. Poignant."

"What's that?"

"Sad. Heart-wrenching."

"Don't you ever read anything cheerful?"

"Sure I do." Then he paused. *Darkness at Noon. The Bell Jar. Sophie's Choice.* Now that he thought about it, there was something depressing about almost everything he read.

"You must have been a good student," Miranda said, wiping down the fridge. "I'll bet you were tops in your class."

"Not really. I just like fiction."

"Frank does too, except he's a western fan. Let him get started on one, and you practically have to fire off a cannon to get his attention."

She sprayed the little fridge with disinfectant and began refilling it. A few apples. Some yogurt cups. A loaf of whole wheat bread. Pickles, olives, cheese slices. "This thing is too small for four people," she complained. "Either we buy a bigger fridge or stop eating."

"I vote for the fridge," Len said.

"Me too."

As Len wiped toner from his hands, his office phone rang. He was still on the call when Miranda left for the weekend, waving a cheery goodbye. A perfectly ordinary Friday. Nothing to herald the impending disaster.

Mom was droning on. "Running around with Jed Latham and Buddy West, that's what got him in so much trouble. Stealing hubcaps and selling them to the junkyard so they could liquor up. Hanging around that ramshackle dance hall outside of town every night, picking up girls. Hardly a week passed without the sheriff's car pulling up to the house, and all the busybodies in the neighborhood peeking out their windows and phoning each other. 'Guess what? Garth Holder's in trouble again!' And after all I did for him!"

As a boy, Len had wished he could trade mothers with Woody Lazenby. Sometimes Len and Joey stayed at their house after school until Mom got off work. Len felt drawn to Barbara and followed her around like a puppy. "You're so considerate, Len!" she exclaimed as he stood beside her at the sink, drying dishes. "Most boys your age won't help with chores."

He hated doing dishes with Mom. "Don't put that towel on your shoulder, it's unsanitary! Don't dry your hands on it, use the hand towel! Don't stack the blue plates with the white ones!" She made him line up all the drinking glasses in neat rows, in case the cupboard police showed up.

One day Barbara listened respectfully as Len read her a story he'd written for school. It was about a lonely boy whose only friend was Fred, his bicycle. Fred's tires whispered secrets to him as he rode along the sidewalk. "That's nice, Len. I'm so proud of you! Do you have any more stories?"

"Sure, lots of them."

"Bring me another one tomorrow after school. I'd love to hear it."

"My mother won't read my stories," Len said glumly.

"Well, maybe she's too tired at the end of a busy day." Barbara hummed a tune as she ironed Milton's shirts.

"Mrs. Lazenby," Len asked, "how come you're always so cheerful?"

"Why shouldn't I be? I have a nice family. A nice home. Nice friends like you to read me stories."

"I wish you were my mom."

Barbara frowned. "Don't ever say that, Len. Sharon has a heavy load, trying to be both mother and father to her children. Someday you'll be grateful for all the sacrifices she's made."

Len wondered what these could be. She didn't have to stand outside freezing on the corner each morning, waiting for the school bus. Or struggle through boring math classes. Ask permission to go to the bathroom. Be yelled at by teachers, hissed at by the librarian, ridiculed by the P.E. coach, picked on by bullies, live in constant fear at school and at home. What did grownups have to worry about? They were the bosses and did as they pleased.

The phone rang, interrupting his reverie. Mom had finally run out of venom and returned to the living room. "Mister Holder, this is Walter Garrett at the medical examiner's office."

"Oh, yes. Did you make any progress?"

"Your mother's fingerprints check out, and I've been able to verify most of the information she gave me. Now, the next step would be exhumation, if you're prepared to go through with it."

"What do I have to do?"

"Normally I'd order it on my own authority, but this case is unusual. So I'm filing a petition with the county court. That'll require the signatures of anyone with power of attorney."

"I have sole power of attorney," Len said.

"Even that may not be good enough. Any relatives who object can sue to block the exhumation, which would force another hearing. You might want to get their permission in advance."

"Yes, I'll do that. Can you start the paperwork? I'll talk to my brother and sister in the meantime."

"All right. By the way, Mister Holder. When I phoned your office, I got an answering service. They referred me to Winslow & Grant headquarters. They have you listed as retired."

"What?" Len exclaimed. "That's impossible!"

"Maybe you should call them."

"I certainly will!"

A woman in the Los Angeles office confirmed it: Leonard Holder, retired on December 31, 2013.

"That's not right!" he insisted. "I've got a dozen open claims, and I'm still getting paid every two weeks." He gave her his Social Security and agent ID numbers.

"I'll look into this," she said, "but it may take some time. Don't expect to hear back from me before next week."

Disturbed, Len opened his laptop and tried the claims database again. It still wouldn't accept his password. His online banking account for the last six months showed no payroll deposits. Only his Social Security allotments.

He went to the living room. "Mom," he said, "you were right. Let's go shopping."

They sauntered through the mall, Mom window-browsing while Len struggled to digest the morning's news. She paused outside a women's boutique. "What beautiful designs!" she said. "Let's go in."

The salesgirl who greeted them bore a strong resemblance to Chelsey West. She caught Len staring at her, smiled, and began offering Mom some outfits to try on. Len wandered about the store, trying to imagine life in retirement. A life without Miranda.

Mom traipsed in and out of the changing room to pose in front of a mirror. As a young man, he'd found her obsession with appearances irritating. Vietnamese peasants were dying at American hands while she fussed over dresses, scarves and jewelry. Her whole generation was so materialistic! Who was she trying to impress?

It certainly wasn't men. When she took the VA job, she was still in her late twenties. Ex-soldiers visited her office every day. As receptionist, it was her job to update their files and check them in for appointments. Some of them must have asked her out.

"A woman with four kids, chasing after men?" she said when Len raised the subject. "Not on your life! I don't need the gossip." Widows, it seemed, were supposed to mourn forever.

Len knew his mother was attractive. Men on the sidewalk stared as she escorted her kids to the grocery store each Saturday. One guy walked right into a parking meter. It wasn't until his teen years that she accepted a few dates. The first was Duke Logan, an assistant coach who also taught Len's history class but wasted most of the time telling football stories. One Monday after a loss, he spent the entire hour berating students who didn't attend the games. "You ought to be ashamed of yourselves!" he shouted. "Those boys bring honor to this school. They should be treated like kings!" Len fumed through the whole lecture, relieved when Mom ditched the coach after their third date. "Men!" she huffed. "They all want the same thing!"

Zeke Wallis, a divorced carpenter, took Mom out to dinner once. Joey liked him because he knew a lot about sports and promised to take him to a baseball game. It didn't happen. On their second date, he appeared at her door smelling like Rolling Rock. Mom sent him packing.

The idea of a stepfather used to frighten Len. He'd heard stories about classmates with abusive ones. He imagined himself and Joey at the mercy of some drunken ogre. Mom must have read his mind. She eventually gave up dating altogether.

When Len was about eight, a mystery man used to call occasionally. He could tell it was the same guy because Mom always stretched the phone cord into the kitchen and spoke in whispers. The conversations lasted a half-hour or more. After hanging up, she went to her room and closed the door. When she returned, her eyes were red. Eventually, the calls stopped. Len never found out who he was.

While Mom was in the changing room, Len approached the salesgirl. "Do you know a woman named Chelsey West?" he asked.

"No sir. Should I?"

"She was a girl I knew in high school. You look so much like her."

She smiled. "I hope that's a compliment."

"It sure is! Of course, she'd be much older now. I thought maybe she was your grandmother."

"Actually, I just moved here from Arizona. I'm still learning my way around town."

Mom emerged with an armload of clothing. "Can I show you something else, Mrs. Holder?"

"I think I'm ready to check out."

Suddenly, Len remembered that her credit cards were invalid. "Uh, Mom, you'd better let me handle this."

"No, I've got it." Before he could stop her, the Chelsey twin zipped her card through the machine. Len braced himself for alarm bells and larceny cops. Instead, she handed Mom a receipt. "Thank you, Mrs. Holder. It's been nice visiting with you." Len was dumbfounded. He'd closed all Mom's accounts seven years ago while settling her estate.

She grabbed his sleeve. "Now, I don't want to hear another word from you! I'm going to buy you a couple of new suits. Maybe some shirts and ties. And look at your shoes, they're worn out! We should have done this a long time ago." She dragged him across the concourse to the men's shop.

Len spent an hour getting dolled up like a Wall Street power broker while wondering if he still had a job. In a few days, Mom's charges would bounce and he'd have to pay for all this finery himself. He supposed it was worth it. Shopping always made her happy.

They lunched at a Chinese place in the mall, Len gambling that the spices wouldn't rekindle his indigestion. Mom chattered gaily about the change in women's fashions. He was too preoccupied with Miranda to listen, imagining Frank, their two kids and four grandchildren in tears. Death was so arbitrary. It kept the elderly dangling in misery but snatched away sweet souls like Miranda while they were still in their prime.

Sometimes death was sneaky. Barbara Lazenby was eighty-five when Milton awoke one morning to find her still lying beside him. That was unusual. Barbara always got up before he did. He thought she'd overslept until he nudged her. When she didn't respond, he turned her over and saw the truth: her soul had simply departed during the night. She hadn't even been sick.

Len was almost as upset as Milton and their children. "I wish I could remember the last thing I said to her," he told Woody at the funeral. "I hope it was something nice."

Perhaps Cindy had had similar thoughts when she returned home for Len's high school graduation. She and Mom hadn't spoken in the four years since her flight to Hazleton with Brandon. They exchanged embraces and pretended their parting argument had never happened.

Cindy's appearance shocked Len. She'd always been skinny, but now she was so thin her dress almost slipped off her shoulders. Her hands trembled. She looked pale and exhausted.

Since the elopement, Mom had risen to administrative assistant at the VA. She bought a new home, taking advantage of a residential building boom in oil-rich Texas. The house was bigger than their old slum rental. Len and Joey had their own rooms and shared a separate bathroom, with a sparkling clean shower stall and new linens. The living room had paneled walls and a fireplace flanked by windows opening on a cozy backyard. The kitchen was all-electric and featured a dishwasher and garbage disposal. Next to it was a laundry room with a washer and dryer. "No more clotheslines!" Mom sighed thankfully.

She had sold her parents' shabby furniture in a yard sale, replacing it with a cream-colored sofa, matching chairs, an oak dining table, and a matching dinette cabinet. She watched nervously as Cindy's two daughters toddled around the house. "Joey, keep an eye on them. Don't let them break anything."

She turned to Cindy. "What's happened to you? You look starved. Aren't you getting enough to eat?"

"I'm all right. Just a little tired from the bus ride."

"Why didn't Brandon come with you?"

"He's on the road, selling vacuum cleaners door-to-door. He sends money when he can, but things are slow right now. He thinks he can get a second job —"

"Joey, I told you to watch them!" Mom leaped up to pull LeAnn away from the coffee table, where she was banging her rattle. She returned to her seat with the grandchild in her lap. "What were you saying?"

"The Fuller Brush man in our neighborhood has a chance for promotion if he can find a replacement for his route. Brandon's on the application list. He figures he won't have to travel so much if —"

"Wait a minute," Mom grimaced. LeAnn was squirming and whining. "Joey, I can't handle this child. Take her to your room. Where's Laurie?"

"In the kitchen."

"Give them those building blocks and puzzles you and Len used to play with." She turned back to Cindy. "What about the Fuller Brush man?"

"Brandon says Fuller Brush products are very popular with housewives. He figures the ones who don't buy vacuum cleaners are still good prospects for Fuller's line."

"Doesn't sound like much of a future. Is that the best he can do?"

"Some men make a career of Fuller Brush. They have these very nice sample cases —"

A loud crash erupted from the kitchen. Both women jumped up. Laurie sat bawling on the floor beside the waffle iron. "I'm sorry," Joey explained, "she grabbed the power cord while I wasn't looking."

"She's not hurt, just scared," Cindy said, cradling the child.

"Oh no!" Mom cried, kneeling on the floor. "One of the tiles is cracked!" She phoned Jake Hardeman, the installer. "You've got to come over right away! I'm expecting guests for Len's graduation party tomorrow. I can't have the floor looking like this!"

While Mom dealt with Jake, Cindy wandered out to the back porch. Len joined her. "How do you like being a mother?" he asked.

"It's … different," she sighed wanly.

"Do you like Hazleton?"

"It's okay."

"Do they have mountains and forests, or is it flat, like here?"

"What I've seen is beautiful, but we don't get out much. Brandon's gone a lot, and I have the house and the girls to take care of."

"What are his parents like?"

"Very nice. His father's a coal miner on the night shift. He usually makes good money, but lately he's been sick a lot. He coughs all the time."

"What about his mother?"

"She got a part-time job as a seamstress after we moved in with them. It's hard, supporting themselves and our family too." Cindy closed her eyes, took a weary breath, then smiled at Len. "Tell me about yourself. Have you got a girl?"

"I did have, but we broke up."

"Oh? What happened?"

"Give me that! Cindy, get in here!" They followed Mom's voice to find her standing over Laurie. "This is not a toy!" she shouted, replacing a flower vase on the window sill. "Cindy, why haven't you taught these children some manners?"

"They're just kids, Mom," Joey protested after Cindy cut the visit short.

"She ought to watch them more carefully. What's the point of having nice things if you don't take care of them?"

"What's the point of having nice things if they come between you and your family?"

"Don't you get smart with me!" she warned. "Who do you think paid for all the nice things *you've* got?"

Len spent most of his graduation party sitting in a corner with a glass of punch while Mom hobnobbed with her friends. The whole thing was really an excuse for her to show off the house. Even the fireplace was a decoration. She refused to let Joey build a fire in it. Too messy.

Barbara Lazenby came over to him, smiling brightly. "It's graduation time, my favorite writer! Why the long face?"

"It's nothing."

"Oh, I see." She sat beside him. "What's her name?"

He smiled sadly. "Loretta Weaver."

"Ah! Well, that explains everything." She patted his hand. "Don't lose heart, Len. She'll come around if she's worth anything."

Barbara returned to the party, a medley of church friends, Bridge club members, and new neighbors. All of them talking simultaneously. Joey wandered about the room in a white shirt and tie, serving hors d'oeuvres to the guests. "Sharon, your boys are such gentlemen!" Carol Harper remarked. "How do you do it?"

After Len's ceremony, Cindy telephoned her congratulations from Hazleton. "I'm sorry I had to leave," she said. "It just wasn't working out."

"Are you all right?" he asked. "Mom's worried about you."

"I'm okay. I've got to go. We can't afford long-distance calls."

"I think you should wear the dark blue suit," Mom said as she cracked open her fortune cookie. "You look good in blue, and it'll go nicely with that patterned maroon tie."

"Wear it where?"

"To church Sunday!" she said, exasperated. "What else have I been talking about? Why do you always tune me out?"

He pulled himself together. "I'm sorry, Mom. I can't get my mind off Miranda. She was so outgoing and bubbly. You could introduce her to someone, and five seconds later they'd be prattling away like old friends."

"Sounds like Beth." She frowned at the fortune slip.

"That's right. No matter how busy she was, Miranda started every morning sitting by my desk and telling me about her family. Sometimes she brought her grandchildren to my office. They sat on the floor and drew pictures for me."

Len had a soft spot for little children. They were so honest and direct. One day, Sheila tottered over to him with a crayon drawing. "I made you a wife, Mister Len," she lisped. It was a stick figure wearing a dress. He taped it to his wall beside Matisse's *Woman with a Hat*.

"You were lucky," Mom was saying. "The other clerks at the VA gossiped about me behind my back. They didn't think I deserved a government job. Wanda Beatty made this tacky remark one day, suggesting I only got it because Bob Sharp pulled some strings for me. I worked twice as hard as any of them, but who do you think got promoted when Bob retired? Howard Davis, the laziest nincompoop you ever saw, and they only picked him because he was a man."

Len groaned. What good was being resurrected if you didn't bury the past? "Mom, why are you like this?"

"Like what?"

"Why do you keep harping on things that happened decades ago? You're only making yourself miserable."

"You'd be miserable too if you had to work with people like that. It took me five years to earn a promotion to secretary and six more before they made me administrative assistant. I was past fifty when I became manager, and by then you boys were grown up and on your own. Everything was stacked against me because I was a woman."

"But you don't work there anymore! So why dwell on it?"

"Well, I'm sorry!" she snapped. "I won't say another word if it makes you happy!" She threw down her napkin.

"Come on. Tell me what's really bothering you."

"You wouldn't understand."

Wordlessly, they left the table. Len paused to examine her fortune slip. It was blank.

They drove home in silence. Mom marched to the bedroom to unpin and de-tag the new clothes.

Len carried his despair to the back porch. Dead leaves from the red oak tree littered the ground. Another chore waiting to be done.

Scenes with Mom always made him feel guilty. His anger would dissolve as he remembered a Christmas morning at the old house when he arose to find a new Schwinn bicycle parked beside the tree. "Must be from Santa," Mom smiled as he admired the handlebars, the pedals, the sleek white frame with red trim. He spent the morning learning to ride it, Mom running alongside him, holding him steady until he got his balance. She clapped her hands as he glided away from her, proudly in control.

Or the time the circus came to town, and Mom bought the kids popcorn and Cokes to enjoy while they watched the clowns and jugglers and performing elephants. Or Joey's tenth birthday party, when she invited all his friends from Sunday School, decorated the backyard with crepe and balloons, and served pound cake with ice cream on card tables borrowed from the church.

Or the day an ambulance took Cindy to the hospital with acute appendicitis, Mom sitting up all night with her after the surgery while the boys stayed with the Lazenbys. Mom skipped work for three days to nurse Cindy until the soreness went away, propping her up on the sofa to watch *Art Linkletter's House Party* and feeding her soup and Jell-O.

Why didn't he remember all this seven years ago, when Jacob Lawson came to the house to take notes for her eulogy?

"Tell me some things about your mother," the pastor prompted her children.

They looked at each other. "She grew up on a farm during the Depression," Cindy offered. "They were very poor."

"She had a lot of friends," Len added.

"She always got her own way," Joey muttered.

Lawson eyed him uncertainly. "Do you have any special memories of her? Maybe something nice you all did together?"

They stared at their feet.

"Olivia, what about you?" Lawson asked.

"She kept me from getting fired."

"Oh yes, that's right!" Len exclaimed.

"What's wrong?" Mom asked as Olivia staggered into the house. Len arose from the breakfast table and helped her to a chair.

"Mateo's dead," she croaked.

"What happened?"

Olivia's eyelids fluttered. "I don't feel so good."

"Len, get her a glass of water."

Olivia's left cheek was swollen. There was a large purple bruise on her jaw. "It's time for your pills, Sharon," she said dazedly. "And I have to take your vital signs." She tried to stand.

"Never mind that now," Len insisted. "Are you hurt anywhere else?"

"That noise ... it was so awful! And the blood ..." She shuddered.

"Mom, I think she's going into shock. I'll call the EMTs."

"No, don't!" Olivia gasped. "Please! I don't have any insurance and I can't afford to miss work. I'll be all right. Could I just sit here for a few minutes?"

"Take all the time you need."

Gradually, the story seeped out of her. Around 2:30 in the morning, Mateo had burst through the front door, wild-eyed on Speed and paranoia, demanding to see his grandchild. Olivia's reminder that the baby had died only stoked his fury.

"After he hit me, he grabbed Delia and started slapping her around, calling her filthy names in Spanish. I was trying to pull him off her when there was this loud crack. Mateo fell over like a rag doll."

"What happened?"

"It was Lucas. I guess he was sleeping on the porch swing again. He hit Mateo in the head with his baseball bat."

"Oh, precious Lord!" Mom exclaimed.

"Where is Lucas now?" Len asked.

"The police took him to jail." Olivia broke down. "Oh Sharon, this thing is all over the morning news! What if my boss hears about it?"

"Len, you go on to work," Mom urged. "Come child, you lie down on the sofa and rest. Don't worry about money. Len and I will pay you just the same." Ignoring her walker, Mom wrapped an arm around Olivia and led her into the living room. Len couldn't tell who was propping up whom.

That night, Olivia's supervisor came to the house. "I'm sorry one of our employees inflicted her personal problems on you," the woman said. "We'll send someone to replace her."

"What do you mean?" Mom asked. "Don't tell me you're going to fire her."

"Let's just say we're handling her case in a professional way."

"What does that mean?"

"Mrs. Holder, we can't tolerate this kind of thing. We have a reputation to maintain with our clients."

"*I'm* your client, and I want Olivia! Nobody else!"

The woman looked to Len, who nodded. "Well ... I suppose I could speak to the owner about putting her on probation."

"That's not good enough," Mom declared. "Olivia's not to blame for what happened. If you want my business, you'd better respect my wishes and treat her right!"

Olivia was back at work the next day. It was one of the few times in his life that Len felt proud of his mother.

Three years later, Len sat at the front of the chapel with Olivia and the rest of Mom's family. Behind him sat a half-dozen people from her Sunday School class. Miranda, Frank, Chad and Sylvia had an entire row to themselves.

"Where is everybody?" Danny whispered. He had flown fifteen hundred miles to be here.

"This is what happens when you live too long," Len answered. "Mom attended all her friends' funerals. Nobody's left to attend hers."

Danny scowled at the grandchildren giggling and poking each other. Their parents took turns shushing them while mumbling into their cell phones. Joey and Cindy stared indifferently at the coffin.

"I'm sorry, Uncle Len. I should have come around more often."

"You did what you could, Danny. You had your own family to take care of. Your birthday cards and phone calls made her very happy."

Danny covered his eyes. "I should have done more. She was all I had left of my dad. But I was always too busy. I'm so ashamed!" The kids quieted as he sobbed, the only person crying besides Olivia.

After the burial, Len drove Cindy to the airport. "Did you love Mom?" he asked.

"No," she admitted. "But I wanted to."

"Len? What are you doing out here?" Mom stood forlornly in the doorway.

He turned away from the tree. "I was thinking how nice that blue suit looked in the store. And you're right about the tie." She smiled gratefully. "How about you? Which dress do you like best?"

"The pink one. It makes me look younger."

He put an arm around her. "Mom, I've got an idea," he said, escorting her inside. "Let's make you a teenager. We'll get you some of those ripped jeans and cold-shoulder tops. You can tie a sweater around your waist, hop on a scooter and ride around chewing gum, texting, and bumping into things. You'll fit right in."

142

"Oh, stop it!" she blushed. "I thought I'd bake some brownies from your grandmother's old recipe. Want to help me?"

"Love to. I'll chop the nuts."

He watched carefully as she set the oven temperature and measured the ingredients. She couldn't remember being dead, or the house she'd been so proud of. But she could still whip up a batch of brownies from memory.

Len thought of Miranda in her elf hat, doling out baskets of Christmas fudge. On impulse, he seized his mother and wrapped his arms around her.

"Well, what's all this?" she mumbled into his chest.

"I just thought you deserved a hug."

Gently, she squirmed free of him. "Now look what you've done," she said. "Made me spill flour on the floor." She dabbed at her eyes.

"I'll get it." Len cleaned up the mess with wet paper towels. "Mom, did you make brownies for Dad?"

"Not that I remember. Probably not. Sugar was a luxury during the Depression." She poured the mixture into a baking pan.

Even as a child, Len could see how the 1930s had traumatized Mom's generation. They never threw anything away, and they fixed whatever got broken. Avery Swann, their neighbor at the old house, had a storage shed full of junk treasures. Phone line insulators. Lengths of barbed wire. Balls of string. A push mower missing one wheel. A hammer head with no handle. Bent nails, rusty bolts, and screws. "You never know when something might come in handy," Avery said.

Mom herself had saved her mother's old canning jars, using them to preserve the black-eyed peas, tomatoes and squash she grew in the backyard of the old rental place. She cut up worn-out clothing for use as cleaning rags. She saved her paper shopping bags for trash can liners; the small ones she used to pack the kids' school lunches, sandwiches wrapped in sheets of wax paper that she cleaned and reused. She taught her kids how to peel potatoes and carrots, which she made into hearty winter soups. Bob Sharp, her boss, invited Mom, Cindy and the boys to his farm to pick elderberries, which she cooked up for jams and jellies. Sometimes Avery brought her some venison from his deer hunting trips. Mom turned it into the best chili Len ever tasted.

The day Len turned twelve, his mother placed a half-dollar coin in his hand. "You'll get one of these each week," she promised, "as long as you mow the lawn, wash the dishes and keep the windows clean." It surprised him, as miserly as she was. Only years later did he realize it was her way of teaching him responsibility.

At first, he blew his allowance on science fiction movies, awed by the spectacle of giant mutant crabs devouring scientists, and an interplanetary vampire with empty eyeballs that fried people's brains. Then one Saturday, he stopped by the Army Surplus store across from the movie house. The display window featured a mannequin in combat helmet, fatigues, and boots.

Len went inside. The store offered a collection of ammo belts, field jackets, gas masks, and mess kits. For a penny, you could buy a U.S. Army shoulder patch. Zippo lighters cost twenty-five cents. A canteen cost twenty. Len browsed for an hour, his fingers fondling the half-dollar coin in his pocket. Finally, he selected a soldier's field cap, a lighter, and a rectangular metal box with a clamp.

The man at the cash register was scary-looking. He had a burn mark across half his face. His right eye was seared shut. A deep red scar ran from the socket to his jawbone.

"Mister, what's this thing for?" Len asked, placing the box on the counter.

"It's an ammo box. It holds fifty-caliber shells in a belt that feeds into a machine gun."

"Do you have the gun that goes with it?"

"Not hardly! You could wipe out a whole battalion with one of those things."

Len placed his coin on the counter with his purchases. "Is this enough?"

"Is that all you've got?"

"Yes sir."

The clerk swept Len's money into the cash register. "Kid, what do you want with this junk?"

"My dad was in the war. I want to know more about it."

"No, you don't!" The man scowled at Len with his undamaged eye. "What theater was your dad in?"

"He wasn't in a theater. He was in the Army."

"Dummy! I mean where did he serve?"

"I'm not sure. He went missing somewhere in the Pacific."

"Oh." The clerk studied Len briefly, then turned to a display case on the wall. "Here, take this."

"What is it?"

"A World War II Victory Medal. If your dad died fighting the Japs, you ought to have something to show for it."

"How much is it?"

"Never mind. Come here." He pinned the medal on Len's shirt, tugged the cap over his head, and dropped the lighter into the ammo box. "Go on, get outta here."

"What's that on your shirt?" Mom asked when he got home.

"A medal. The man at the Army Surplus store gave it to me."

"Oh." She bent to examine it.

"Mom, which battles was Dad in?"

"I don't know. Why?"

"Did he kill anybody?"

"That's not a nice thing to ask, Len. Take that thing off before it tears a hole in your shirt."

The Zippo didn't work, but Avery fixed it with a flint and some lighter fluid. "Don't let your mom catch you smoking," he winked solemnly. Len carried the lighter around in his pocket to make him feel manly. He used the ammo box to store his collection of science fiction paperbacks.

The brownies came out warm and chewy, just as he remembered them. Len poured two glasses of milk. "We're spoiling our supper, you know," he teased, taking a seat at the table. "You'd never let me get away with this if I was still a kid."

"I suppose you think I mistreated you because I made you eat healthy meals."

"Now Mom, I didn't say that. Actually, you were a great cook."

"That's not what you said when you were little," she reminded him.

He grinned. "I didn't like anything that was good for me."

"My mother wouldn't teach me how to cook," she said. "We were so poor she was afraid I'd waste food. She wouldn't even show me how to make chicken and dumplings, Papa's favorite. I had to learn all by myself after your father and I got married, and mine was never as good as hers."

"Dad's letter from the war said he missed your cooking," Len said.

"Oh. Well, he worked so hard in the fields he'd eat anything I put in front of him."

Len helped himself to another brownie. They were delicious, but he wondered where she'd found the ingredients. He couldn't remember the last time he'd cooked from a recipe.

"You should learn to cook like Olivia does," she continued. "You're going to ruin yourself with those frozen dinners."

"It's too much trouble, especially after I've been working all day."

"Be glad you've got a choice. I didn't, not with a husband and kids to feed. There weren't any frozen dinners or fast-food places back then. You ate what you could grow or went hungry."

Mom was mystified when Starbucks stores began to appear around town. It didn't make sense, she said. Why would anyone pay three dollars for a cup of coffee when they could make it at home for pennies? But at the mall today, she'd spent twelve hundred dollars on clothes without batting an eye.

"What was it like on the farm, Mom?" Len asked. "Did you and Dad slaughter your own livestock?"

"The chickens we did. Will had an arrangement with Ned Sorensen about the cattle and pigs. We supplied the feed, and Ned butchered the animals. Then Ned decided that wasn't enough. He wanted to charge us thirty cents a pound for our share of the meat. Will said that wasn't fair, and besides, we couldn't afford it. So we just did without. Those Sorensens were a greedy bunch anyway. They never brought any food to the church socials, but you can bet they ate their share, all six of them. And on top of that, Nelly Sorensen had the nerve to criticize my squash casserole! Said it needed more cornstarch and less salt! Well, that didn't stop her from gorging on it. And those kids of hers were the noisiest bunch you ever saw. One morning, right in the middle of church …"

Len tuned her out. In his mind's eye, Miranda sat beside him, chattering happily about her grandchildren.

After supper, they watched the news. Len was trying to explain Facebook to Mom when Joey appeared on the screen.

"My remark following last night's NFL game was a spur-of-the-moment attempt to describe a coach's job situation. I had no intention of offending anyone, especially senior citizens, for whom I have the greatest respect. Many callers to my radio broadcasts are seniors who know more about sports history than I do. I'm keenly aware of what elderly people suffer because my own mother passed away under hospice care. It was the dedication of those skilled professionals who made her last days easier. I hope anyone who feels hurt by my remark will accept my sincere apology."

The anchorman was speculating that Joey would keep his job, given his popularity. But Mom gaped at the screen. "What's he talking about, Len? What does he mean I passed away?"

"Uh ... well," he stammered, "you know how TV people are, Mom. It's just Joey's way of getting off the hook."

"I didn't bring you children up to lie! What's going on?"

"Mom, I'm sure —"

"That man at the courthouse, taking my fingerprints and talking about paperwork mistakes. Does Joey think I'm dead?"

"Mom, it's like I told you. We got this letter —"

"I might as well be! He *acts* like I'm dead. When was the last time he came to see me? Or even called to see how I'm doing? What kind of son treats his mother that way?"

"Mom, Joey has a demanding job. And like I told you, the paperwork thing is probably some computer glitch."

She pressed her hands to her temples. "You're hiding something. You think I'm just an empty-headed old woman, too dumb to understand anything. Who do you think took care of you and made all the decisions for you kids? Where would you be if I hadn't done all your thinking for you? Well, I'm still Sharon Holder and I've still got my wits about me! All of a sudden, you've stopped going to work, hanging around the house all day, pretending everything's normal. But it's not! Now you tell me what's going on!"

Maybe she was right. "Mom ... do you remember waking up last Monday morning?"

"What about it?"

"When I found you here in the living room, I was surprised. Do you know why?"

"What's surprising about that?"

"Please, concentrate. What was happening right before you came into the room?"

Her eyes turned cloudy and distant. "I remember dreaming of your dad, holding me in his arms. It was 1934. We were kids again, just married, off by ourselves for a little while. There was no war yet. Just the two of us. I felt loved. Cherished." She hugged herself. "I haven't felt that way in a long time."

"Mom," he asked gently, "what about Sunday night, or the day before? Where were you then?"

She stood and gathered her robe around her. "I'm tired. I'm going to bed."

"Now? It's only 6:30, time for *Wheel of* –"

"You're trying to confuse me! I'm tired! Leave me alone!" She disappeared into the bedroom.

She knows, Len thought.

He watched tonight's movie by himself. Lionel Barrymore had Death trapped in an apple tree so he could remain alive to protect his grandson from a scheming aunt. Len, his heart still raw over Miranda, wept when Grandma passed away while knitting and listening to Stephen Foster tunes on the radio. He dissolved again when Grandpa and the boy strolled off to Heaven together. Sappy and emotional, but tonight Len was a sucker for weepy endings.

"I'd never have become a father if it weren't for Miranda," Chad confided to him once, "much less a husband or a Christian. Until she introduced me to Marylou, I didn't realize how empty my life was. She taught me to look beyond the present moment." Chad had changed almost overnight, from party animal to family man. He even became a youth counselor at his church.

Things didn't work out so well for Sylvia. Three years after her marriage, Demetri asked for a divorce.

"I warned him it wasn't going to work," she sighed one morning as Len drove her to a client meeting. "I've been afraid of men my whole life."

"I don't get it," Len said. "Demetri seems so crazy about you."

"That's why I have to let him go. He wants children, and I ... I can't help it, Len!" she cried. "I can't bear to be touched that way!"

"Sylvia, something terrible must have happened to make you like this."

"It did!" she wept. "It did, and I can't talk about it! I won't!" She shrank into the passenger seat.

"Have you thought about getting some help?"

"You mean a psychiatrist? I already tried that."

So fragile and sensitive. You'd never know it to look at her.

"I'm sorry, Sylvia. I hate to see you so unhappy." Len was silent for a moment. "You're not afraid of me, are you?"

"Oh no, Len!" she sniffed. "Not you. You're a nice guy. Anybody can see that." She leaned over and kissed his cheek.

Nice, he thought. Harmless is what she means.

He moped about Miranda for a while, feeling lost. She was the best friend he'd ever had. Not that he'd had that many. Breaking through Len's defenses was too much work for most people. Miranda had never met anyone she couldn't win over.

Abruptly, he seized his laptop and browsed through his incomplete stories. Since taking up writing again he'd played around with some new ideas. A comic murder mystery combining characters from Jane Austen and Danielle Steel novels. The rise and fall of a 1950s jazz combo. A satire about TV news reporters. All of them defective eggs that wouldn't hatch. The farm novel remained his only promising effort. But he'd been bogged down in it for weeks.

Following the computer revolution, Len had retyped all his manuscripts into an IBM PS-2 and stored them on floppy disks. But they didn't look any better onscreen than they had on paper. Now, on his aging laptop, they seemed as hopeless as ever.

"Don't let your failures discourage you," a successful author once wrote. "Start by accepting the fact that basically, every story has already been told by someone else. Love, hate, jealousy, fear, greed, ambition – the difference is in the way *you* tell it. Let your passion for the subject lead you where it wants to go. That's how you make an old story *your* story."

Len decided he was passionate but conventional; clever but superficial; imaginative but ineloquent. Why did God instill those qualities in him if he had nothing worthwhile to say?

Throughout five decades of paper shuffling, Len had felt himself spinning his wheels. Sure, other people had mundane jobs, but they found compensation in family or friends. Len lived in a world of imaginary characters, none of them aware that he existed.

Before he met Miranda, his relationships with real people had always ended in failure. This one had ended in death.

On his way to bed, he stopped by Mom's room. Seven years ago he would have welcomed an evening like this, Mom asleep and untroublesome. His personal freedom had seemed so important at the time. Now, he couldn't remember one night from another, or what he'd accomplished on any of them.

He sank into the bedside chair, listening to her deep, regular breathing. This was the woman who taught him how to brush his teeth and tie his shoelaces. Who bought Len and Joey a little record player and a collection of Disney tunes that they played, over and over. Who occasionally whipped up a batch of Grandma's brownies on her day off.

Brownies.

To make brownies, you needed things like eggs, flour, cocoa and sugar. Where did Mom get all that stuff for her baking this afternoon?

He went to the kitchen and opened the pantry. It contained vegetable oil, baking soda and various spices that Olivia had used to prepare their meals. There was a Hershey's cocoa tin and a small bottle of vanilla extract, both of which Mom had used in this afternoon's recipe. The flour and sugar canisters atop the cabinet were half full. All this stuff must be eight or ten years old. Even the nuts should have been stale by now. He hoped Mom hadn't accidentally poisoned them both.

Len returned to her bedside. Interesting, how innocent sleeping people looked, all their personality quirks suspended. Sharon Denise Holder lay at rest, ninety-six years of life experience stored in that slumbering brain, none of it evident on her face. No joy, sorrow, laughter, tears, pleasure or pain.

He settled deeper into the chair, watching his mother breathe until his eyes closed and his own respiration matched hers.

The Farm Tree

BY LEONARD HOLDER

Doctor Hogan shook his head. "There's no way we can save that leg. Too much bone and tissue damage. I'm very sorry."

Annie Brady stifled a sob. Ruth helped her to a chair beside Matt's hospital bed. John stood at the foot of it, his face haggard, his shirt and jeans smeared with blood and dirt. "Is it my fault? Maybe I should have left him out there and run for help."

"John, you're the only reason he's still alive," Hogan said. "He'd have bled to death if you hadn't gotten him here when you did."

Matt heard none of this. He lay unconscious beneath sheets hiding the mangled remains of his left leg. His breathing was steady. An IV dripped fluid into his arm.

"John, that tractor must weigh over a ton," the doctor said. "How did you get him out?"

"I had to dig a trench under him with a plow blade so I could pull him loose. It was the only thing handy."

"Did he say how it happened?"

"He swung around too fast at the end of a turn row and it flipped over. Annie, I'm so sorry." She nodded, too upset to speak.

The door opened and Charley appeared. "I came as soon as I heard. How is he?"

"We'll be taking him to surgery any minute now." The doctor's nose wrinkled. "What's that smell?"

"Sorry. I was delivering a baby colt when Mom called. I didn't stop to shower." Charley washed up in the sink, then went to place his hand gently on Matt's forehead.

"Doctor, may I see you outside for a moment?" John asked. They stepped into the hallway. "Are you sure about this? Maybe if we sent him to the Mayo Clinic."

"We don't have time. That leg's got to come off tonight or the infection will kill him." He studied John closely. "You don't look so good yourself. I'm going to admit you for observation. Carrying a man on your back for two miles is enough to –"

"I'm all right." Through the doorway, he watched Ruth and Charley comfort Annie. "He's a proud man, doctor. He's going to wish I'd left him out there to die."

Saturday

Len dreamed he was writing a play. It was awkward, because he was also driving down the street, balancing his old portable typewriter on the steering wheel. His scene depicted a pianist, playing with his back to the audience. To his left, a glamorous actress in a long black dress perched on a stool, her legs crossed, a cigarette holder in her hand. When the pianist struck the right chord, the actress was supposed to fall off the stool and shatter like a porcelain vase. The scene had a symbolic perfection that Len needed to explain to the actress. But suddenly she was sitting on his lap, obscuring his vision, criticizing his driving and his typing.

The car crashed into a tree, jerking him awake. "My dreams are more interesting than my stories," he muttered.

He hauled himself upright. Two nights in a row, he'd slept in the chair beside Mom's bed. Two mornings in a row, she was still there, snoozing away. How long do resurrections last? he wondered. According to the Bible, Jesus had lingered for forty days.

Not that Len had anything else to do. Miranda was dead. Chad and Sylvia had vanished. The new people at Winslow & Grant didn't know him. His writing was stalled. All he had left was his undead mother.

Joey sounded groggy when he answered the phone. "Sorry," Len said. "I didn't mean to wake you."

"That's okay," he yawned. "I need to get up anyway."

"Joey, I'm calling about your hospice apology last night."

"What about it?"

"That remark you made was from a game played seven years ago."

"Seven years?" he mumbled sleepily. "What are you talking about?"

"Mom heard what you said. She got very upset."

"Oh Len, give me a break! I spent all day yesterday trying to salvage my career. The Twitter trolls are after me, plus I've got jetlag and a houseful of grandkids. Your fantasies aren't my problem."

"I'm not making this up, Joey! If you don't believe me, call Cindy. She's been getting —"

"Come on, Len! Ever since she died, you've been telling me about these dreams of yours. Why don't you sell Mom's house so you can stop living in the past?"

Beth said something in the background. "It's okay, honey, it's just Len. Hey, I'd better go. This is the first Saturday I've been home since football season started. I promised to take Tori and Kathy to Magic Land."

"Joey —"

"Len, Mom's dead. The sooner you accept that, the sooner you can start living a normal life." He hung up.

"Who were you talking to?" she asked, wandering into the kitchen.

"Oh, uh, just one of my clients."

She opened the refrigerator. "I wish we had some bacon. When are we going to the supermarket?"

"This morning," he said, scribbling on a pad. "I'm making a grocery list now."

"Well, write down bacon. And key lime pie."

"There's still some in the freezer."

She came to the table with a carton of milk and a box of Cheerios.

"Mom," he began cautiously, "about last night —"

"I don't want to talk about it."

"The reason I asked —"

"I DON'T WANT TO TALK ABOUT IT!" She stood abruptly. "I'm not hungry. Let's go to the store. I'll get dressed." She left the room.

Joey couldn't fool Len with his remark about living in the past. He was the oldest active announcer in America. A place of honor awaited him in the Sports Broadcasting Hall of Fame. He had nothing left to prove. Seven years after Mom's death, he was still trying to make her proud of him.

Unlike many sportscasters, Joey wasn't an ex-jock. In high school, he was too short for basketball, too skinny for football, too slow for track, too uncoordinated for baseball. So he hung around the practice field after school, cheering for his classmates. The football coach took pity on him and appointed him team manager. He made friends with the players while shagging towels, laundering jerseys, and mopping the locker room.

Even as a boy, Joey was quick to appreciate the drama that announcers added to sporting events. He would sit up late at night, searching the radio dial for the faint voices of Red Barber, Harry Caray and Vin Scully. He kept a little notebook of their colorful phrases and sat in front of the TV every Sunday, practicing his play-by-play routine. Mom scoffed at him. "Why should people need announcers to tell them what they're looking at?"

Joey's rich voice and crisp enunciation earned him A's in speech class. They also got him a job broadcasting high school games on a local radio station. For someone so young, he had a knack for spontaneous commentary.

People at church complimented Mom on having such a talented son. She remained indifferent. "He'll talk to invisible radio audiences," she complained to Len, "but he won't talk to his own mother." It was true. After the breakup with Beth, he avoided Mom, biding his time until he could finish high school, get a job and move out of the house.

One Friday night, a TV producer driving through town heard Joey describe the opposing team as "Popeye in a spinach drought." The man invited him to New York for an audition. The timing couldn't have been better. It was the early 1960s, the genesis of the TV sports boom. The networks needed fresh faces and vibrant voices.

Joey came up in the days before mobile TV cameras. The fixed units were bulky monsters, set so high in the stadium that onscreen, the players looked like ants. Worse, their jerseys displayed no names, only numbers. Each week Joey had to memorize new team rosters so he could quickly identify the ball carriers and tacklers. There was no instant replay, so he had to be on his toes. Sportswriters loved to reprint an announcer's blunders.

On camera, Joey had an authoritative air. He was analytical without being intrusive, witty without being offensive, and his enthusiasm for the games he covered was infectious. His handsome face attracted female viewers. Soon after his debut, fan mail began to pour into network headquarters. Within two years he became the lead announcer for college football games. By the 1970s he was covering NFL Football, Major League Baseball, and NBA Basketball.

Through it all, Joey remained a family man. Between his divorce from Whitney and remarriage to Beth, he always made time for the kids, despite his grueling travel schedule. On non-game days, he worked at the local network affiliate, filming interviews, compiling statistics, and tracking developments in off-season sports. Only Len and Beth knew how hard Joey worked at his job, and why he needed her. Beth was both wife and surrogate mother.

The prices at the supermarket astounded Mom. "A dollar twenty-nine for a pound of oranges? A dollar forty-nine for grapes, and that's a special? It's robbery!"

"It's inflation," Len laughed. "You just haven't been grocery shopping in a while."

While she picked over the fruit, Len watched a stock boy arrange apples in tidy rows to make them more appealing. It reminded him of his own first job.

"You're too old now to need an allowance," Mom declared the day he turned sixteen. "See if you can get a job at Turcot's Market."

"They'd probably turn me down," he shrugged.

"You'll never know unless you ask."

"I don't have any experience."

"So? How do you think other people get experience? I wasn't born working at the VA, you know."

"What if they hire me and I make a mistake?"

"Then you'll learn from it and do better next time. Go on, give it a try."

It was either that or risk one of her bad moods. She still hadn't forgiven Joey for turning down a summer car washing job. He preferred to hang around the radio station, ripping news bulletins from the teletype machine for the DJs to read on the air.

Len shuffled over to the store and found Mister Turcot on his knees, stamping prices on canned goods. "Excuse me, sir," Len said timidly, "have you got any kind of work I can do?"

The man looked up. "How old are you, son?"

"Sixteen, sir. Today's my birthday."

"Well, happy birthday." Turcot got to his feet. "You got any objections to wearing an apron?"

"Sir?"

"You'll need one unless you want your mother complaining about meat stains and fruit smears on your clothes."

"Oh! Right."

"Can you work from six to eleven on Friday nights and eight to three on Saturdays?"

"Yes sir."

"Good. I'll start you at seventy-five cents an hour. Bagging, carry-outs, and cleanup. Any questions?"

"No sir!" he grinned. "Thank you, sir!" He ran all the way home. Seventy-five cents an hour times twelve hours was – nine dollars a week! Eighteen times his allowance! And his new boss's handshake to go with it. All at once, he felt grown up.

Len spent his weekends following housewives out to their cars, his arms laden with paper bags. During shopping lulls, he wiped down the checkout counters and sorted empty soda bottles. Before going home each Friday night, he swept and mopped the entire store.

Three weeks after he started, Mister Turcot said, "Well, Len. Looks like your mother was right."

"My mother?"

"She said you'd make me a good hand if I gave you a chance. I'm glad I did." He patted Len's shoulder.

Len worked at the store through high school to earn money for college. On his last day, Mister Turcot wrote him a letter of recommendation. "Always prompt," it said. "Good at following orders and adjusting to a routine."

They should carve that on my tombstone, Len thought now. Along with "He was a nice guy."

As Mom added bacon to her shopping cart, Len's phone rang. "Hi, it's Beth. I couldn't help hearing what Joey said. I waited until he left the house to call you. Len, I'm sorry. Talking about his mom still disturbs him."

"Did he tell you what I said?"

"Yes. I thought he was joking."

"See for yourself." He handed Mom the phone. "Hi, Beth! I can't believe what they charge for fruit these days! Listen, if you're not busy later, why don't we go out to lunch?"

Beth was waiting in the driveway when they returned, dumbstruck to see her dead mother-in-law emerge from the car. Mom went inside to change clothes.

"Len, this isn't possible!" Beth whispered as he put away the groceries.

"No, but there she is."

"How did it happen?"

"I don't know. Monday morning, I came into the living room and she was standing there, looking out the window."

"Did she say how she got here?"

"She's been evasive. When I tried to pin her down last night, she got upset."

"Len, Cindy and I picked out her burial clothes! That two-piece Ann Taylor suit she was so proud of."

"And now it's back in her closet with all her other clothes."

"How?"

"I don't know. Crazy things have been happening all week. I keep hearing Joey's radio show in his old bedroom."

"What's unusual about that?"

"There's no radio in there. Nothing but his bed, the one he hasn't slept in since high school."

"Are you sure it wasn't a dream?"

"I wish it was. I wish this whole thing was something I could wake up from."

Beth glanced nervously toward Mom's bedroom. "What am I supposed to do? Act like everything's normal?"

"That's what I've been doing."

"I'm ready!" Mom chirped, reappearing in a sunny yellow dress and high heels. Len suppressed a smile. Only Mom would dress up for lunch on Saturday.

"Len, are you coming with us?" she asked.

"I think I'd better get the leaves raked up. We're supposed to get a cold front tomorrow night. Bring me a takeout order."

They left, Beth looking back at him uneasily as she closed the door.

He fetched a rake from the toolshed and began working the leaves into a large pile. The exercise felt great in the crisp autumn air.

Mom always acted as though she and Beth were best pals, conveniently forgetting her reaction to Joey's second marriage. "I knew it!" she exclaimed after visiting their home. "She puts her dishes in the washer without rinsing them first. There's a layer of dust on the dining table. The kids' clothes are scattered from one room to another. And Janie's socks don't match!" It was a lot of smoke. Mom was hurt that Joey deliberately shut her out of the wedding.

Her attitude changed one Saturday when Beth drove up to Mom's house with a load of flowers, shrubs, and mulch bags. "Surprise!" she cried when Mom answered the door. "There's a spring sale today at Robinson's Nursery. I got you some great bargains." They spent the day together, transforming Mom's front yard into a gardener's showcase. After that, they began hanging out together regularly.

Len admired Beth. She had bounced back from traumas that would devastate most people. Her chaotic childhood. The stigma of being an orphan. Her first husband's death. A hysterectomy that prevented her from having children with Joey. She never seemed to get angry or depressed. And she never criticized Mom for wrecking her high school romance.

The kids from their first marriages adjusted to each other, once they resolved differences over which toys belonged to whom. By then, Mom was eager to play grandmother. She bought them yo-yos, a pogo stick, a dollhouse, and a ring-toss game. She made Kool-Aid and seated them at her dining table with jigsaw puzzles and Play-Doh, covering it with a linen cloth to protect the finish.

Everything was fine until Joey returned from a road trip one day and learned that Beth had left the kids alone with his mother. He raced over to her house and herded them into his car. "Why is he like this?" she cried to Len. "Don't I have the right to see my own grandchildren?"

One Sunday afternoon the adults relaxed on the back porch, watching the children hunt Easter eggs in the shrubbery. Beth's youngest girl wandered over and crawled into Mom's lap. "Tilly, go play in the yard!" Joey ordered. "It's okay, I can handle her," Mom protested. Wordlessly, he snatched Tilly away and seated her on the lawn.

Mom was the only subject Joey and Beth fought over. "She's good with the kids," Beth insisted. "And she's the only grandmother they've got."

"You don't know her like I do," he said stubbornly. "Just wait till they break a dish or spill something on the carpet."

Eventually, the tension created a wall between the children and their grandmother. They concluded from Joey's attitude that she was some kind of witch. Len's presence didn't help. He was a mystery, an odd-duck uncle who hung around his mother because he had no life of his own.

After Mom retired from the VA, she tried filling her time with Bridge parties, crafts and church activities. It wasn't enough. Lonely and blue, she invited Len, Joey and Beth over for dinners and birthday celebrations. Joey resisted at first, but Beth urged him to let bygones be bygones. Eventually he relented, though he mostly kept quiet during the visits, forcing Beth to fill the silence.

Then Mom decided that everyone should come over for Thanksgiving dinner. "It's been ages since I put out my guest tablecloth and dinnerware," she told Len. "There's plenty of room if we add extra leaves to the dining table. I'll cook a turkey and Millie Dawson's stuffing recipe. Beth can make her sweet potato casserole."

Joey absolutely refused. "She can bring the darned turkey to our house," he said to Len. "She's not going to criminalize my grandkids because one of them puts a nick in her gravy boat!"

Beth smoothed things over. "Why don't you let Joey cook the turkey outside in his smoker?" she suggested to Mom. "You and I can do the rest in my kitchen."

Thus, Joey and Beth's house became the focus of Thanksgiving dinners. The grandkids ran in and out all morning, burning up energy. Mom put Eric's oldest daughter to work chopping celery and onions as she told stories of her girlhood on the farm. Joey lurked nearby like a cop, waiting for her to say something hurtful.

Years passed. The Thanksgiving crowd grew bigger as the grandchildren grew up, got married, and spawned more grandkids. Beth bought card tables and seated the youngest ones in her living room. "I've got a perfectly good dining table and plenty of space," Mom grumbled to Len. "It's just going to waste!"

But as the new millennium dawned, age began to drain away Mom's stamina. Now she was just a tired old lady, slow, arthritic, and sensitive to noise. On Thanksgiving Day Beth and Janie bustled about the kitchen while Mom sat in a corner, wincing as the latest crop of rug rats tore through the house. Len took her home immediately after dinner. He put on some Christmas music, dragged the artificial tree out of storage, and decorated it while she dozed in the recliner.

One day she phoned Len at his office in a panic. She'd backed into a parked car while leaving the hair salon. Len handled the insurance settlement, but a month later she got a ticket for running a stop sign. "I've been driving down that street for almost fifty years," she said tearfully, "and there wasn't any sign there before!"

"Mom, I think it's time you stopped driving."

"Why? Because nobody warned me about a new stop sign? Because that car I hit was parked illegally? I've been driving since I was eighteen, and I've never had an accident before."

"Remember what Doctor Lane said about your vision getting worse? What if you hit somebody? What if a child runs into the street and you can't stop in time?"

Reluctantly, she surrendered her car keys. Len added chauffeur and errand boy to his duties. On Saturdays, he took her grocery shopping, then to the beauty parlor.

He also began driving her to church. It was the first time he'd attended services in forty years. To his surprise, the hard-boiled church of his youth had passed into history. Jacob Lawson portrayed God as the essence of love, and His Church as a refuge. Sometimes people he'd counseled came onstage to reveal how faith had helped them through alcoholism, drug addiction, or marital problems. Len was impressed. At last, the Church was nurturing people instead of condemning them.

Mom and Len grew set in their ways, like an old married couple. After Sunday services they lunched at a restaurant, then went home to watch whatever sport Joey was covering. Later, she napped while Len worked on his novel until supper time. When she went to bed, he refilled her prescription dispenser for the coming week: Micardis for high blood pressure, Pantoprazole for acid reflux, lutein for her failing eyesight. After her first hip replacement, Doctor Kirby added Tramadol for post-surgical pain, and Namenda to fight her growing dementia.

The house, once a merry hub of ladies' lunches and card games, grew silent as Mom's old friends died or became housebound themselves. Beth seldom had time to visit anymore, too busy babysitting and driving grandchildren to soccer practice. Joey found reasons to avoid his mother entirely. Her only weekday companion was Olivia.

Her infirmities worsened. She grew reluctant to leave the house except for church, where she was embarrassed to be seen struggling with a walker. Olivia's weekend absences made her despondent. The grandchildren, immersed in their own lives, forgot about her. At Christmastime, Beth dropped by with gifts from herself and Joey. Cindy mailed a few more from Hazleton. But with only Len and his mother on hand to open them, Christmas morning felt as bleak as a Dickens novel. On Mom's final Christmas day, her only companions were Len and the tree. The tarnished star drooped above the winking lights.

Len packed the leaves into plastic bags. "How dare you clutter up my nice, clean lawn!" he scolded the tree in his mother's voice. When she bought this house, Mom planted the red oak in memory of the one shading the farmhouse where she grew up. She would sit on the porch, watching the red leaves fade and drift down to carpet the lawn. Majestic though it was, the tree created a lot of work for Len each year.

The season always reminded him of Mom's funeral and her brief graveside service. As Jacob Lawson read the Twenty-Third Psalm over her coffin, Len felt uneasy. For the first time in his life, he had no parents at all. It was like surviving an earthquake, but no longer trusting the ground beneath him.

As the small crowd dispersed, Miranda threw her arms around Len and hugged him so tightly that his joints popped. Gently, Frank pulled her away. Now, her own funeral loomed, another crack in his foundation.

The cemetery! he thought suddenly, standing erect. With Mom gone to lunch, this was a perfect time to check her gravesite. He tossed his rake at the leaf pile and headed for the car.

Holder	**Holder**
Pfc. William Earl	**Sharon Denise**
Beloved husband of	Beloved wife of
Sharon Denise Holder	William Earl Holder
Born March 14, 1914	Born September 10, 1917
MIA Pacific 1944, U.S. Army	Died November 2, 2013

The earth over Mom's grave was undisturbed, so he needn't fantasize about midnight excursions, shovels, and empty coffins. Maybe the exhumation would be futile. But he had to make sure.

Even without the dates, you could tell which one died first. Mom's gravestone was still pristine. Dad's showed seven decades of weathering. It was small and plain, due undoubtedly to the family's poverty at the time. Cindy had suggested replacing it with a new stone to match Mom's, but Len was adamant. The old one was a tenuous link to his father.

Mom and Len used to visit the cemetery each Memorial Day. "Tell me something about Dad," he urged as she placed flowers on his marker. "Something you haven't mentioned before."

She smiled. "I wish you could have known him those first years. Will would come in from the fields at sunset, stand in the doorway, and say, 'Where's my chipmunk? I want chipmunk for supper!' It was a game he and Garth played. Garth would find a different hiding place each night and make Will search the house for him. 'Where's my dinner?' he'd growl, and Garth would get tickled and give himself away. Will dragged him out of the closet or from under the bed and carried him around on his shoulders while I put supper on the table. When Cindy came along he was thrilled, even though we couldn't afford another mouth to feed. He assured me that times would change, the Depression would end, and he could make the land work for him. He dreamed of building a modern farmhouse, with electricity and indoor plumbing. He wanted you kids to have it better than we did."

Her eyes lingered on Dad's marker. "If only he hadn't gone to war."

Gradually, the cemetery visits became part of a general pilgrimage to honor the many friends Mom had outlasted. She wandered among their graves, reliving old memories. It was the only time Len heard her talk about the past without griping.

Once, they ran into Woody Lazenby, praying over his parents' graves. "Barbara and Milton meant so much to me," Mom said, patting his arm. "I'm so glad they lived long enough to enjoy their grandchildren." The couple had died two years apart, in their eighties. Len envied Woody, whose parents took in stride the trials of marriage and family life. He had never seen them quarrel or abuse their children. Fifty years after their marriage vows, Milton and Barbara still held hands in church. Len wished he'd thought to grab some flowers on his way here. From now on, he'd never be able to visit Barbara's grave without thinking of Miranda.

In the seven years since his mother's death, Len had dropped by the cemetery often, trying to picture himself in a two-parent boyhood. The gulf between Will Holder's death in 1944 and Mom's in 2013 seemed unnatural, like a huge chunk of family history cruelly hacked away. From his reading, Len knew a great deal about the Pacific war that took away his father. The Bataan Death March. Midway. Guadalcanal. Leyte Gulf. Iwo Jima. "MIA Pacific" wasn't much of an epitaph for a soldier. It would be interesting to know how Will Holder contributed to the Allies' victory, and how he met his end.

Len once asked Cindy if she remembered anything about Dad. "All I remember is his absence," she said.

As he returned to the car Len noticed a plastic bag fluttering from somebody's tombstone. He wandered over to rip it away. Then he noticed the name on the stone:

Chelsey West
March 3, 1943 – August 11, 1963

Len was shocked. He'd last seen Chelsey back in college, the day Link Endicott dragged her from the cafeteria. According to those dates, she was only twenty when she died. What could have happened to her?

He'd heard little news of his classmates since graduating from high school. Marilyn Travis, his pizza date, moved to San Francisco, where she was arrested in 1968 during an antiwar protest. Whitey Jones, one of Len's bullies, went to law school and started a non-profit legal service for indigent clients.

In the spring of 2011, Len got a postcard in the mail. It was an invitation to his fifty-year class reunion. The old bitterness arose in him. He ripped the card to pieces and threw them away.

A few weeks later the *Chicory Gazette* published a reunion photo. Marilyn and Whitey posed in a small group that included Loretta Weaver, whose last name was Kelly now. She was still slender, with the same auburn hair, but her teenage allure was gone. Whitey's stomach hung over his belt buckle. Marilyn was gray and wrinkled. Now he felt childish for tearing up the invitation. But what could he have said to Loretta? Or to any of them?

Ironically, Chelsey West had died about the same age as Emily Webb, the character she played in the senior class production of *Our Town*. Len still remembered the audience's breathless silence during the final scene, when Emily's spirit rose from the graveyard to wander among the townspeople. "They don't understand, do they?" she lamented to the other dead souls around her.

Mom and Beth were still gone when he returned. As he resumed raking leaves, his phone rang. "Mister Holder, this is Ron Stokes. I have some information for you about Miranda's funeral."

"Oh, good. Hang on a second." He dashed inside to grab a pen from the kitchen counter.

"It's going to be Monday at 2:00 o'clock, Ward Street Presbyterian Church. Burial will be in Silent Repose Cemetery."

"Have you heard from Chad Norris or Sylvia Baros?" Len asked. "They're the people I work with."

"Miranda did mention a guy who left the company on some sort of missionary campaign. There was also a woman who got hurt in a bike race. I guess it was pretty serious. Miranda said her ex-husband came and took her home with him."

"And you say all this happened a few years ago?"

"That's what Miranda told me."

Len felt dizzy. "Mister Holder? Are you still there?"

"I don't understand this," he said. "Last week I was sitting right where you are. Now my coworkers are gone, and the home office thinks I'm retired. Mister Stokes, would you mind checking the claims database? See if there are any pending claims with my name on them."

"I already thought of that. There aren't any. Mister Holder, I've got to go. I'm working overtime this afternoon, trying to catch up. Maybe I'll see you at the funeral Monday."

Len lingered at the counter. It was only last Friday that he was telling Miranda about *Jude the Obscure* while she cleaned the minifridge. Then a phone call interrupted them. It was Darren George, a client who wanted to give Len the serial numbers of some items stolen from his house.

The update should be in Len's work file, proof that he was still employed last week. He hunted up his laptop and tried logging into the claims database again.

INVALID USER NAME OR PASSWORD

ACCOUNT LOCKED

Please contact W&G technical support for assistance

"I'm sorry," a technician responded to Len's call. "I show no account under the name Leonard Holder."

Now he remembered something. Shortly before Mom died, Miranda had finally gotten frustrated with the minifridge and replaced it with a full-size Amana. She donated the minifridge to the Salvation Army Thrift Store.

So why did Len remember her cleaning it last Friday?

Disturbed, he returned to the leaves. I may be old, he thought, but I'm not senile. My office has two artificial plants. There's a print of Monet's *Water Lilies* next to my computer. I have twelve claim files open: seven roofing jobs, three totaled cars, and two burglaries.

And a partridge in a pear tree.

He was still raking leaves when Beth returned. "Well, she seems like her old self. Acts like nothing has changed."

"I know," Len replied. "Did you ask her what it's like to be dead?"

"I was afraid to mention it. We just talked about family stuff. But Len, she seems confused about my grandkids. When I mentioned Toby starting high school next fall, she thought he was still in fifth grade."

Len frowned. "I thought Toby graduated two years ago. Didn't you tell me he got accepted to Yale?"

She laughed. "Toby's a smart kid, but not that smart!"

"I guess I'm as confused as Mom," Len sighed. "She thinks this year is 2010."

"What are you going to do about her?"

"Take it in stride, I suppose. Right now, I'm working on restoring her benefits. Tell Joey I may need his permission to exhume the body."

"Oh, Len! Don't you think that's going too far?"

"I have to, Beth. What if she needs medical care or expensive drugs? It could bankrupt me."

"But how can she need medical care if she's already dead?"

"Does she seem dead to you?"

"No," she admitted. "Quite the opposite. Have you told your sister about this?"

"Yes, and that's another thing. Cindy says Mom's been phoning her. But I canceled Mom's landline when she died, and she doesn't know how to use a cell phone."

"Len, what do you think all this means?"

"I don't know."

A shadow crossed Beth's face. "Sharon was the closest thing I ever had to a mother of my own. All during lunch today I was thinking it was like old times, the two of us shopping and running errands together. I still have dreams about her."

"So do I." Len paused. "Beth, I've always meant to ask. How could you bury the hatchet with my mother, after what she did to you and Joey in high school?"

She shrugged. "Forgive and forget. That's what families do."

"I wish I could be like you."

Beth smiled. "Joey wishes he was like you."

Mom appeared in the doorway. "Len, we brought you some fettuccine Alfredo."

"Keep it warm for me, will you? I'd better get this done in case the wind picks up."

Beth followed her inside. As he returned to the leaves, he pictured himself phoning Medicare. "Hi there, my name is Len Holder. Say, my mother came back to life the other day and I was just wondering ..." How did one stumble into such quandaries?

By the time he finished the leaves, Beth was gone and Mom had settled down for a nap. He bolted his lunch, then went to his room to phone Cindy, hoping she'd turned her ringer back on. It wasn't every day that you asked your sister's permission to dig up her mother's coffin.

Cindy had seen more than her share of trouble. Brandon was working for an exterminator service when his father died of lung cancer. He had no life insurance, so his mother took in extra sewing. Cindy got a job in the cafeteria at her daughters' school. But it wasn't enough. In desperation, Brandon replaced his father in the coal mine. The night shift paid an extra fifty cents an hour.

Their daughters were eleven and thirteen years old when Laurie, the youngest, ran away from home. Cindy and Brandon searched frantically until a cop found her beneath a highway overpass. She had nothing with her but her Heidi doll and a peanut butter sandwich. Sobbing, she complained that her schoolmates called her "tunnel brat," made fun of her threadbare clothes, and asked if she got coal in her Christmas stocking.

It seemed every time Len spoke to Cindy, there was a new crisis. LeAnn fractured her ankle playing volleyball. A family of skunks moved into the crawlspace beneath the house. An ice storm caused the pipes to freeze after the city shut off the gas for non-payment. The whole family came down with flu. Each time, Cindy swore Len to secrecy. She didn't want to give her mother the satisfaction.

One night Brandon was loading an underground rail cart when a methane explosion trapped him and four other men beneath fifty tons of rock. By the time the survivors dug them out, it was too late. Brandon was only thirty-three.

"It's so unfair!" Cindy cried to Len over the phone. "He tried so hard to be a good provider."

"I'm sorry, Cindy. Have you called Mom yet?"

"No. She'd just say 'I told you so.'"

"What are you going to do now?"

"I don't know. We were barely getting by when it happened."

"Should I send you some money?"

"Oh … you know what Mom would say. 'Neither a borrower nor a lender be.'"

"Forget Mom! How much do you need?"

"Would fifty dollars be too much? Just to cover this week's groceries. I'll pay you back when I can."

That happened much later. Cindy had only her high school diploma and a year of college to her credit. Nobody in Hazleton was hiring. Eventually, she managed to land a secretarial job at a Wilkes-Barre meatpacking company, twenty-nine miles away. The family car had been repossessed, so she arose early each day and commuted by bus. The job didn't pay much, but after four secretaries in two years, Mister Fitzgerald was relieved to find someone who showed up on time, followed orders, and typed flawlessly. After a few months, he added bookkeeping to her duties, with a small raise.

When the chief accountant went on maternity leave and didn't return, Mister Fitzgerald recommended Cindy for the job. This time her raise was substantial. Len hardly recognized her voice when they spoke on the phone. Now, it had a tone of self-confidence.

Two years later, the company hired a new production manager. Kevin Weeks was forty-two, widowed, and lonely. He started spending a lot of time in Cindy's office and insisted on driving her back to Hazleton each evening to save bus fare. Eventually, he asked her to marry him. LeAnn and Laurie liked Kevin, who had a teenage son of his own and took the whole bunch on camping trips. The marriage ended the family's financial crisis. Soon, LeAnn and Laurie were among the best-dressed girls in school.

One summer, Kevin accompanied Cindy and her daughters on a visit to Chicory. To Len, she appeared healthy and serene, in contrast to the high-strung teenager of old. LeAnn and Laurie didn't remember their grandmother, but they sat politely on either side of her as Len photographed them with a Polaroid camera. Mom smiled wistfully as they told her about their boyfriends and their college plans. She took a shine to Kevin, who shared his family's Great Depression stories with her. Mom and Cindy avoided talking about the past. As everyone said goodbye, they embraced each other awkwardly.

After their kids were grown, Cindy and Kevin took in Brandon's mother, who could no longer manage the old house by herself. She continued her little sewing business until her eyes began to dim. She died peacefully in bed.

Cindy and Kevin stayed with the packing firm until their retirement. They joined an RV club and toured the country every summer until Kevin became too ill to travel. He died of kidney failure a month short of their thirtieth anniversary. Cindy bore her grief privately. She didn't even tell her mother until after the funeral.

"Do you ever regret dropping out of college?" Len asked her once. "You were the best student in our family."

"Sometimes, I guess. I did enjoy the classes."

"Have you ever been sorry you married Brandon?"

"No," she answered firmly. "He was always sweet to me. Kevin was, too. That's all I ever wanted."

Kayla answered Cindy's phone. "Hi, Uncle Len!"

"What are you doing there?" he asked. "I thought you'd be in Pittsburgh." Kayla was LeAnn's daughter. She was on the arts faculty at Carnegie Mellon.

"I took a few days off to visit Grandma."

"Is she all right?"

Kayla lowered her voice. "That's why I'm here. She wasn't answering the phone, so I got worried. She's been acting funny. Keeps talking about your mother. Sometimes she talks *to* her, like she's still here."

"Talking on the phone?"

"No, into empty space! Uncle Len, I think she's getting dementia."

Must run in the family, Len thought. "Has she had any other calls while you've been there?"

"Yes, but she won't answer the phone. I answered it myself once, and there was nothing but silence. Telemarketers, I guess."

"Well, thanks for looking after her. Tell me about yourself. What's happening with art school?"

"Oh, I've been so busy! Three of my paintings are on display this fall at the university gallery, and I'm revising my spring curriculum. Next year I'm going to Berlin University of the Arts, as a guest lecturer."

"That's wonderful!"

"I'm driving all my friends crazy, practicing my German on them."

"Well, save some time for your fiancé."

"My what?"

"Greg. Aren't you two getting married next month?"

"Married? I don't even have a boyfriend now. I'm too busy. Who's Greg?"

"Wait a second." Len looked around for the wedding invitation. He couldn't find it. "Sorry," he improvised. "I must be thinking of someone else."

"Oh. Well, here's Grandma. *Auf Wiedersehen*, Uncle Len!"

Cindy took the phone. "Hi, what's up?"

"Just so you know, I've got Beth as a witness that Mom's alive. Not to mention the chief medical examiner, who's working on revoking her death certificate. I may need you and Joey to sign an exhumation permit."

"Exhumation?" She sank to a whisper. "You want to dig up her body?"

"I don't want to, but if she's here to stay, I'll have to restore her benefits. Will you sign it if I fax it to you?"

"Well ... what does Joey say about all this?"

"He's still in denial."

"So am I."

"Then talk to her, Cindy! Let me put her on the phone."

She hesitated. "Len, suppose you open the coffin and there's no body. Or even if there *is* a body, what are you going to do? Put it back in the grave, then sit around waiting for her to die again?"

"How should I know?" he flared. "You think I'm some kind of resurrection expert?"

"Well, don't take it out on me!"

"I'm sorry." Suddenly, he felt tired. Tired of worry. Tired of grief. Tired of mysteries piling up like oak leaves. "Look, can you fly out here for a few days?"

"Why?"

"To visit. So Mom has somebody around besides me."

"Len, you know how it was with us."

"Maybe it'll be better this time. Besides, you're retired. What else have you got to do?"

"Has she changed any?"

"Not a bit," Len acknowledged. "But there must be some reason why she came back."

"Like what?"

How to express his feelings? "Cindy, I've been thinking a lot this week about the Lazenbys. Remember them? They grew up in the Depression, like Mom, but they had a great relationship with their kids."

"Of course they did! They were a two-parent family. All we had was a tyrannical mother."

"Maybe she wasn't strong enough to handle the four of us by herself."

"That was no excuse for treating us like scum! I don't know why you're taking her side anyway. Look how you turned out."

"What's that supposed to mean?"

"You've got talent, Len! You could have been a great writer if she'd given you some encouragement."

"I've been thinking about that, too. It's easy to blame your failures on somebody else. Maybe I should have tried harder."

"Well, what's your point?" Cindy asked impatiently.

"All I know is, she's my responsibility again. Maybe I'll have to take care of her for the rest of my life. If I do, I want to get it right this time."

Kayla spoke up in the background. "Grandma, are you okay?"

"I'm fine, sweetie." She returned to Len. "I'd better go. Kayla thinks I've got a screw loose."

"Call me when you decide about the exhumation," he pleaded. "And think about what I've said."

They hung up. Len searched his desk drawers in vain for Kayla's wedding invitation. Come to think of it, Mom's medical diary was still missing, too.

In the living room, Mom was fiddling with the TV remote. The screen was snowy again. "Why do they make these things so complicated? Used to be, you had only three channels."

Len restored the cable settings. "What show were you looking for?"

"I've forgotten now. Who was that on the phone?"

"Oh. I was, uh, checking on Miranda's funeral. It's set for Monday afternoon."

"What did you say happened to her?"

"A car accident." Len flopped on the sofa. "It's terrible, Mom. She was only fifty-four years old."

"Well. That just goes to show you. I guess I should be thinking about my own funeral." She gazed out the window. "I wonder what people will say about me?"

"Mom," he asked over supper, "what did you dream about doing with your life when you were a kid?"

"In my day, girls didn't have many choices. You grew up, got married, and raised a family."

"Did you have any playmates?"

"The only one I remember was Patsy Lohan. She stayed with us during the day while her mother kept house for someone in town, I forget who. Patsy wanted to be an athlete, like Babe Didrikson. We used to race each other up and down the farm road until my mother told us to start acting like young ladies. So we built little castles out of rocks and pretended we were debutantes, dancing at fancy balls with tall men in tuxedos and white gloves. We took turns being the boy or the girl, waltzing around the yard."

Len smiled. "What else did you do?"

"Mama drew some squares in the dirt behind the barn and taught us how to play hopscotch." She chuckled. "I never could beat Patsy. She hopped twice as fast as I could, and she never stepped outside the lines."

"What happened to her?"

"One day she stopped coming over. That's all I remember."

"Did her family move away?"

"Who knows? The Depression destroyed a lot of families. Sometimes children were forced to go live with relatives because their parents couldn't feed them. We were poor too, but at least we had land to farm until the bank took it during the war. Papa always said land was the best investment a man could make. It was something you could feel with your hands and make use of. It broke his heart to lose it."

"Did you ever think about going off on your own?" Len asked. "To Dallas or Houston, someplace where you could find a job?"

"Goodness, no! In those days you hung onto what little you had. Besides, I got what I really wanted."

"What was that?"

"To be Will Holder's wife, and mother to his children."

Later, they watched *Here Comes Mister Jordan,* a romantic comedy about a boxer returning from death to fight for the championship. When it was over Mom said, "I'd better get some sleep. We've got church tomorrow morning."

"Why don't we stay home and rest?" Len said. "You've had a busy week."

"We never missed church in the old days, even during cotton harvest. I'm not starting any lazy habits now." She headed for the bedroom, leaving Len to worry about What Other People Will Think.

Tonight's reading from *Catch-22* was about the bomb squadron's commander, Major Major Major. He gets his name from a mischievous father and his rank from "an IBM machine with a sense of humor." Servile and insecure, he orders the sergeant to admit visitors to his office only when he's absent.

Meanwhile, Yossarian continues his private campaign to survive the war. He forces postponement of a bombing mission by sabotaging the target map, and by adding laundry soap to the mess hall food, causing a diarrhea epidemic among the crewmen.

The novel gave Len an idea. He opened his laptop and began typing.

> As a child, Teddy Buford pictured his father as a war hero, flying dangerous missions over enemy territory, parachuting behind the lines, stealing enemy secrets, and winning big battles for the Allies.
>
> "Your dad spent the war patching truck tires and greasing axles," his mother rasped over a washtub of laundry. "That's all he knows how to do now, and that's why we're so broke. So don't get any big ideas."
>
> "I don't care," Teddy insisted. "He'd have been a hero if they gave him a chance."

"He'd be a hero if he got a decent job and stayed home at night. The next time I catch him behind the barn playing hopscotch with Patsy Lohan ..."

"Mister Tuttle never finished high school, and he's on the radio."

"Billy Tuttle thinks he's special because his father owns the radio station. I'm sick of hearing his voice."

"Well, I like him!"

"You would! Go to bed. We've got church tomorrow."

[Chapter Two: Teddy runs away from home. Chapter Three: Parents search frantically. Chapter Four: Teddy found safe at Billy Tuttle's house. Tears and reconciliation. Stupid idea. Go to bed, Len. You've got church tomorrow.]

EXCERPT FROM

The Farm Tree

BY LEONARD HOLDER

"You're no Rembrandt," Terry smiled. "But you've come a long way in eleven months."

Matt Brady's painting depicted a tall man in jeans and a straw hat leaning on a fence rail with the setting sun behind him. From a tanned, leathery face, his blue eyes surveyed a field of ripened grain.

"Looks like the Marlboro Man, don't he?" Matt grinned. "That's the way I've always thought of your dad. The last of them Old West pioneers."

"Idealized and immortalized," Terry agreed. "I couldn't have done better myself."

He pulled up a chair. The two men sat in the sunroom John Driskill had tacked onto the old farmhouse while Matt recovered from his amputation. Watercolors and charcoal sketches of Charley and his patients filled the shelves around them. Doctor Driskill bottle-feeding a lamb. Doctor Driskill stitching up a cow's flank. Doctor Driskill giving injections to a litter of piglets.

Matt's landscapes stood out against the room's white walls. A pastel drawing captured John and Gene striding together through rows of grain. In another, Ruth and Annie sat together on the porch, shucking corn. Pencil images of Laura and her kids on horseback filled his sketch pad.

"Where are you going to hang it?" Terry asked.

"In their livin' room. It's a surprise for his sixtieth birthday party. Annie and your ma are workin' out the details."

"Well, I think it's great, Matt. He'll be awfully embarrassed, though."

"He'll survive." He turned to face Terry. "So how's things at the college? They made you the boss yet?"

"Actually, I've got a big decision to make. Professor Folger's recommending me to replace him as dean of Arts and Sciences when he retires next year. But I've also had a very tempting offer to be curator of the new Ames Institute in Chicago. What do you think I should do?"

"You're askin' me, an ex-farmhand? What kinda doctor is a curator?"

Terry chuckled. "Curators don't cure anything. They're sort of ... well, custodians."

"Custodians? You mean like janitors?"

"Now, you're making me have second thoughts," Terry laughed. "No, they run the gallery and schedule exhibits. It's a great chance to promote new artists."

"Like that book of paintin's you gave me, huh? That book changed my life." Matt surveyed his own gallery. "Terry, I never dreamed I could do somethin' like this."

"You're a natural-born artist, Matt."

"I had a good teacher. Without you, I'd be mopin' around in this chair all day." He turned serious. "Terry, I hate to ask anything else of you, but I need a big favor."

"Name it."

"Help me convince Mistuh John that the accident wasn't his fault."

"Hoo-boy! That's a tall order."

"I 'preciate all your dad done for us, but it's gotta stop. I never took a handout from nobody my whole life before this. Now, Mistuh John's on some kind of crusade. The car he bought Annie so she can drive us to church. New furniture. A new stove. A college trust fund for our kids. I don't want to hurt his feelin's, but I hate takin' charity. Will you talk to him?"

"Matt," Terry said gently, "you don't give yourself enough credit. As Dad's business manager, you've taken a big load off his shoulders. Now, he doesn't have to worry about payrolls and paperwork for the three farms. Thanks to you, he can concentrate on what he loves – working in the sunshine, growing things, and feeding the world."

Matt turned back to the painting of John at the fence. "This is the best piece I've done since you started teachin' me, but it don't come close to sayin' how I feel about your dad. Nobody 'roun' here was hirin' colored people when I come lookin' for work. He took us in when we was desperate."

"And you helped make him the richest man in the county. You deserve anything he can do for you."

"It ain't gratitude. He's tryin' to buy my forgiveness when there's nothin' to forgive. The man saved my life!"

"He blames himself for giving you too much plowing to do."

"Aw, I got in too big a hurry, that's all."

Through the window they watched Ruth and her granddaughters pick squash and tomatoes in the garden. "When's the weddin'?" Matt asked.

"August 9, if I can get my desk cleared by then."

Annie entered the room with a paper bag that she thrust into Terry's arms. "I couldn't let you get away without somethin' to take home."

"Mmm!" He savored the aroma of fresh peaches. "These look great! Thanks, Annie." He kissed her cheek.

"Now you be sure and save some of these for your fiancée."

"I will." Terry checked his watch. "I've got to run. My plane leaves at five. A couple of art professors are coming through from New York tomorrow." He bent to embrace Matt. "Your work's better every time I see you. Keep it up."

"Sure thing. Maybe if you take that gallery job, you'll save a corner for my paintin's."

"A corner? I'll schedule a whole exhibit!"

Sunday

"Sharon, you look so beautiful! I love your dress!"

The church lobby was filled with people greeting each other. Mom traded hugs with Crissy Jenkins and Lynette White. Both had attended her funeral. Len was mystified, yet relieved. So much for What Other People Will Think.

They joined the crowd heading for the auditorium. Len waved at Gavin Strong and Mason Toliver, two of the church elders. They didn't seem to notice him.

Lynette White threw her arms around Len. "I'm so proud of you," she whispered in his ear. All the ladies thought it was sweet, an elderly man driving his elderly mother to Sunday services.

Much had changed about church since Len's boyhood. Business suits and fancy dresses were long gone. Even the preacher wore a sport shirt and slacks. Len felt conspicuous in his new suit.

The old hat shelves in the foyer now contained a collection of inspirational DVDs. The songbook pockets on the backs of the pews were empty. Instead, two video screens flanked the stage, flashing the lines of each hymn.

"When did all this start?" Mom winced as the band struck up a raucous version of "This Is Amazing Grace." He should have thought to warn her. Shortly after her death, the church had introduced Christian Rock, under pressure from younger members. Len himself missed the old pipe organ. It radiated a warmth that the electronic music couldn't match.

All around him, people joined in song. Len stood silent, feeling like a hypocrite. If not for Mom's infirmities, he might never have set foot in a church again. God wanted people who believed in Him and showed it by their works. Driving your mother to church each Sunday didn't count. Her accusation was right. Len had always treated her as an obligation.

Jacob Lawson's sermon today was titled "Good Intentions," a theme built around Saul's conversion. "Saul was so zealous in persecuting the early Church that Jesus' followers must have wondered why God didn't strike him down. But God looked into Saul's heart and said, 'Here's a man I can use. He just needs a push in the right direction.' So God sent Jesus to confront Saul on the road to Damascus. When Saul realized he'd been wrong, he did a complete turnabout. He devoted the rest of his life to serving Jesus with the same passion he'd used to oppose Him."

Jacob paused for emphasis. "It's been said that the road to Hell is paved with good intentions. I don't believe that. I believe God smiles on us when our hearts are in the right place. And even if we make wrong turns, He is always willing to redirect our steps."

After the service Mom was chatting with Lynette and Crissy when Len's phone rang. "Can you and Mom come over for lunch?" Joey asked.

"I guess so. Something on your mind?"

"Beth and I have been talking about Mom. About a lot of things, actually. She thinks we should get together."

"Don't you have a game today?"

"Roger Toland's covering for me until that hospice controversy dies down."

"All right. We'll be there in a little while."

As he hung up, Ellie Stewart placed a hand on his arm. "Len, I heard about your boss. I'm awfully sorry."

"Thanks, Ellie."

"You always spoke so highly of her. How are you handling it?"

"Not so good. I dread seeing her in that coffin tomorrow and facing her family."

"You haven't talked to them?"

"I didn't want to intrude. They must be overwhelmed with relatives and funeral plans."

"Probably so." People brushed past Len and Ellie, heading toward the parking lot. "Sharon certainly looks spry for her age."

You don't know the half of it, Len thought. Ellie was a high school classmate whose own father died in the war. She worked in the school library during study hall. Len used to hang around the checkout counter, pretending to read the dictionary so he could smell her perfume. Another girl he wasn't good enough for. Ironically, she had married Hal Stewart, a quiet, studious boy. They'd been together fifty-six years.

"Ellie," Len asked, "do you remember Chelsey West?"

"Sure, why?"

"There's a salesgirl at Doreen's Fashions who looks just like her. I saw her at the mall Friday while Mom was shopping."

"Gosh, who could forget Chelsey?" Ellie said. "It was such a shame, what happened to her."

"What?"

"Didn't you know? Link Endicott killed her. Two years after we graduated."

"Oh no!" Len gasped. "Why did he do it?"

"The way I heard it, she broke up with him and ran away to her sister's house in Tucson. He followed her out there and shot her to death."

"Oh, that's terrible!"

"Yes. She was so beautiful and talented."

"What happened to Link?"

"Still in prison, as far as I know. So mean-tempered. I knew he'd come to a bad end."

What a waste, Len thought. Chelsey was an A student. She played clarinet in the band, danced in ballet recitals, and sang solos in the choir. Len still remembered her duet of "Tonight" with Michael Jeter in the spring musical.

"There isn't much left of our class, Len," Ellie reflected. "Several of the boys got killed in Vietnam. Ted Withers. Coy Jones. Ronnie Hudson."

"Ronnie Hudson? I never knew that."

"His father was very bitter about it. He said the Army ordered Ronnie's unit to capture a hill occupied by the North Vietnamese. A month later, the Army abandoned that hill and the enemy took it back."

"That was Vietnam, all right." Len had never thought of Ronnie Hudson as somebody's son. Just a bully who made his life miserable.

"Ellie," he asked. "What was your mother like?"

"What do you mean?"

"Did she have any hang-ups? Things she took out on you and your brother?"

Ellie considered. "No. Mom was pretty strict, but I knew it was because she loved me. Actually, she was a lot like your mother."

"In what way?"

"Thoughtful. Generous. Remember that time Marjorie Cates was recovering from surgery? Your mother drove her kids to school every day for two weeks."

"I'd forgotten that," Len admitted.

"Sharon was always so good about visiting sick people and running errands for them."

Len remembered heating canned spaghetti for himself and Joey when Mom was busy with charity work. "You're both old enough to fix your own meals," she told them. "If you don't like canned food, open the cookbook and follow the directions. How do you think I learned?" She marched out to the car with a casserole destined for some other family.

Ellie was still smiling at him. She was gray now, a little stooped, but her eyes were as bright as ever.

"Ellie, let me ask you something else. Did your mother ever forbid you to date somebody?"

"No, not exactly. She wouldn't let me go out with a boy unless she knew him, or he came to the house for dinner first so she could check him out." Ellie laughed. "Hal was so nervous! He said he felt like a defendant in the Spanish Inquisition." She studied Len curiously. "Why do you ask?"

"No reason. I've been reminiscing a lot lately."

She stepped closer and whispered in his ear. "Len, just between us, I always liked you best of all the boys in school."

"Me?"

"Your essays about nuclear disarmament and civil rights inspired me to join the peace movement during Vietnam."

"Gosh, I'm surprised," he said. "I didn't think anybody read the school paper."

"I did. I read everything you wrote. You should have made a career of it."

"That's what I wanted to do."

"Why didn't you?"

"Well … it just didn't work out."

"You always seemed more mature than the other boys. Except for Hal, of course. That's why I married him."

Hal stood nearby in the middle of a crowd. He seemed to be the center of attention. Dolly McCormick embraced him. "I'd better go defend my turf," Ellie smiled and left to join her husband. What a fool I've been, Len thought.

Mom appeared beside him. "What did Ellie have to say?"

"Oh, she was admiring my new suit."

"See? What did I tell you?"

As they left the church, one of Ellie's remarks stuck with him. How did she know about Miranda's death? There had been nothing in the news all week.

Mom complained about the rock hymns all the way to Joey's house. "I don't know how God could hear the singing through such a racket!" For once, he had to agree with her.

Ronnie Hudson's arrogant face floated up from his memory. Good at football but unqualified for college, he must have been drafted. Another victim of the war that ripped America apart in the late Sixties. Nobody made heroic movies about Vietnam. Nobody even liked to talk about it anymore.

Judging by his neighborhood, you'd never know Joey was a celebrity. He and Beth still lived in the same modest brick house two blocks south of the old lumberyard, now a Home Depot store. When their kids were growing up, the two boys had to share a room with bunk beds. The three girls were crammed into the master bedroom. Joey and Beth made do with the smallest one.

"Why don't you get a bigger house?" Len asked him once. "Something in Laurel Acres or Buena Vista. You can afford it now."

"We've talked about it," Joey said. "But our kids grew up in this house. The laundry room still has pencil marks on the wall, where Beth measured their heights each birthday. Eric's room still has my autographed pictures of Gayle Sayers and Bart Starr. The grandkids like to sleep in their parents' old beds when they spend the night. This place has a lot of good memories."

"So what do you do with your money?" Len asked. "I know the network pays you a fortune."

"Most of it goes into a college trust fund for the grandchildren. They're all going to have career opportunities if I have anything to say about it."

Beth escorted Mom and Len through the house and into the backyard, where an odor of charcoal wafted through the air. Joey stood on the patio in a red chef's apron, grilling steaks.

"I'll have to stick with the side dishes," Len told him. "Meat's been giving me some sort of indigestion lately."

"That's okay. It's so nice and warm out, I couldn't resist."

"Enjoy it while you can. There's a big cold front coming through tonight."

Joey watched Beth seat his mother at a picnic table across the yard, next to the flower garden. Without his styled hair and magnetic blue eyes, he might have been any old guy puttering around in his backyard. To Len, he looked like an actor rehearsing a commercial for charcoal lighter.

"How was church?" he asked.

"Unusual, under the circumstances."

He nodded. "I miss it sometimes. I have an excuse on game days, but otherwise … I don't know. I guess it reminds me too much of Mom and her rules." He studied her. "She looks younger than I remember."

"That was my reaction," Len said.

"And you're saying she just showed up last Monday? For no reason?"

"None that I can figure out."

Doggedly, Joey shook his head. "There has to be some rational explanation."

"The last time I saw her, she was in a coma. Olivia and I watched her slip away. *That* sure felt real. But then, so has everything in the past week."

Joey poked at the steaks with a barbecue fork. "Len, I'm sorry for being grouchy on the phone yesterday. Sometimes I forget how you must have felt when Mom died." He closed the hood on the grill. "Does she seem any different?"

"No. She's the same old Mom, except she can walk again. Feed herself. Dress herself. She's chewed me out once or twice like she used to."

"What do you make of all this?"

"Now that I'm used to it, I keep remembering nice things about her. The bicycle she gave me for Christmas one year. The telescope she bought for my birthday when I got interested in astronomy. Sunday picnics in the park. All the hours she spent ironing our clothes before wash-and-wear came along." Len smiled. "Remember how the house reeked of ammonia whenever she gave Cindy one of those Toni home permanents? And how she made us polish our shoes every Saturday night?"

Joey snorted. "She was just trying to impress those snooty old church ladies."

"I think you're being too hard on her."

"Maybe I am." He put the meat fork aside. "Len, I wasn't exactly straight with you on the phone yesterday."

"About what?"

"About dreams. Last week I kept having the same one. That I was in my old bedroom, doing my radio show."

Len gaped at him. "You're kidding!"

"What?"

"I've been hearing your voice in that room for the past week!"

"Really?" he blinked. "What did I say?"

"Once, you were talking about Aaron Rodgers as most valuable player. Then you had a discussion about Ben Roethlisberger as comeback player of the year."

"Roethlisberger?" Joey frowned. "He's not making a comeback. He's just having a solid season, although the Steelers are going to miss the playoffs. And everybody knows Peyton Manning's going to be the MVP."

"Peyton Manning's retired," Len said. "And the Steelers have already clinched a playoff spot."

"Hey, who's the sportscaster here?" Joey laughed. "For someone who hates football, you sure talk like a fan."

"Joey," Len persisted, "you were talking about Roethlisberger as a sentimental favorite. I heard every word of it."

"And this was in my old bedroom?"

"Yes!"

"Well," he shrugged, "you must have some kind of ESP. Or ESPN."

"Tell me, Joey," Len asked, "what game did you cover Thursday night?"

"Saints at Falcons. Weren't you watching?"

"Yes, and that's another thing. That game was played seven years ago. Mike Smith got fired at the end of the following season."

Joey suppressed a smile. "Len, you're all mixed up. Mike's still with the Falcons, although he's on life support – well, he's in big trouble anyway. Mike was Coach of the Year last season. You must be thinking of somebody else."

"I'm not! Check the NFL records. Arthur Blank fired Mike Smith on December 29, 2014."

Worriedly, Joey studied him. "Len, what year do you think this is?"

"2020."

"How old are you?"

"Seventy-eight. Why?"

"I hate to break this to you, Rip Van Winkle, but this is 2013 and you're only seventy-one. And if you know who's going to win the next seven Super Bowls, there are several thousand bookies who'd like to meet you."

Dizzily, Len put a hand to his head.

"Are you all right, pal? Beth thinks you've got a touch of senility."

"Where's your cell phone?" Len asked.

"Right here." He drew it from his pocket. The date read December 6, 2020.

"That's weird," Joey said. "Must be something wrong with the settings."

"There's something wrong with everything! Joey, I verified all this football information on the internet. Look it up yourself."

"All right," he surrendered. "I'll do that after lunch if it makes you feel better."

He opened the hood to flip the steaks. "How's your book coming along?"

"It's stuck. I don't think I'll ever get it finished. Besides, the market's glutted these days. Everybody with a laptop is writing the Great American Novel."

"Well, let me know if you do finish it. I've got some contacts in the publishing business."

He watched Beth pour Mom a glass of iced tea. "Len, have you ever wondered if you're really yourself?"

"Huh?"

"Think about it. What if you'd been born in a kind of vacuum, where there was nobody to influence you? Teach you about God and Jesus. Drill good manners into your head. Tell you what to eat, how to dress, what to read. All that stuff we get from our parents, teachers and friends. Could there ever be a Joey who was his own person, not the result of family or social pressures?"

"But you're not," Len said. "Not entirely, anyway. You're free to decide which influences to accept or reject. We all have a natural sense of self."

"I'm not so sure." Joey's face darkened. "Len, I'm one of the biggest names in sports. I've got a video game named after me. Snack foods and soda cans with my face on them. What if my audience knew that my mother still runs my life, like some kind of football coach? No matter what I say or do, on the air or in private, I get this nagging voice in the back of my head asking what Mom would think. That's ridiculous at my age!"

"I know what you mean. For me, there was always something missing in Mom. Something I needed from her. She didn't exactly disapprove of the choices I made. She just didn't seem interested."

"Oh, she was interested, all right! You just escaped the worst by staying single." Joey stared moodily at tendrils of smoke rising from the grill. "In high school, she did everything she could to come between me and Beth. Then when I married Whitney, Mom practically moved in with us. Buying us curtains, dishes, lamps, rugs, towels and stuff. Taking the kids shopping for clothes and toys behind my back. Like I wasn't able to provide for my own family."

"Maybe she was trying to buy your forgiveness," Len said.

Joey sighed. "Pathetic, aren't we? Two old men still hung up on their mother. Look at them!" Mom was chattering to Beth about something. "You'd think they'd be mortal enemies after the way Mom kept us apart as kids. Beth has a great heart, and that's why I love her." He raised the hood and began forking the steaks onto a platter. "Well, I didn't ask you to lunch so I could reopen old wounds. Somehow or other, she's back. Maybe she can tell us why."

They dined outside, Beth's potato salad and baked beans complementing the meal.

"What were you two arguing about?" Mom asked.

"Sports," Joey said.

"What a silly thing to get worked up over!"

Joey's face reddened. He attacked his steak.

"Why didn't you tell me you had diabetes?"

"Diabetes?" he frowned. "What are you talking about?"

"Len said that's why you've gained so much weight."

Joey peered curiously at Len, who cleared his throat. "How's your steak, Mom?"

"Very good."

"I guess anything's better than those nutrient drinks."

"What drinks?"

"You know. Ensure. Boost. Carnation."

"I wouldn't know," she shrugged. "I've never tried them."

Beth glanced meaningfully at the two men.

"What have you been up to lately, Mom?" Joey asked.

"There's some sort of paperwork confusion at the courthouse. Len's taking care of it."

"That reminds me. Did you ever follow through on that cemetery plot?"

"Hmm?"

"A while back you said something about buying the space next to Dad's marker. Did you do it?"

"I don't suppose there's any hurry about it."

"Well, you know how it is. If you don't choose your location in advance —"

"Don't be so anxious to bury me, Joey!" she blurted. "I know we don't get along so well, but I do try to stay away from here so I don't say anything to upset you."

"Mom, all I meant —"

"You and Cindy hardly ever call or visit! You're always too busy with sports, too busy with grandkids, blah blah blah! The truth is, you wish I'd dry up and blow away!"

"Mom, that's not true!"

She began to cry. "All my life I've never understood why my children hate me. I've done everything I could to please you. I never remarried so you wouldn't think I was disloyal to your father. Do you have any idea what it's like, no one to lean on, never a break from kids wanting this, wanting that, only to see you grow up angry and resentful like I'd abused you or something? Do you know how much that hurts? What did I do that was so wrong, Joey? What?"

She sobbed into her napkin. Joey strode into the house and slammed the door. Len followed him. "Joey, why did you do that?"

"Do what?" He whirled about, his face aflame. "You want me to go back out there and apologize now? All I did was ask about the cemetery plot!"

"Why?"

"If she was real, she'd remember she bought that plot after Barbara Lazenby died."

"Joey, she's been confused and forgetful all week. The cemetery's not a good subject to bring up right now."

"It's the same old script, Len! She *looks* for reasons to attack me. Then I end up saying I'm sorry when I don't even know what I'm supposed to be sorry about!"

"Okay, you're right. She wasn't perfect. She took her problems out on us, treated us like worms. But that was a long time ago."

"I heard all this from Beth last night," he fumed, pacing the room. "She's got this mystical notion that Mom came back for a reason. Is this it? To pick up where she left off?"

"What she said out there is a symptom of something else," Len said. "I think she just wants us to love her."

"Well, she's got a strange way of asking for it!"

"Maybe she doesn't know how."

"Don't pretend she doesn't drive you crazy, too. Admit it, Len!' Joey turned on him. "You could have retired years ago, but you hired Olivia so you didn't have to be around Mom all the time."

"That's not true, Joey. I love my job."

"You always let her push you around. Put up with her moods, feel guilty for despising her. That's another reason why I quit coming around those last years. I couldn't stand to watch her drain the life out of you." He collapsed on the settee. "Len, how did you stand living with her all that time?"

"Somebody had to."

"Well, you're a better man than I am."

"No, Joey. You're a good husband and father. I was just available."

Through the window Len watched Beth try to comfort his mother. "Look, I hate to bring this up now, but it's important. I can't get Mom's benefits restored without a judge's ruling, and that's going to involve exhuming the body. If there is one. Will you go along with it?"

"Beth mentioned that, too." Joey sighed. "Len, I'm already in the doghouse over that hospice remark. What if the news media find out I'm digging up my mother's body? The tabloids will have a field day. My sponsors will drop me, the network will can me, and I'll go down in sports history as a graverobber."

"The hospice thing will blow over in a couple of weeks," Len said.

"How do you know?"

"I'm speaking from the future, remember?"

Joey chuckled dryly. "What was all that talk about diabetes?"

"Oh! I'm glad you reminded me. Have you seen your doctor recently?"

"No. Why?"

"Take my advice. Have him check your blood sugar."

"More mysteries, huh? All right, I will." He joined his brother at the window. "Len, I know you dislike what I do for a living, and I understand your reasons. But Mom's different. She judges me on what I'm not, instead of accepting me for what I am." He studied her through the glass. "You think I should apologize, don't you?"

"I can't tell you what to do. But I wish you wouldn't leave it like this."

"Len, it's always been like this."

"I shouldn't have said those things," she confessed on the way home. "What did you and Joey talk about?"

"He feels as badly as you do."

"He still hates me for separating him from Beth in high school. He looks for ways to hurt me." She gazed at the passing scenery. "Len, I've always felt unwelcome in my own family. I know I made some mistakes, but do I have to be punished forever?"

"Nobody's punishing you."

"Yes, you are. All you kids think I'm a monster."

"Oh, Mom." They rode the rest of the way in silence.

He pulled into the driveway and started to get out. "Len." She touched his arm. "Am I the reason you never married?"

"What?"

"We've never talked about it. I was afraid to ask. I thought maybe it was my fault because you didn't have a father to help you grow up." She hesitated. "Len ... you're not ... gay, are you?"

Astonishment boiled up in him, then anger. But her timid expression made him laugh. "No, Mom, I'm not gay. I was always just shy and awkward with women."

"You were such a handsome boy! Several ladies at church told me their daughters were interested in you."

"Really? Who?"

"Diane Kinsey, for one."

"Diane Kinsey!" he snorted. "She'd go out with anybody in pants!"

"Len, that's unfair. Maybe she wasn't beautiful, but she was the most sweet-natured girl I ever saw. That's the trouble with you men. You can't see below the surface."

She was right. In high school, Diane always had a smile for Len whenever they passed in the hallway. By then he'd become distrustful of everyone, except Loretta. Who then proceeded to dump him.

"Well, that's interesting, Mom. Who else thought I was hot stuff?"

"Let me see. There was Betty Rayford ... Chelsey West ..."

"Oh, come on now!" he scoffed. "Chelsey West? You're pulling my leg!"

"Really! Her mother liked you, too. She urged Chelsey to show you she was interested. She was afraid of what the other kids would say. Some of them thought you were gay, too."

"Good grief! And you've wondered about it too all these years?"

"Well, it's not the kind of thing you can ask your own son. I was afraid of what the answer might be."

Chelsey West, he marveled. Am I really that dense? "If you knew about all those girls, why didn't you tell me?"

"You always got so huffy when I gave you advice about anything. Whatever happened to Loretta Weaver? You seemed serious about her."

"Oh ... we just sort of broke up."

"I liked her. After what happened with Cindy and Joey's marriages, I thought —"

"Mom, it wasn't your fault." He imagined himself back in school, classmates whispering insinuations behind his back. "I guess you're disappointed in me, ending up a bachelor."

"I just never understood you. You were always so private and ... sullen or something. That's why I wouldn't read those stories of yours. I was afraid they were about me."

"Why would you think that?"

"I could tell you resented me. That the stories were your way of saying so."

The remark contained a grain of truth that made Len squirm. "Well, it doesn't matter now. Come on, let's go inside."

"Wait!" He turned back to her. "Len," she asked warily, "do you kids blame me for your not having a father?"

"No, of course not. We all knew he was lost in the Pacific."

Mom lowered her eyes. "That's ... not exactly what happened."

"What do you mean?"

She hesitated. "Remember that card you were asking me about the other day? The one you found in my clippings?"

"Yes. *USS West Point.* April 14, 2300 hours."

"That's when Will was supposed to report back to the transport ship. April 14, 1944. He, uh ..." she swallowed. "He never showed up."

"What?"

She drew a deep breath. "Len ... on his last leave, your father came home looking like a ghost. Pale, unshaven, his eyes all wild and bloodshot. He could hardly sit still. He'd wander around the house all jittery and irritable. Loud noises, like cars backfiring, made him jump out of his skin. Garth and Cindy were scared and hid from him. After a couple of days, Will started picking at me. He said he felt like a stranger in his own home. He accused me of turning his kids against him, said I married him to get his father's farmland. Demanded to know who I'd been dating while he was away. Kept calling me a cold fish, asked where was the sweet girl he'd courted during cotton harvest." She choked on tears. "It wasn't true! He wasn't the same man that last time home. He's the one who turned cold and distant, sitting on the porch half the night, chain-smoking, staring into space. One night I found him out there with his father's shotgun on his lap, like he was waiting for something. I said Will, what's happened to you? And all he could talk about was dead soldiers. Heads with no faces, bodies with no heads, bloody pieces of arms and legs with flies crawling over them."

"Weren't you able to help him?"

"I tried! I told him how much I missed him, how much I needed him, how hard it was to handle four kids by myself. That just made him madder. He said I had no idea what hardship was, wading onto beaches with bullets whizzing past his ears, American boys dropping dead all around him. Always hot, feverish, fighting mosquitoes, lying awake all night in foxholes, afraid the enemy would creep up in the dark and slit his throat. He went on and on, about sadistic Japs, cowardly officers, and dirty-minded bunkmates. Then he turned on me again, called me weak and selfish. So I got mad and said some things I wished I could take back. Two days before his leave ended, I woke up and he was gone."

"Mom …" Len's head swam. "You're saying he deserted! How do you know?"

"It was about a week later. A couple of MPs came to the house looking for him." Her hands tightened into fists. "Those brutes! They questioned me for over an hour, accused me of covering for him, threatened to put me in jail if I didn't tell them where he was. I told them everything I knew. They said I could lose custody of you kids if I was charged with harboring a fugitive. I was terrified!" She shielded her face, unable to bear the expression on Len's.

"Why didn't you tell us this before?" he asked.

"You have to know how it was back then! The neighbors … people looked out for each other, especially families with soldiers overseas. Somebody saw the MPs knocking on my door and started a rumor that Will had been killed in action. People came to the house to comfort me. They brought food and flowers. They told Garth's friends his daddy died a war hero. The church held a candlelight service. Edith Scofield even brought a gold star to put in our front window."

"You didn't tell them the truth?"

"How could I?" she cried. "I hadn't recovered from those MPs when I thought what would happen if people learned he was a deserter. His service pay was cut off. Your grandparents were gone and we'd lost the farm. All I had was the drugstore job. While other young men were dying overseas or coming home crippled, Will was off hiding somewhere. Disgrace could ruin you in those days! If the truth came out, I might have gotten fired. You kids would be humiliated and bullied at school. Everybody in the family would be shunned!"

"But … Mom," Len stammered, "you got a telegram that Dad was missing in action. Was that a lie, too?"

"Not exactly. The telegram was part of the rumor. I just never denied getting one. When you kids got old enough to ask questions, I told you I lost it."

"What about his marker in the cemetery?"

"The church took up a collection," she confessed miserably. "I went along with it."

He slumped over the steering wheel. "Oh, Mom! All my life I've believed my father was a hero!"

"Len, that war with Japan was brutal. Whole platoons were being slaughtered on the beaches. Entire ships were going down with all hands. Some of the boys just couldn't handle it. You hear all this talk about 'The Greatest Generation,' but there were over fifty thousand deserters in World War II."

It couldn't be true, Len told himself. Dad was John Wayne in *Flying Leathernecks*. Audie Murphy in *To Hell and Back*. Van Johnson in *Thirty Seconds Over Tokyo*.

"Over the years I've tried to understand why he did it," Mom was saying. "When I put myself in his place, I imagined the choices Will had. He could go back to the war, crack up and return home as a mental case and a burden to his family. Or he could run away. What would you have done?"

Len thought back to Vietnam. His high lottery number had saved him from the draft. He'd never been forced to choose.

"Garth must have been eight or nine by then. Did he know about all this?"

"Oh, Garth. That's another story." She dug through her purse for a handkerchief. "Garth used to fetch the mail from the roadside box every day after school. I told him never to open it, but when I got home from work one evening, he was waving a letter at me. It was from your father. Some ranch place in Idaho. I don't remember what he wrote. Garth wanted to know why I lied to him about Will being dead. I tried to explain that his father was sick, that he had to go away someplace to get well. He didn't believe me. He threw the letter in my face and said it was my fault Will left home. Then he ran off and stayed missing for two days."

"I don't remember that," Len said.

"You were only four at the time. You and Joey stayed with Mrs. Swann next door while I was at work and Cindy was in school. Oh Len, that was the worst night of my life! I couldn't go looking for him. We didn't have a car then, and I couldn't leave you kids alone in the house. I didn't dare call the sheriff for fear of gossip getting started. So I sat up all night waiting for him, and the next night, too."

"But he did come back."

She nodded. "When I got home the next evening, he was ransacking the house for Will's letter. He wanted the return address, so he could hitchhike up to Idaho to live with his father. I said Garth, you can't do that, you're only eleven years old! He wouldn't listen. When I refused to give him the letter, he started digging through the kitchen drawers, the bureau drawers, the closets, under chair cushions and mattresses. Finally, he gave up and collapsed in the middle of the floor, crying. I tried to comfort him, but he shrugged me off. After that, he became impossible, and ... well, you know the rest."

"Where was the letter?"

"Under the stove. I burned it after he went to bed that night."

"Were there any more letters from Dad?"

"Lots of them. I asked the mailman to hold everything for me at the post office so Garth couldn't get to them. Each one came from a different town up north. He couldn't seem to hold a job very long. All of them were full of nightmares and anger. It was like Will was writing down everything that had happened to him, so he could get the war out of his head. I burned those letters too when Garth wasn't around. But he knew I was doing it. 'Why are you ashamed of my Dad?' he kept asking me. But I wasn't ashamed. I wanted to protect him. I didn't want him to see what his father had become."

"I wonder why Garth never mentioned this to me?" Len said. "Or Cindy, or Joey?"

"I guess he didn't want to hurt you, the way he'd been hurt."

Pieces of the puzzle were coming together. Garth as an ex-Marine, tall, tanned and muscular. Playful with his brothers, gentle with his sister, spiteful of his mother. Arrogant to everyone else. Constantly drunk. Always in trouble.

"Mom, why are you telling me this now?"

"I don't know," she said helplessly. "I suppose I wouldn't be if things had gone better with Joey today."

Len felt like he'd been sitting in the car for years. "Come on. Let's go inside."

The confession followed them into the living room, clouding it like a dark fog. "Mom," he asked as they took their seats, "how did you get a job with the VA? They must have had the AWOL report on Dad."

"Oh, Len, haven't you heard enough?"

"Tell me."

She studied the floor so long he thought she wasn't going to answer. "Even the drugstore job couldn't support me and four kids. So one day I went to the VA to see if they had any openings. The personnel manager's eyes lit up when I came in. He gave me some papers to fill out. When I finished, he invited me to lunch. After I got the job, he started hanging around my desk, flirting, asking me out. When I finally reminded him that he had a wife, he took me into his office and said he knew all about Will, that there were plenty of real widows who needed my job, that he'd done me a big favor, and I'd better show some appreciation."

Len's jaw dropped. "Oh Mom, no! Tell me you didn't ..."

"I couldn't risk it, son!" she cried. "Jobs were scarce with all those soldiers coming home. The VA offered us a future."

"Oh, God!" Len felt sick to his stomach. "How long did it last?"

"Four months, six months, I don't know." She began sobbing again. "It seemed like forever!"

"Did Garth and Cindy know?"

She shook her head. "We met at a motel on our lunch hour. But everybody at the office knew what was going on. I could see it in their faces. It was humiliating!"

"Oh God, Mom!" He sat there, listening to her cry. "Is that why you never remarried? I know some guys were interested."

"I never knew if Will might show up again. I couldn't divorce him without revealing the truth. Anyway, you kids idolized your father. Or what you knew about him. I thought it would help you grow up, thinking of him as a hero." She raised her streaming eyes. "Now I wish I hadn't told you this. Do you hate me?"

"I don't know how I feel," Len said.

Teardrops spilled onto her new pink dress. "You don't know what that job was like, Len. That man constantly hovering over me. Everyone else's eyes condemning me. And day after day, year after year, ex-soldiers coming up to my desk. They had the same haunted faces Will had on his last trip home. Every day I expected to look up and find Will himself staring down at me."

"You should have moved away. Gotten another job."

"Where? How could I find one that would support me and four kids? I had no qualifications. I'd never even finished high school, we were so busy farming."

Len went to fetch her some Kleenex from the kitchen. "I know what you're thinking," she mumbled into the tissue. "Your mother's a hypocrite. Putting on airs, making you go to church, teaching you manners, while all the time I was hiding a dirty secret. I always meant to take it with me to the grave. But the way things turned out with all of you ... living a lie didn't do me any good, did it?"

"Mom," he said, "when I was in third grade, you had these long, secret phone conversations with somebody. Was it ... him?"

Dismally, she nodded. "He wanted to come home. 'I'm all right now, Sharon,' he said. 'I'm sorry for everything. I love you.' We couldn't figure a way to work it. He was still a fugitive. Sooner or later, he'd have been arrested. We finally agreed it was best to stay separated. He gave me a postal address in case I needed anything. Sent me a little money. I mailed him some pictures of you kids from time to time."

"So that's why you bought that Brownie camera," Len said.

"That wasn't the only reason. I wanted us to have a family album."

"Whatever became of him?"

"I don't know. In my last letter, I asked him to stop calling, so you kids wouldn't start asking questions. After that, I never heard from him again."

Len sat quietly, letting it all sink in. "Mom ... I don't know what to say."

"I'm sorry, son. I guess I should have told you everything a long time ago and trusted the consequences to God." She came to sit beside him. "Len, your father was a good man. You'd have loved him. The Will Holder I married *did* die in the war."

Wordlessly, she went to change clothes. Len wandered into his own room, tugging at his necktie. His only pictures of Dad hung on the wall.

The smiling groom with his bride. The austere soldier in khakis. In both, he looked strong and confident. His blacked-out war letters painted a more truthful portrait.

Len sat on the bed and opened his laptop. A web search turned up several Will Holders. A youthful-looking foundation trustee. An English typographer. A twenty-nine-year-old rugby player. There was a seventeenth-century clergyman and music theorist named William Holder. And several William Earl Holders, none with his father's birthdate.

He narrowed his search to "William Earl Holder. U.S. Army. AWOL." No results. Undocumented and forgotten by all but his wife.

She was napping in the recliner when the phone rang. Outside, daylight was waning. "Len, is Mom still there?" Cindy asked.

"Yeah, right here." Mom sat up.

"Do you think it would be all right if I talked to her?"

"I guess so. Mom, it's Cindy."

She took the phone from him. "Hi, Cindy … No, I was just dozing. We had a cookout at Joey's. It's been quite a day." Len tried to read her face as she listened. "Cindy, it's funny you should say that. We've both been talking about the past … No, I didn't … I don't, I never meant … I know you didn't, Cindy … You're right, we should have … That was all my fault, I wish I … Well, that's very big of you, honey … No, I don't blame you a bit. Cindy, let me say something. What happened with Brandon – I had no right to interfere. I just thought you deserved better. I'm so sorry." She put a hand over her eyes. "Yes, he did. Kevin was a wonderful man. You had some hard knocks, honey, but you stood up for yourself. I'm very proud of you … Thank you, Cindy … Yes, here he is."

She returned the phone to Len. Cindy was crying. "Are you all right?" he asked.

"Yes … no … I don't know. I've wanted to say so many mean things all these years, and all I can say now is, I'm sorry."

"I know. We had quite a talk ourselves a while ago."

He waited as Cindy composed herself. "Len, what about Joey?"

"He's still … I don't know."

"Listen, maybe I'll fly out your way for Christmas. We can all get together, like the old days."

"That would be great. We haven't done that in a long time."

"Good night, Len. I'll talk to you soon."

They hung up. Mom was gazing out the window. In the deepening twilight she looked older, the kind of old he remembered from her deathbed.

"Mom, when are you going to tell Cindy and Joey about Dad?"

"Now, I'm afraid to. Will you tell them for me, after I'm gone?"

"It would be better coming from you."

"I don't know if I've got the strength." She turned to him. "Len, I hope you'll remember the circumstances before you pass judgment on me. Even with the gold star in our window, a bad reputation could destroy you in those days. What other people thought really mattered."

"There's still something I don't understand, Mom," he said. "If everybody at the VA knew about the affair, how did you keep from getting fired?"

Her eyes softened. "Do you remember Barbara and Milton Lazenby?"

"Sure, Woody's parents. Two of your best friends."

"Better than you know. Barbara could tell something was bothering me. When I told her about that … that awful man, she asked Milton to talk to Bob Sharp, my boss. You remember him."

"Yeah."

"Milton and Bob were in the Elks Lodge together. Bob called me into his office and told me not to worry. 'We take care of war widows,' he said. After that day, I never saw the personnel man again. They transferred him to San Diego and made him regional manager."

Len gasped. "He got a *promotion* after what he did?"

"I guess it was the only way they could get rid of him quietly."

"But … didn't Mister Sharp know the truth about Dad?"

"He never mentioned it, but Bob ran the VA office. He must have known. Bob was a very kind man. The best boss I ever had." She flopped back in the chair. "I just had a nap and I'm exhausted."

"Do you think you could eat something?"

"I'm cold. Is there any soup in the pantry?"

"I'll go see."

Tonight's movie classic was *Stairway to Heaven,* with David Niven as a combat pilot trapped in limbo after being shot down. Len was too preoccupied to concentrate on it. Mom's eyelids drooped. "Are you okay?" he asked.

"I feel sort of weak or something. Will you help me up?"

She gripped his arm as she wobbled toward the bedroom. "I guess I'm tired from all this talk today. I feel like I could sleep the clock around."

Len paced outside the room while she brushed her teeth, cleaned her face, and put on her nightgown. "May I go to the funeral with you tomorrow?" she asked as Len pulled the bedcovers up to her chin.

"Sure. I'd appreciate some company."

"Len ..." She reached for his hand. "Do you hate me for what I told you this afternoon?"

He hesitated. A lifetime of moats and battlements stood between them. "I guess I understand you better now. You must have loved us all very much to keep such an awful secret."

"I do love you, Len."

"Good night, Mom. Sleep well." He kissed her forehead.

He sat in the living room a long time, wishing he could forget everything he'd heard today. Finally, he picked up *Catch-22* and flipped idly through the pages. The "catch" was a military regulation for bomber crews. It required them to keep flying combat missions unless they went crazy. But if a man asked to be grounded, that meant he *wasn't* crazy, because only a crazy man would want to continue flying missions; therefore, he couldn't be grounded. Now, the paradox didn't seem so funny.

Len lingered over the chapter about Snowden. Yossarian was in the rear of the plane, trying to patch up the young man's wound while the pilot dodged through enemy flak. "I'm cold," Snowden kept whispering. "I'm cold."

Then it struck him. *Catch-22* was the book he'd been reading the night before Mom died.

The Farm Tree

BY LEONARD HOLDER

Twilight was upon him, but Gene wanted a few minutes alone before joining the crowd back at the house. He was remembering an evening long ago, when Dad patted his shoulder and declared, "Tomorrow we'll start harrowing." Now, a tractor crawled slowly across the dimming horizon. This machine was guided by a GPS that made plowing more efficient. Still, the occasional drought or flood reminded God's farmers who was really in charge.

Charley strode up beside him. "Those things put the old plow horse out of business. Time was, you couldn't run a farm without a horse or a mule to do all the heavy work."

"And you'd prefer it that way, I suppose?"

"Tractors are dangerous. Look what happened to Matt. They add to air pollution, and they cost twenty times what you'd pay for a pair of mules."

Gene smiled. "Charley, you were born into the wrong century."

"People don't respect animals anymore. In the Garden of Eden, their relationship with Man was harmonious. Now we use them for food. Poachers kill them for their hides and tusks. The rest get penned up in sanctuaries and zoos. It's not fair."

"Spoken like a true vegetarian. Maybe you should write a book about it."

"I might do that when I retire. Right now, I've got more patients than I can handle."

"Gene!" Laura beckoned distantly from the porch. The two men headed toward her, past the tractor barn, the expanded hen house, the machine shop, the corral. A half-dozen wind turbines stood watch over the farm, silhouetted against the darkening sky.

"Your mom's asking for you," Laura said as they entered the kitchen.

The dining room was full of relatives and friends. They helped themselves to fried chicken, potato salad, fresh vegetables, peach pie, and iced tea. Everyone was dressed casually despite the occasion. Farmers, merchants, church members, and their families stood around in groups, talking and remembering.

"She's in the bedroom," Laura said. "I wanted her to lie down and rest awhile, but she insists on seeing you now."

"Thanks, honey." Gene weaved his way through the crowd, pausing briefly to accept handshakes and embraces.

A small child approached him. "Grandpa! Come see what Uncle Terry painted for me!"

"All right, Cassie. I'll be there in a minute." He slipped into the hallway and knocked on a door. "Mom? Are you decent?"

"Come in, Gene." Still dressed in black, Ruth stood at the window, watching the sunset. She wheeled her walker around to face him and lowered herself into a chair. "As you're the oldest, I wanted you to be the first to know. I've decided to stay."

"I understand. It's not a problem."

"All you children were kind to offer, but I was born on this land. I wouldn't feel at home anyplace else. Annie and Matt are just across the yard. They'll look after me."

"Mom, I'd still feel better if you had someone living in the house with you. It would be easier on Annie, too, so she doesn't have to be running back and forth all day, tending to you and Matt both."

"I thought about that. But Matt's got the farm business and his painting to keep him occupied. Annie spends half her time over here anyway since their children moved away. You and Laura are good about visiting regularly. I'll manage."

Gene sat on the bed. "Are you missing him, Mom?"

"I guess it hasn't hit me yet," she smiled sadly. "It's as though he's out there working late. Cutting wheat, or fixing the fence, or working on the harvester."

"You look tired out. Why don't you take a nap? All those folks outside will understand."

"There'll be time for resting later. Who knows when we'll all be together again? Help me up, will you?"

The crowd quieted as she emerged from the hallway. "You all look like you just came from a funeral!" Ruth scolded. "Lighten up!" Relieved laughter swept through the room. Gene seated her in Dad's favorite chair, where she held court to the crowd of well-wishers. On the wall behind her hung Matt's painting of John Driskill leaning on a fence rail. It drew Gene's attention every time he entered the room.

Ricky approached, holding a glass of tea. "How are you holding up, Gene?"

"I'm okay. How's the family?"

"Good. I wish all the grandkids could have come. Josh is still stationed in South Korea. He tried to get away for the funeral, but there wasn't time. Wes had two open-heart surgeries he couldn't reschedule. At least Rhonda made it. She's about to make us great-grandparents again, as you can see." A very pregnant blonde was propping a cushion behind Ruth's back. "Dina's trying to persuade her and Patrick to move here permanently. I sure hope they do. We don't see them often enough."

"Dina never seems to age," Gene said. "She's as beautiful as she was at eighteen."

"That's what I keep telling her. Folks at church accuse me of robbing the cradle."

Small fingers tugged at Gene's. "Grandpa! You promised to come look at the painting!"

"I'm sorry, Cassie. Lead the way."

The child bounded noisily up the stairs, Gene following on creaky knees. Years ago, Terry had converted his old bedroom into a family gallery, taking advantage of the skylight Dad installed during his senior year. Terry's portrait of Mom at forty accompanied others of Dad, their children, Matt and Annie.

"What do you think?" Terry asked, stepping away from the easel. His new canvas showed John and Ruth seated side by side in the gazebo, wearing their Sunday best. Cassie perched on a stool between them. Their clasped hands lay on the child's lap, her hands resting atop theirs. Cassie's face, framed by blonde curls, beamed sweetly. Her great-great-grandparents smiled fondly.

"It's beautiful!" Gene exclaimed. "How long did Uncle Terry make you pose, Cassie?"

"Forever! My bottom hurt by the time it was over!"

"Terry, this is your best one yet."

"Thanks. Hard to believe it was only six weeks ago. Who'd have thought Dad would go so quickly?"

"Uncle Terry, where's Grandpa John now?"

"Well Cassie, he's gone to be with his own mom and dad. And his grandparents. And his grandparents before them."

She pondered that for a moment. "Can we take the painting downstairs? I want everybody else to see it."

"That's a good idea. Why don't you ask Aunt Dina to clear a space for it? We'll be down in a minute."

"Okay!" She scampered away.

"When do you have to be back, Terry?" Gene asked.

"No hurry. Mandy Paulson's taken over most of my old duties. The gallery pretty much runs itself now. I'm just a figurehead."

"You're too modest."

"How about you? Thinking about retirement yet?"

"Gosh, no!" Gene chuckled. "I'm busier than ever. Besides, I've got all those guest lectures to do at the university. Maybe you ought to stick around and give me some pointers. I'm not used to public speaking."

"You'll do fine. Remember, you're the land management expert. They're just a bunch of agriculture students."

Gene's eyes drifted back to the painting. "I'll never understand how you do it, Terry. It's not just their faces you captured. It's the people inside."

"That's the nicest compliment a critic ever gave an artist."

They stood quietly for a moment. "Terry, do you ever wonder what our lives might have been like if Dad hadn't survived the war?"

"I never thought about it. He was always here for us."

"Not always. You're too young to remember, but before he came home, the farm was a wreck. Mom was struggling just to feed us." He ran his fingers along the frame. "More than four hundred thousand Americans died in World War II. Whenever I think about it, I thank God for sparing Dad."

"Amen!" Carefully, Terry lifted the painting. "Carry the easel, will you? I'll be right behind you."

Dina directed them to a space in front of the living room window. The mourners gathered around, some aiming their phone cameras at the painting. Gene watched, wishing there was a way to capture the moment itself on canvas.

"Gene, I want you to meet somebody." Laura led a woman into the room. "This is Heather Jordan, all the way from Bloomington, Indiana. Her father served in the Pacific with John."

The lady gripped his hand. "I tried to catch you at the church, but the crowd was so big I decided to follow you to the house."

"Oh, I'm sorry for the inconvenience. Thanks for coming all this way. May I offer you some refreshment?"

"Your wife already did that. I'm here at my father's request. He wanted you all to know how much he admired Mister Driskill."

"Really? What did he say?"

She drew an envelope from her purse. "After Dad was diagnosed with leukemia, he wrote me this letter while he was still able. I promised to deliver it personally."

Puzzled, Gene took the letter from the envelope and unfolded it.

Dear Heather,

You were always curious about my war experiences when you were a child. I kept the worst of it from you because you were too young to hear such stories. Now, I want you to know something I've never told anyone, not even your mother.

It was at Okinawa in April 1945, four months before the Hiroshima bomb. A bunch of us were mopping up from an all-night battle with the Japs. Shortly after sunrise, we came across a crevice in the hillside with several enemy bodies. I won't upset you with descriptions. Just know that it was a scene as horrible as you can imagine. We were checking to make sure they were all dead when one of them groaned. Two of our guys, John Driskill and Manny Lomax, pulled the Jap out of the hole. John kneeled beside him to check his wounds. He couldn't find anything wrong, so he tore open the soldier's uniform. He was a kid, nothing but skin and bones. His ribs stuck out, and he seemed to be groaning not from injuries, but weakness. We'd heard reports about the Japs starving for lack of supplies, but this was the first one we'd seen for ourselves.

There was a guy in our platoon named Derek Hodge who hated the Japs. Every time he shot one, he carved a fresh notch on his rifle butt. He yanked this kid away from John and started to slit his throat. John yelled

"No!" He drew his service revolver and pointed it right at Derek's head. Derek cursed John and threatened to report him to the Colonel. John didn't say a word, just stood his ground until Derek put the knife away.

John sat the boy up and gave him a sip of water from his canteen. As he was opening a packet of K-rations, the Jap screamed "Banzai!" and yanked a grenade from John's belt. Just as he pulled the pin, John batted it away. It landed right in Derek's lap and exploded.

John scrambled over to Derek and checked his pulse. I'll never forget the look on his face. Nobody knew what to say.

Without a word, John lifted the Jap in his arms and carried him down to the beach with the other prisoners. Manny and I followed him with Derek's body.

The war didn't end until four months later. But that was the moment when I knew the Allies were going to win.

Heather, I want you to give this letter to John's family. He was a man of great character. I hope I've been as good an example to you as he was to me.

Your devoted father,
Gerald Marks
Pfc., U.S. Army
27th Infantry Division

Gene looked up from the letter, his eyes moist. "Did you make a copy of this?"

"Yes," Heather said. "Dad wanted your family to have the original."

"Thank you. Thank you very much." Gene embraced her. "Let me introduce you to my mother." He led Heather to Ruth's side and brought a chair for her.

Gene drifted away from the crowd, re-reading the letter through a blur of tears. "You okay?" Terry asked.

"Round up Dina and Charley, will you? There's someone here you should meet. And read this." He handed Terry the letter and wandered over to the new portrait. Annie stood before it, her own tears trickling down her cheeks. "Oh, Gene, he's gone!" She leaned against him. "I loved that man like my own father!"

He put an arm around her shoulders as John Driskill's image smiled back at them. These are family pictures, too, he thought. Annie and me comforting each other. Mom tickling Cassie on her lap. Rhonda's belly with the promise of a new generation. Dad, I sure hope you can see them.

Monday Redux

"Two little clouds, one summer's day,
Went flying through the sky . . . "

Len was dreaming about yesterday's cookout at Joey's house. The steak he had declined now lay on the plate before him, so juicy-looking that he wolfed it down. It stuck painfully in his chest. "Always chew thirty-two times before you swallow," his mother cautioned.

"They went so fast they bumped their heads,
And both began to cry."

The dream faded as he awoke to a howling wind. The predicted cold front must have blown in during the night.

"Old Father Sun looked out and said:
'Oh, never mind, my dears,
I'll send my little fairy folk
To dry your falling tears.'"

The clock read 6:47 a.m. Len sat up in the dark, disoriented. He remembered settling into Mom's bedside chair last night. Now, he was back in his own room.

Tossing the covers aside, he plodded down the hall toward her voice. "Olivia, is that you?"

She lay sprawled on the floor in her nightgown. "Mom, what happened? Did you fall?"

"Where's Olivia?"

"Come on, I'll help you up." He offered his hand but she squealed, trying to rise. "Leave me alone, that hurts!"

"What happened?"

"I was getting dressed for church and lost my balance."

Church? "Here, put your arms around my neck and I'll help you stand." He bent forward and tried to pull her up.

"Stop, stop!" she cried. "It's no good, it hurts too much."

"Where?"

"My leg … my hip."

"Oh gosh, you must have broken something." Len pulled a blanket off the bed and wrapped it around her. "Mom, relax and don't move. I'll call 911."

He dashed to his room for the phone. As it rang, the date on the screen caught his eye: Monday, November 30, 2020. "What in the world?" he muttered.

There was no response from 911. He tried again and waited through a dozen more rings.

He returned to his mother. "They don't answer. Let's get you back in bed until I figure out what to do."

"No, don't! Wait till Olivia gets here."

"Olivia doesn't work for us anymore," he said, kneeling beside her. "I'm looking after you now."

"Why?" She squinted at him. "Len, you didn't fire her, did you?"

"No, of course not."

"Then I don't understand! Is this Sunday?"

"Sunday was yesterday."

"But Olivia always stays with me on weekdays." Her eyes surveyed the room. "Is this my house?"

"Yes, Mom." He felt her forehead. No fever. "Listen, I've got to put you back in bed." He pulled the blanket away.

"No, don't! It'll hurt!"

"You can't stay on the floor." Squatting behind her, he hooked his elbows under her shoulders. "Just three seconds and it'll be over. Ready? Grit your teeth." Standing, he heaved both of them backward onto the bed as she yowled in agony. "Okay, good girl! We did it!" He slipped out from under her. "Now, one more move." She gasped as he gently scooted her legs into place and tucked a pillow beneath her head. "There! That wasn't so bad, was it?"

"We're ... going to miss ... church!" she panted.

"Church was yesterday, remember?"

"So this is Monday?"

"That's right."

"Is Olivia here yet?"

"Mom, I think you're confused. Let me check you over." He probed her hip joints. The left one felt swollen. "Don't do that!" she winced. "It hurts!"

"I'm sorry. Hang on, I'll get you some Tylenol." She moaned as he went to the bathroom, returning with pills and water. "Let's sit you up so you can swallow. Put your arms around my neck. Hold tight, now. I'm going to pull you backward, very gently. Here we go." She yelped as Len slid her toward the headboard. He stuffed two pillows behind her, straightened her nightgown, and pulled up the blanket. "There now. That's better than the floor, isn't it?"

She swallowed the pills and sank back. "Joey, where's Beth?"

"It's Len, Mom. Joey and Beth aren't here now."

"Len?" she blinked. "Why are you here? You're supposed to be at work." Her eyes searched the room. "I can't see anything. Where are my glasses?"

"Right here, on the lamp table." He helped her put them on.

"I still can't see. Must be dirty."

He fogged them with his breath and polished them with his shirt. "Try them now."

"I still can't see you, Joey. Are we at home?"

"It's – yes, Mom. We're in your bedroom. It's Monday morning."

"Monday?" She became agitated. "I have to get up! Make breakfast for the kids." She pushed the covers aside.

217

"Mom, keep still. Lie back and rest."

"They'll be late for school!"

"I'll go take care of them right now. I promise. Don't try to move."

In the living room, he tried 911 again, in vain. He phoned the main number at Paxton Memorial. Still no answer. Must be an outage somewhere.

There was no reason to panic. She'd be okay with painkillers until he got her to the ER. That was one problem. The other was Miranda's funeral at 2:00 o'clock.

He opened the curtains. The wind whistled through the red oak tree, dark clouds making the dawn tardy. In the gloom, he could see leaves whirling thickly across the lawn. Len frowned. He thought he'd raked them all up on Saturday.

He searched the TV for a weather update, but every channel was snowy. This time his attempts to restore the settings didn't work. Maybe the wind had knocked out the cable service, too.

Back in the bedroom, Mom gazed vacantly at the wall. Now, Len remembered that she couldn't have a broken hip. Implants had replaced both of them before her death. The injury must be elsewhere.

This morning there was no voice from Joey's room. Len shaved quickly, pulled on some clothes, and sat in Mom's bedside chair, trying to think. Maybe he could take her to the ER in Beth's minivan. They could make a sling out of her bedsheets.

He tried Beth's phone but got only ringtones. The wind must have disrupted the cell network.

The clock read 7:30. Soon, Frank and his family would be up and about, getting ready for Miranda's funeral. Len imagined them, red-eyed with grief and exhaustion. They'd be pleased that he came, though. Maybe Chad and Sylvia would be there! They could talk to Ron Stokes, straighten everything out.

Mom stirred as gray light emerged through the windows. "It's daytime, Len. Why aren't you at work?"

"Miranda's funeral is today. The office will be closed."

"Who's Miranda?"

He smiled sadly. "My boss."

"Oh. Are you going?"

"I hope so. I'm having trouble finding someone to help you."

"What for? I'm not a baby, you know. Get out of here so I can get dressed and I'll go with you. AHHH!" she screamed as she tried to move.

"Take it easy, Mom. You've got an injury."

"Oh, that hurts!" she moaned, shutting her eyes tight.

"Try to relax. That should help."

The wind screeched against the window panes. He sat on the bed and took her hand. "How bad is your pain, Mom? Has the Tylenol kicked in yet?"

Her brow knitted. "Tylenol? What are you talking about? It's just morning sickness."

"What?"

"I had it with all three of you. Now, this one's acting up. Get me some water, will you?"

Len stared at her blankly, then fetched the water. She drained the glass. "That's better. Whew! Four kids are enough, Will. What do you think we ought to name this one?"

"This one?"

She smiled affectionately. "You named Garth after your uncle. I named Cindy and Len after my grandparents. You get to choose the last one."

A knot formed in Len's throat. "How about Joey? That suits a boy or a girl."

"Joey. I like that. A sweet name." She looked around. "Are they up yet? I'd better fix their breakfast."

"That's my job, Sharon. You rest and take care of the baby while I'm home."

"Thanks, Will. I do feel a little weak. Maybe I'll sleep a while longer." She closed her eyes. Len's were wet as he sank back in the chair.

Around 9:00 o'clock he tried 911 again. Then the home health agency. Beth and Joey. None of them answered. The date on his phone was still a week behind, and the TV was still out.

Len watched his mother sleep. Seven years ago, she'd at least known Len and Olivia until the last few days, when she sank into unconsciousness.

The swaying tree branches reminded Len how much Miranda enjoyed thunderstorms. Whenever the sky grew dark, she dashed outside the building and took cell phone pictures of lightning strikes. He doubted that she'd like this storm. No fireworks, only blustery gloom. A miserable day for her funeral.

He needed to leave by at least 1:30 to get there on time. He supposed he could run across the street to see if Mabel Darby had phone service. But he was afraid to leave Mom unattended. Technicians must be working on it. Give them a chance.

Yesterday's revelations returned to haunt him. A father who deserted his post. A mother who compromised herself to cover it up. She was right. What other people thought *did* matter. It mattered to him.

All his life, Len had wondered how things might have turned out if Will Holder had survived the war. But he ran away from it. All of us went AWOL, he reflected. Garth into wildness. Cindy into rebellion. Joey into bitterness. Me into myself. Only Mom stayed and did her duty. She was the real hero.

He tried to concentrate on things he could do something about. Even if he no longer had a job with Winslow & Grant, his prospects with other insurance agencies were good, despite his age. Lots of people started over late in life these days. The AARP magazine was full of stories.

He leaned forward to check Mom's pulse. Sixty-seven beats, but without her wrist cuff, he couldn't be sure. Strange that all her clothes and bedding had reappeared last week, but not her medical devices.

Restless, he fetched his laptop. It showed the same date as his phone: Monday, November 30, 2020. What was it with these electronics?

He scrolled through the yellow folder containing his abandoned stories. The closest he'd come to finishing one was his novel about the farm family. But he'd never found that intangible element that would tie everything together.

I never wanted to be anything but a writer, he thought. *When you can't be what you want to be, does that make you a failure?*

Something was missing from Len's desktop icons. *The Farm Tree* had its own folder. It was gone.

He scanned the C drive to see if he'd accidentally moved it elsewhere. No luck. He opened the recycle bin. It was empty. "Oh no!" he moaned. He'd never printed any hard copies. His novel was lost! All that work down the drain!

Wait a minute, he paused. *The last time I checked was Tuesday morning. Mom was watching her TV shows. I opened up the folder and wrote a new scene for ...* which chapter was it?

It didn't matter. The point was, on Tuesday morning *The Farm Tree* was still there. And he hadn't deleted anything since.

He rebooted the computer, praying it would resurface. Mom dozed beside him as the laptop hummed and clicked.

The log-in screen reappeared, still reading November 30. The folder containing *The Farm Tree* was still missing. Len's heart sank. He didn't think he could rewrite it all from memory.

A violent gust battered the house. The tree branches rocked.

With the phone service out, Len hoped Walter Garrett wasn't trying to reach him. He needed to get the exhumation business out of the way so he could restart Mom's benefits. But he still didn't have permission from Joey or Cindy. And even if they approved, even if there was no body in the coffin, how would he ever convince Medicare?

What if he took Mom to the hospital, but they wouldn't admit her because her Social Security number was invalid? What if they did perform surgery, but the rehab facility wouldn't take her? Or what if she woke up tomorrow, healed and healthy again? There was no natural order anymore. Just some Wizard of Oz hiding behind a curtain, pulling levers.

No natural order ...

On a hunch, he clicked on the Winslow & Grant shortcut. In the log-in field, he typed one of his old passwords:

J@ne&yre

INVALID USER NAME OR PASSWORD

At least his account wasn't locked anymore. He tried another one:

Wa$hington$quare

INVALID USER NAME OR PASSWORD

M!ddlem@rch

That one worked. The claims database appeared. He typed in his agent number:

ACCOUNT CLOSED

He began entering dates, working backward from 2020. At 2013 he got results:

Holder, Leonard

CLAIM NO.	CATEGORY	STATUS
5703817	ROOFING SETTLEMENT	CLOSED
5703772	ROOFING SETTLEMENT	CLOSED
5703623	VEHICLE SETTLEMENT	CLOSED
5703572	PROPERTY THEFT SETTLEMENT	CLOSED
5703148	ROOFING SETTLEMENT	CLOSED
5702936	ROOFING SETTLEMENT	CLOSED
5702891	ROOFING SETTLEMENT	CLOSED
5701633	VEHICLE SETTLEMENT	CLOSED
5701572	PROPERTY THEFT SETTLEMENT	CLOSED
5701283	ROOFING SETTLEMENT	CLOSED
5700931	VEHICLE SETTLEMENT	CLOSED
5700742	ROOFING SETTLEMENT	CLOSED

Seven roofs, three cars, two burglaries, as he remembered. But the year should be 2020, and the status should be "PENDING" on all of them.

Time had been mixed up all week. Conversations confused, familiar faces transposed. The only people who seemed to belong were his relatives and the people at church yesterday. Ellie Stewart, Crissy Jenkins, Lynette White.

A disquieting suspicion arose in Len's mind. In the browser window, he typed "Ellie Stewart, Chicory, Texas." A single result appeared.

https://www.chicorygazette.com/local/obituaries/2020/12/03
Chicory Gazette Local Obituaries
Eleanor Faye Stewart, 78, died Wednesday, December 2, 2020, after a brief illness. Services are pending.

Len's heart froze. His laptop slid to the carpet with a thump.

Mom stirred beneath the bedcovers. "Who's there?" she asked.

"It's Len, Mom."

"Len? I'm hungry. Is there any key lime pie?"

"I don't think you should eat anything until the doctor sees you."

"Please? Just a little piece?"

"Well ... okay." With a sense of dread, he went to the kitchen, debating whether to do a search on Crissy and Lynette.

He opened the freezer. The leftover pie was gone.

The refrigerator section was empty. So was the fruit bowl on the countertop.

He searched the pantry. All the groceries he'd paid for Saturday were missing. The cocoa tin, Olivia's spices, the flour and sugar canisters – all vanished. The cupboards were bare of dishes and glassware. The utensil drawers were empty.

Now Len was frightened. Some things couldn't be rationalized away.

He glanced around. Mom's cross stitches were gone from the walls. So was the Plains State banner. The cartoon magnets on the refrigerator, the ceramic turtles above the stove – all had disappeared.

He seized his phone and called 911. Then Beth, Joey, Cindy, every number on his menu. Nothing but desolate ringing.

Returning to the living room, he found it bare. The snowy TV, Mom's precious living room furniture, the Noah's Ark print – nothing remained except for a book lying on the fireplace mantel. It was Len's copy of *Jude the Obscure,* with a small envelope for the bookmark: Kayla's wedding invitation.

Terrified, he rushed outside. The wind tore at him. Across the street, Mabel Darby's porch was vacant. Her windows were dark. So were all the neighbors' windows. No dogs barked, no cars drove past. Turbulent blue clouds swept across the sky.

Turning back to the house, he tripped over a metal signpost stuck in the lawn:

FOR SALE
ESQUIRE REALTY
3BR, 2BA, Utility
2100 sq. ft.

"What? … *What?*" Len stumbled backward, almost tripping again on the porch steps. Closing the door against the gale, he staggered into Mom's room. Her closet was empty. Even the clothes she'd bought at the mall on Friday were gone.

Now, her medical diary lay on the lamp table beside the bed. He paged through it. All of Len's notes were intact except for November 2, 2013. His final entry, noting the time of her death, was missing.

Trembling, he sank into the chair. Mom lay asleep on her back. She was wearing the Dallas Cowboys warmup suit.

"It's a dead-end job," Olivia remarked dolefully.

"What is?" Len asked. It was mid-afternoon, the last day of his mother's life. They sat by her bed, listening to her shallow breathing.

"Now I know what that phrase really means. Dead-end job. That's what this is. Waiting for one client to die so I can move on to another one."

Len had never heard Olivia talk this way. He was weary from being up all night with Mom and the hospice nurse.

A tear slipped over Olivia's cheek. "Len, this is my fourth terminal case in nine years. I spend hours and days and weeks sitting up with them, feeding them, taking their vital signs. Getting more and more attached until they fade away." She choked. "I can't do this anymore, Len. Watching them die and leave me to grieve. I've got to find something else to do."

"But you're good with people, Olivia. What else would you do if you gave up home health?"

"I don't know. Len, how do you get to be a claims adjuster? Does it require a college degree?"

"Not necessarily. But don't fool yourself into thinking it'll be easier than this. There are lots of tears in the claims business, too."

"Maybe so. But at least your clients don't die on you."

"Actually, sometimes they do."

Olivia sighed. "Death. There's no escaping it."

She placed her hand tenderly on Mom's forehead. "Len, you're a writer. Tell me something. Mateo's dead, and my grandson never had a chance. Is that what you'd call a tragic ending?"

He thought about it. "I suppose so. But you and the girls managed to survive. Delia's back in school now, and Lucas is out on probation. I guess I'd call that a bittersweet ending."

"Do you think there's any such thing as a happy ending?"

"I wouldn't know. I've never seen one."

They watched over Mom silently as the afternoon wore on.

"Will … Will?"

Len emerged from his stupor. The clock read 1:45. "I'm here, Mom – Sharon."

"Will, something's wrong. I can't move."

"Relax. You've fallen and hurt yourself."

"I did? When was that? We were over at Cindy's house only yesterday."

"Joey's. We were at Joey's."

"I know where I was! Cindy and Kevin invited us to lunch after church. All they had was turnips and mustard greens because the corn crop failed."

She closed her eyes and reached out, her fingers grasping at the air. "I'm so tired, Papa. Picking cotton, hoeing weeds, milking cows, and there's never enough to eat. I can't do anymore today. Please let me rest."

"It's okay, Sharon," Len soothed. "You lie here and sleep. I'll take care of the chores." Gently, he took her hands and settled them in her lap.

"I'm so hungry, Papa. Is there any food in the house?"

"Maybe tomorrow. Think about something else."

"All right, Papa." She drifted off.

Len tried his phone again. Now, it didn't even ring. He looked around for his laptop but couldn't find it.

He curled up on the bed beside his mother and listened to the wind howl, trying not to think.

"Two little clouds … went flying … through the sky …"

He sat up and looked at the clock. It was after 4:00. Miranda was in the ground by now. Frank and the family would be at home, receiving visitors. What must they think of him, not showing up for his boss's funeral? And Ron Stokes. Chad and Sylvia. He'd missed his chance with them, too.

"They went too fast… they bumped their heads …"

Len touched her gently. "Mom?"

"Who's there?" she asked.

"It's Len, Mom."

"Len?" The glasses had disappeared from her nose. Her eyes, rheumy and unfocused, searched his face. "I was remembering something my mother used to sing when I was scared of the thunder."

"Yes. I know that one."

"She sang it over and over until I went back to sleep. It was something like, 'Two little clouds … they bumped their heads …'"

Len sang softly:

"Two little clouds, one summer's day,
Went flying through the sky;
They went so fast they bumped their heads,
And both began to cry."

She sang with him.

"Old Father Sun looked out and said:
'Oh, never mind, my dears,
I'll send my little fairy folk
To dry your falling tears.'

"One fairy came in violet,
And one wore indigo;
In blue, green, yellow, orange, and red,
They made a pretty row.

"They wiped the cloud-tears all away,
And then from out the sky,
Upon a light of sunbeams made,
They hung their gowns to dry."

She squinted at him. "Joey?"

He took her hand. "I'm here, Mom."

"Where are we, Joey?"

"We're home, Mom. Safe and warm in your nice, cozy bedroom."

Sightlessly, she looked around the room. "It *is* nice, isn't it? I've always loved this house."

"Me too."

"Is it mine?"

"It sure is. You worked hard and paid for it all by yourself."

She smiled. "Your father's going to be so pleased. Where is he, anyway?"

"He's, uh … he's off fighting the war, Mom."

"Gosh, is it ever going to end? It's so hard without him. You kids need him. I try my best, but I can't do everything by myself."

"You're doing a good job, Mom. I'm proud of you."

"You are? You never … you kids don't seem to understand, none of you. Mama and Papa are gone now, there's nobody to help me. You're all so demanding and ungrateful." She sighed deeply. "But it's not your fault. You're too young to understand."

"I understand, Mom. I didn't for a long time, but I do now." He kissed her. "I love you."

"You're a good boy, Joey."

Len patted her face. "How do you feel? Any pain?"

"I feel pretty good. Papa let me take a nap in the cotton wagon. I can go back to work now."

"The cotton's all picked. We finished while you were asleep."

"Oh, that's good. Did he get it to market on time?"

"He sure did. We won the first bale prize again. Three years in a row!"

"That's wonderful! Fifty dollars! We sure can use the money."

"And you're all done with the harvest for this year."

"Thank God! I'm so tired. Papa let me nap in the wagon, but I'm … still so … tired."

Her eyes closed. Len held her hand until the gentle rise and fall of her chest ceased.

It was dark outside when his eyes opened again. The storm had passed. Beside him, Mom lay still, her face a mask of serenity.

"Well, it's about time you woke up!"

He turned, startled. Miranda smiled at him from the bedside chair.

"Miranda! You can't be here. I must be dreaming after all!"

A soft light surrounded her plump figure. She wore a red plaid suit and an elf hat. Her favorite Christmas outfit.

"I'm so confused, Miranda," he moaned. "Everything's falling apart. And I missed your funeral!"

"That's okay," she laughed. "I missed yours."

"What?"

She spoke gently. "Your time came this morning, Len."

Fear seized him. "You mean I'm ... But that's impossible! I've just lived an entire week!"

"I'll say! You sure kept me waiting a long time."

Her gentle glow began to envelop him, easing his anxiety.

"Why did I have to go through all this, Miranda?"

"I guess God thought you both deserved a second chance."

"What about all those people I met? Walter Garrett, Ron Stokes, Ellie Stewart. And all those familiar faces."

"Angels, to help you along. I think you writers call them supporting characters."

All around him the room was dimming slowly, blending with the night.

"Miranda, what year is this?"

"What year do you want it to be?"

He hesitated. "I wish it was 1945. With the war over, and my Dad back home. But it's too late for that."

"Maybe not." She nodded at the bedside table. The medical diary was gone. In its place lay a hardback edition of *The Farm Tree*. The dust jacket showed a tall man leaning on a fence rail, the setting sun behind him.

"My novel! I finished it! Why don't I remember?"

"You've had other things on your mind."

Now the only light in the room was the one they shared.

"Why are you here, Miranda?"

"To take you home. Your work is done."

He reached for the book but couldn't seem to grasp it. He turned back to the bed. "I can't just leave her here."

"Joey will know what to do. Listen." His brother's voice murmured from down the hall. "You and I have other paths to follow."

"Where?"

She arose and took his hand. "Let's go find out."

CPSIA information can be obtained
at www.ICGtesting.com
Printed in the USA
BVHW031039100122
625870BV00010B/331/J

9 781087 997377